## MY ROOM HAD BEEN TRASHED!

I looked around—at the suitcases I had yet had time to empty now spilled on the floor, at the books that were once a neat TBR pile and were now strewn everywhere, at my notebook computer, open and running, even though I knew I'd shut it down before I left that afternoon.

But who could have done such a thing?

And why?

I'd barely had a chance to wonder when all the lights flickered.

They winked.

They blinked.

And they finally went off.

# Haunted Homicide

## LUCY NESS

**BERKLEY PRIME CRIME**
New York

BERKLEY PRIME CRIME
Published by Berkley
An imprint of Penguin Random House LLC
penguinrandomhouse.com

Copyright © 2020 by Connie Laux

ISBN: 9781984806772

First Edition: September 2020

Printed in the United States of America
1  3  5  7  9  10  8  6  4  2

Cover art by Oscar Perez
Book design by George Towne

*For the real Bill Manby, and for
Sally Manby, too. It's a pleasure sharing
in-law honors with you!*

# Chapter 1

"You're not wearing *that*, are you?"

Just inside the massive double doors that led into the Portage Path Women's Club, I froze, dropped the suitcase I was carrying, and automatically looked from where Muriel Sadler stood tapping the toe of one expensive pump against the marble floor down to my outfit.

Black pants.

Red scoop-necked T-shirt.

Black flats.

Yes indeed, it looked like I was wearing *that*. In fact, I'd been wearing it since early that morning when I loaded up my car outside of Cassadaga, New York, and drove the 170 miles to Portage Path, Ohio, thirty miles south of Cleveland. The outfit was comfortable and, thank goodness, it was forgiving. Just ask the double mocha latte I'd picked up at a drive-through outside of Erie and promptly spilled down the front of me.

The good news? Mocha blends pretty well with red, and the morning sun was behind me.

"It's nice to see you again, Ms. Sadler." Oh yeah, my voice was as dazzling as the crystal chandelier that hung high above us in the two-story entryway. I added a smile to go with it when I stepped forward, my hand extended. "I didn't think I'd see you until later this afternoon."

"Obviously." She looked me up and down, but she didn't take my hand. In fact, Muriel's top lip curled and left a smudge of rose-petal pink lipstick on her dentures. Muriel was five feet nothing and as big around as a strand of angel hair pasta. She was dressed in a matching brocade jacket and skirt in the same delicate shade of blue as her hair. A touch of understated blusher on her cheeks. A couple rings that were sparkling but not too gaudy. A brooch pinned near her left lapel, a swirling loop of letters crafted in gold that caught the morning sunlight and flashed in my eyes.

PPWC.

Portage Path Women's Club.

My new employer.

I told myself not to forget it and kept my smile firmly in place. I might be the new kid on the block, but I was no dummy. The next day would be my first on the job as the club's business manager, but I already knew the lay of the land—I had impressed every single member of the club's board in the in-person interview that had gotten me the job.

Everyone but Muriel.

Luckily, she was just one vote, even if she was club president.

And I knew I would need her backing if I ever hoped to accomplish anything and keep the job, the decent salary, and the chance to start out fresh in a place that was nowhere near my lovable (but crazy) aunt Rosemary and her lovable (but crazy) friends and the retreat center back in Lily Dale, New York, that they'd just opened and wanted me to run. Don't get me wrong; I like a challenge as much as the next type A person. It should be noted, though, that I do not like challenges that involve Rosemary's wacky ideas about all things woo-woo, including spirit visitations and astral projection. She may be my mother's only sister, and yes, she raised me. I will even go so far as to admit that I share her DNA when it comes to blue eyes, honey-blonde hair, and a soaring height of five feet ten inches, but believe me, that's where the similarities between me and Rosemary end. She's a medium, see. Which has nothing to do with size, and means she talks to the dead.

Me talking to the dead? Not so much.

And let me say, that suits me just fine.

While I was thinking about all this and considering my options (which were basically zero because, like I said, my job was all about keeping the members of PPWC happy, starting with Numero Uno herself), Muriel was watching me closely. She had eyes the color of the massive wooden front desk, where, starting the next day, I'd station myself and make sure the club ran like a well-oiled machine. I'd welcome members and their guests, schedule club activities that included everything from book discussion groups to a classic movie club, work to bring in revenue by securing outside conferences and events at the old mansion that was the club's home, and deal with staff and members.

Including Muriel Sadler.

Yeah, by this time, my smile was a little stiff around the edges.

No matter. Smiling to beat the band, I grabbed my suitcase. "I'll just head upstairs to my suite and get settled,"

I told Muriel. "I'll meet you back down here and we can have lunch together like we planned last time we talked."

"Oh no!" She latched onto my arm. "There's no time for that. And no time for you to change, either." Another look at my outfit. Another curl of the lip. "We need to get up to Marigold and be ready when he arrives."

"It's a little soon to be badgering Avery, don't you think?" The front door opened and slapped shut, and in spite of the fact that Muriel's fingers dug into my skin, I was able to turn just in time to see Patricia Fink sail into the entryway like the *Queen Mary* approaching the dock. She, too, was one of the club's board members, one of the women who'd supported my hiring. I certainly didn't know her well, but in the times I'd talked to her, I'd learned she was a force to be reckoned with.

Patricia was squat, muscular, and younger (a relative word) than most of the other women I'd met at PPWC. She was dressed sensibly in tweed pants and an ochre blazer, the color a perfect match to the autumn leaves on the tree that shaded the front door. I'd gone through two extensive phone conference calls and one in-person interview before I'd been offered the job and in that time, I'd found out Patricia did not suffer fools gladly.

I was lucky to have her on my side.

"Give the poor girl a break, Muriel." As expertly as if she did it all the time—and for all I know, she did—Patricia saved me from Muriel's clutches by untangling Muriel's hand from my arm. "From the looks of her, I'd say she just got out of the car. It's too soon to start harassing her. And besides, she's not even supposed to officially start the job until tomorrow."

Now that her hands were free, Muriel gripped them at her waist. "All well and good, but we've got to get up to

Marigold. The restorationist will be here in a little while."
Her gaze slid ever so briefly to mine. "It's a business meeting. Which explains why we're dressed appropriately."

I've worked in the hospitality industry all my adult life
and just for the record, I'm twenty-nine. That's a lot of
years of bussing tables, taking orders, working behind the
front desk of a hotel, setting up business meetings and ca-
tering menus, and (the worst of the worst) wedding planning. I was used to biting my tongue. Being gracious.
Keeping my mouth shut and my smile in place.

But honestly, there's only so much anyone can take.

I had just opened my mouth to cut Muriel off at the
knees when Patricia intervened.

"Marigold is a disaster, our records were nearly destroyed, and the only thing you can think about is what
Avery is wearing?" Her snort told Muriel she didn't need
an answer. "By the time we're done up there, we're all going to smell like smoke and Muriel, that pretty little Armani
suit of yours is going to get as ashy as hell. Looks like when
it comes to knowing what to wear, Avery is the only one of
us with any sense."

It was, apparently, the first Muriel thought of this, because her face paled and her hand slipped down the delicious fabric of her jacket—a loving, protective touch.

All well and good. While she composed herself, I had a
chance to turn to Patricia and ask, "What's going on?"

"You don't know, do you? Well, you wouldn't. It happened just last week. After you'd already been hired." The
front door opened again and Gracie Grimm slipped in. Another member of the board, Gracie was proud of telling people she was "older than dirt," and that because of it, she was
the club's historian. "No wonder," I'd heard her chuckle. "I'm
the only one left who remembers most of the club's history!"

Just as I'd seen her the last time I was there, Gracie was dressed all in gray. With her tiny hands and feet and a little bit of an overbite, she reminded me of a mouse.

I'm not sure how, but Gracie knew exactly what Patricia was talking about and jumped right into the conversation.

"It's the fire, dear," Gracie said, closing in on me. I couldn't decide if it was her shoes or her voice that squeaked. "Just a week ago. Up in the Marigold Room. Awful thing." She shook her head, and her neatly styled silver hair bobbed around her chin. "So many of the old papers destroyed."

I remembered seeing the room when I'd toured the club before my final interview. Sure I was a newbie, but that didn't make me feel the loss any less keenly. "That's terrible! What happened?"

Gracie and Patricia exchanged looks. Muriel's left eyebrow slanted.

"Accident," Patricia said.

"So unfortunate." Gracie's eyes were gray too, and they welled with tears.

"Ridiculous." Muriel spit out the word. "If it wasn't for Agnes Yarborough being such a careless—"

When the door opened again, Muriel swallowed her words.

Something told me it didn't matter. From the way Agnes Yarborough's lips pinched when she joined us, I could tell she'd heard what we were talking about.

"Is he here yet?" Agnes asked. Obviously, *he* wasn't, but she looked around anyway, as if the mysterious *he* might be crouched behind my desk or peering at us over the mahogany bannister of the stairway that led up to the second floor. Agnes wasn't as old as Gracie. She wasn't as young as Patricia. In fact, Agnes had one of those timeless faces, wrinkle free, that made it impossible to tell for certain just how old she might be. Then again, I remembered what she'd told me when I was there for my interview—Agnes's mother had once been president of the club. Her grandmother had once been president of the club. Age aside, Agnes had pedigree, and an air about her that said she came from money and privilege.

She was obviously right at home at PPWC.

"He said eleven o'clock," Patricia informed Agnes.

Muriel sniffed. In a ladylike way, of course. "That's what he said last time. And he showed up at nearly half past."

"It's not like it matters." Gracie glanced around. The Carnation Room, where members played cards, was just down the hallway, empty at this time of day. The Rose Garden Restaurant was just beyond that—a place for members and their guests to dine—and from the way the waitress stood at the front reception desk with her hands clutched behind her back and the mother of all bored expressions on her face, my guess was she wasn't expecting anyone for lunch anytime soon. In fact, she might not be expecting anyone at all except me and Muriel, and our luncheon appointment wasn't for another hour and a half.

Gracie's voice was heavy. Her shoulders heaved. "It's not like we're doing anything else around here these days, anyway."

Call me crazy (and just for the record, Aunt Rosemary did when she learned I was taking a real job over the one she'd offered at the woo-woo retreat), but I just couldn't stand there and watch the pall settle. Okay. All right. I knew what these women knew. The once-thriving PPWC was down on its luck. Back in the day, membership stood at more than two thousand. And now? Well, I knew the number because

I'd seen the books, and I'd seen the books because I wanted to know what I was getting into, and once I knew what I was getting into . . .

Well, remember what I said.

I'm always up for a challenge.

These days, the PPWC numbered exactly eighty-nine members.

The mansion went empty and unused for days at a time.

The various special interest groups that used to fill the rooms to put together puzzles or host tea parties or work on their needlework or talk politics and history were down to only a few members, most of them too elderly or infirm to show up if the weather wasn't perfect, the time wasn't just right to work around their naps, or they happened to not be laid up with one ailment or another.

It was a sad commentary on a modern problem—how to make a dinosaur like a women's club relevant in a society that was all about high tech and life that moved at the speed of light.

And exactly what I'd been hired to handle.

I gave myself a shake and a firm reminder not to forget it, and while I was at it, I reminded myself that (well, maybe not officially at that moment, but soon enough) I was in charge. The club was faltering? Membership numbers were abysmal? Nobody cared anymore about things like camaraderie, card games, and the intelligent exchange of ideas?

Well, I was going to change all that.

There was no time to start like the there and then.

My head high and my shoulders back, I scooted behind my desk, the better to peer at the screen of the computer there.

"Jack Harkness." I read the name on the day's calendar, then looked from one woman to the other. "He's the restorationist?"

As one, they nodded.

"We need estimates," Muriel said.

"And a plan," Patricia agreed.

"And he's a looker!" Gracie gave me a wink.

"So until this restorationist gets here," I said, "how about you fill me in. There was a fire last week. I got that much. What happened?"

A tear slipped down Gracie's cheek.

Color rushed into Patricia's face.

Muriel's skin, already pale, blanched even further until I could see every vein in her neck and cheeks like cold blue rivers.

It was Agnes who finally spoke up.

Well, if snuffling, sniffling, then bursting into tears qualifies as speaking up.

"It was all my fault," Agnes wailed. "I did it. I started the fire. And I . . ." She sucked in a breath that made her words bounce around even more. "I nearly got killed!"

# CHAPTER 2

By the time we got Agnes calmed down (it wasn't easy),
it was fifteen minutes past eleven, but since there was
no sign of the restorationist, I took the bull by the proverbial horns, told the waitress in the empty restaurant that we
needed a pot of tea and we needed it pronto, and settled
Agnes in the chair nearest to my desk. One by one, Muriel,
Gracie, and Patricia pulled over chairs too, theirs clustered
around Agnes's in the sort of tight little circle I'd seen Aunt
Rosemary use when the folks she called querents gathered
around waiting for her to tap into the mumbo jumbo that
supposedly connects her to the Other Side.

Thank goodness there was no talk of auras or ectoplasm!

I grabbed a chair too, and the four of us waited patiently
while Agnes pulled in breath after breath, collected herself,
dabbed her nose with a lace-edge hankie, dissolved again
into tears, then repeated the process.

Finally all cried out, she lifted red-rimmed eyes to me.
"I didn't mean it," she said.

"Of course not!" I had just finished pouring tea into a
china cup decorated with rosebuds and I added sugar,
stirred, and handed it to Agnes, who took it from me in
trembling hands. "Nobody means to start a fire. I mean,
most nobodies, anyway. And as upset as you are, I know it
must have been an accident. You're obviously—"

A sharp *tsk* from Muriel cut me off. "I think the word
you're looking for, Ms. Morgan, is *irresponsible*. Agnes
was irresponsible. Not to mention stupid. If she wasn't,
none of this would have happened. Smoking! In the Marigold Room!"

"And after you told us you'd quit." This, to Gracie anyway, was more of a letdown than even the resulting fire.

It was enough to make Agnes hang her head. The tears
started again. "I know, I know. I tried so hard to quit, and I
was doing so well. I knew it was the wrong thing to do the
minute I lit up, but—"

"But nothing," Muriel snapped. "It was stupid. Not to
mention illegal. There's no smoking in this building. You
know that."

"I do. I do," Agnes wailed. "And I did quit for a while; it
was my New Year's resolution. But things haven't been
easy at home, you see, what with me dealing with my mother's affairs now that she's in assisted living. And on top of
that, as vice president I've had to pick up a lot of the club
manager's responsibilities, and . . ." Her explanation dissolved on the end of a sigh and she looked my way. I wasn't
sure if she was hoping for sympathy or just trying to explain herself to the one person there who hadn't already
heard her excuses.

"I was irritable and feeling the strain. I couldn't help

myself. I just had to have a cigarette. Then I sat down on the couch up in Marigold to relax and enjoy it, and I guess exhaustion got the best of me. I fell asleep and the next thing I knew . . ." The memory overwhelmed her and a shiver cascaded across her shoulders. "I'm sorry. I'm so, so sorry. I was weak and it nearly cost me my life. I swear, I'll never, ever light up another cigarette. I could have been killed."

A rush of color stained Muriel's cheeks. "Get over yourself, Agnes! Our records are in that room. The history of this club! And the whole building might have gone up in a puff of smoke. Then what would we have done? Are you listening? Maybe it will finally sink in. Whatever might have happened to you, you deserved it for your carelessness. But what would we have done if the Portage Path Women's Club burned to the ground because of you?"

I'd like to report who said what at that point, but it was a little hard to tell. Voices overlapped—outraged, hurt, insulted.

"How can you be so cruel, Muriel? This is too much, even for you."

"You know the fire was nothing but a terrible accident!"

"It could have been worse. It could have been much worse. We're really very lucky."

Far be it from Muriel to back down from a confrontation, even when it was three against one. "Horse hockey!" She snorted. "No one with half a brain goes sneaking a cigarette in a historic building like this. And in the room where all our valuable documents are kept!" She pinned Agnes with a look and when Agnes squirmed, Muriel's thin lips lifted in a smile.

"It was almost as if you wanted to burn everything in the Marigold Room, Agnes. Is that true? I can't imagine why you'd want to do that. Or maybe you were looking to go down in the annals of the club as some sort of martyr." Muriel's harrumph was both indignant and disgusted. "That would be just like you. Bad enough some of our precious records were destroyed and can never be replaced. You would have died from smoke inhalation, Agnes, if Bill Manby didn't show up to save you."

"Bill." One corner of Patricia's mouth pulled tight. "He's our maintenance man, grounds keeping and such," she told me. "At least he used to be. Last week, he was a hero. He dragged Agnes out of the Marigold Room, used a fire extinguisher to put out the flames, and called the fire department. And how was he rewarded?"

Muriel's smile dissolved, her lips thinned into a tight line. "I had no choice," she grumbled. "In the absence of a business manager, hiring and firing decisions are the president's. It's in the club's charter. I had no choice but to fire the man."

"After he saved Agnes's life?" I know, politically incorrect to sound so outraged, but it's not like I could help myself.

If I needed the reminder, it came in the form of Muriel's icy glare. "There were issues," she hissed. "Once you're officially on the job, you will be apprised of them. Until then—"

"Until then, you expect poor Avery to be here for a meeting when she hasn't even unpacked her bags yet, you criticize the way she's dressed even though she thought all she was going to do today was move into her rooms, but you won't keep her in the loop when it comes to how you sacked Bill? It's just like you, Muriel." Patricia's dark eyes bulged. "You and your damned noblesse oblige. You think you're better than everyone."

"That's because"—Muriel stood—"I am." She glanced over all of us ever so briefly, her gaze landing on Agnes long enough to make her squirm. "I've got the family tree to prove it."

Like her shoes were on fire, Patricia hopped out of her seat. She propped her fists on her hips. "I always knew you were an elitist. I just wish you'd quit trying to prove it."

Muriel glared at Patricia.

Patricia glowered for all she was worth.

Gracie, shaky and breathless, pulled herself up and wedged herself between them. "Now, girls, let's not get carried away. You remember the motto of the club: Friendship, Loyalty, and—"

"Snobbery!" Patricia barked.

"Maybe," Muriel snapped back. "But at least I don't want to open the doors wide and invite every bit of riffraff in the neighborhood in for tea!"

Patricia chortled. "You'd rather see the club go under? Become even more irrelevant than it already is? There are people out there"—she swung out an arm, maybe taking in the neighborhood, maybe indicating the world as a whole—"people out there who could be real assets to this club. People with interesting ideas. People with incredible talents. Just because their blood isn't as blue as yours doesn't make them any less worthy. Look around, Muriel. Wake up! If we don't do something fast, this club is going to go under. How would you like that to be your legacy? Muriel Sadler, the *last* president of the Portage Path Women's Club! We can change that, don't you see? If we open up our doors and become more inclusive—"

"Over my dead body!" Muriel narrowed her eyes, and her hands curled into fists.

Patricia let out throaty growl.

Gracie mumbled something about decorum. Like anyone was listening.

Agnes started up again with the waterworks.

It was at this point I thought of clapping my hands and stomping my feet. It might have at least stopped them in their tracks. I actually would have had the chance if the front door didn't open and a man didn't step into the club.

Our restorationist?

I would have bet any money on it.

With Gracie trying to run interference, Agnes sniffling, and Muriel and Patricia still going at each other like Rocky and Apollo Creed, I rose from my chair and went to the door.

"Mr. Harkness?"

As if he wasn't quite sure, he pushed his dark-rimmed glasses up the bridge of his nose and looked down at me.

Yes, down.

There's nothing I like better than a man who is actually taller than me.

Not that I was thinking of liking Jack Harkness. Right about then, I was only hoping to introduce some sort of voice of reason into what was happening all around me before he caught wind of the knock-down-drag-out and hightailed it for the hills.

I put out a hand. "Avery Morgan," I said. "The club's business manager. I understand you're here to look at the damage in the Marigold Room."

He had a leather portfolio tucked under his right arm, and he shifted it to his left. It bulged with papers and when a couple of them slipped out and fluttered to the floor, he retrieved them, mumbled something about getting organized, and finally shook my hand.

His hand was large. His fingers were long and cold. His palm was warm.

Jack Harkness was six feet three inches of scruffy hair

that was more red than brown, and eyes that were green and had a faraway look in them, like his body was there at PPWC but his mind was a million miles away. He was dressed in rumpled khakis and there was a leaky pen in the breast pocket of his blue-and-white pinstriped shirt. Try as I might, it was hard for me to pull my gaze away from the splotch of black ink.

It was a Rorschach.

A dog.

No, a moose.

No, a fairy-tale cottage complete with thatched roof and stone walkway.

I slipped my hand from his and stepped back. "Since Mr. Harkness is here, I guess it's time to get started," I said nice and loud so the women could hear me over their own sniping. "Muriel . . ." I spoke just in time. She was about to say something to Patricia about the responsibilities of the upper class. "Muriel, since I'm not familiar with the building yet, perhaps you'd like to lead the way to the Marigold Room."

Of course she would.

Her face frozen with the sure and mortifying knowledge that our guest might actually have taken note of her bad behavior, Muriel shook her shoulders and blinked. Her fingers twined together, she nodded by way of greeting, and I couldn't help but think about what I'd just heard, how Muriel thought she was better than everyone else. Here she was, the queen welcoming the peon who'd come to do her bidding.

I just hoped this particular peon, rumpled clothes and all, knew a whole lot about repairing fire damage.

I let Muriel and Jack step past me and go to the elevator first. They got in and stood at the back and Patricia made sure she stayed as far away from Muriel as the tiny elevator allowed. Gracie was next, so small she took up hardly any room at all, then me. I stepped inside and pushed the button for two (the only floor the elevator went to). A few smooth seconds later, we stepped out into the hallway with its walnut-paneled walls, its silver sconces, and the portraits of past presidents of the PPWC watching us parade past.

I swear, I could feel their eyes on me as we walked by, checking me out, judging me. They were a matronly bunch, well-heeled and well connected. They'd married well and devoted their lives to the club. Every one of them was dressed in black, every one of them was wearing pearls and the kind of expression that said being in charge of PPWC was Serious Business.

I wondered what they thought of a kid from a crazy family in Upstate New York and figured it hardly mattered. If they approved, if they disapproved, I still had a job to do.

We stopped in front of the closed door of the Marigold Room at the end of the hallway and because Jack was at the front of the pack, he swung the door open. Even from where I stood at the back of the line, the smell of charred wood and burnt paper caught me by the throat.

Muriel, Patricia, and Gracie stepped back, their hands automatically covering their mouths. Agnes sniffled. When Jack tried the light switch (it didn't work), then stepped into the room, I sidled my way past the members of the PPWC and went right along.

Even if I hadn't seen it before, I would have known the room had once been beautiful. The carpet was (well, once upon a time) a soft beige, and the walls—I leaned forward for a better look—were papered in white with pretty blue ribbons swooping and swirling around bunches of yellow and gold marigolds.

There was a fireplace along one wall, with a couch, table, and reading lamp facing it. One corner of the couch was blacker than the rest of it—testament, I suppose, to Agnes's confession that she had fallen asleep there with a cigarette in her hand. Two of the walls in the room were filled with bookcases, their shelves crammed with books whose leather bindings were blackened and cracked from the heat of the fire and ashy from its smoke.

Though no one had suggested it, I crossed the room, opened the draperies, and flung open a window. A gush of fresh air slapped my face and I pulled in a lungful and felt my head clear.

"Better?" I asked Jack. Except he was so busy snapping pictures of the wallpaper, he wasn't listening.

"Nineteen forty-five," he said, jotting the date in the notebook he opened.

"Nineteen forty-five, as in . . ."

"That's when this particular pattern of wallpaper went into production," he informed me.

"And you know this because . . . ?"

He'd been staring at one particular bunch of marigolds, the gold edges of the flowers blackened and sooty, and he glanced my way. "I'm the restorationist."

I figured he was going for funny so I smiled.

Jack went back to looking at charred marigolds.

I gave him some time to do whatever it is restorationists do and while he did it, Muriel, Gracie, and Patricia stepped into the room. Agnes trailed behind, her expression gloomy and contrite.

We watched him poke at the wall with the tip of his leaky pen. We stood quietly while he jotted notes. We followed along, silent and like we actually knew what we were doing, as he did a turn around the room, checking out the mahogany table next to the couch and the small marble statue on it, one I'd seen on my first visit and knew was one of the club's prized possessions.

"Hortense Dash," I told Jack just as he set down the statue and rubbed his sooty hands on the leg of his pants. "She was the first president of PPWC."

He didn't say if he was impressed. In fact, he didn't say anything, and after a few more minutes of listening to the scratch of his pen against his notebook, I thought it was time to get some details.

When Jack stood in front of the bookcases, tapping his chin with one finger, I asked, "What's the plan?"

He thought for a while longer before he finally said, "I'll need to do an inventory."

It was on the tip of my tongue to say, "No, duh!" but I managed to control myself. My first day of almost being on the job was probably not the time for that.

"After that, I can do an assessment of each object in the room and determine what's worth saving and what isn't," he added.

"You must preserve the club's records." Muriel hovered near the bookcases. "Who knows what kinds of valuable information are in these books. I know they look hopeless, but . . ." Her expression folded in on itself and maybe the harsh reality of what had happened there in the Marigold Room made her feel a little more charitable when it came to Agnes and her part in it all. Muriel actually looked to her for an opinion.

"Don't you agree, Agnes?" she asked. "You're our vice president and we all need to support this effort. Don't you agree that we need to make sure we keep every single historical document that's important to the club?"

Agnes edged over to the bookcases. There were a couple

volumes down at the end that looked unscathed, and she made to slip one from the shelf.

"I wouldn't do that." Jack stepped forward, one hand out to stop her. "The flames may not have touched those particular books, but the heat and smoke may have caused plenty of damage. We need to go through everything one careful step at a time."

"Can you give us an idea of how long it will take?" Patricia wanted to know.

He didn't spare her a look. But then, he was cocking his head left and right, studying the spines of the leather books on the shelf. "Too soon for that. I won't know anything for a while." He'd been so focused on the books, so lost in whatever thoughts fill the heads of restorationists, when he spun my way, I flinched. "Can you give me work space?"

Since I wasn't sure, I glanced over my shoulder to Muriel, who stepped right up. "The Lilac Lounge is right across the hallway," she said, motioning that way. "It's set up as a study right now, a place where our members can read and catch up on their correspondence. We can change that. We can push the sideboard over nearer to the windows, move some furniture around, have a desk brought in for you and—"

"Really, Muriel?" Patricia settled her weight back against one foot and folded her arms over her chest. "Who's going to do that? Bill Manby?"

Muriel's lips pinched. "Obviously not." She turned and swept out of the room. "She's the business manager. Avery will simply have to take over all the maintenance and grounds keeping tasks for now."

I opened my mouth to say something that would have probably sounded a whole lot like, "Are you nuts?" but I never had a chance. Once Muriel was gone, Gracie, Patricia, and Jack followed. Agnes stared at the blackened books for a moment, shifting uncomfortably from foot to foot, before she, too, turned and walked out.

"Well, doesn't it figure?" Not that anyone was listening, but I threw my hands in the air and made sure I added a grumble to my statement. "It's not even my first day on the job and I'm already getting work piled on." I set my jaw and told myself, "Better get to it."

Just as I got out the door of the Marigold Room, though, I stopped cold.

There was music playing somewhere in the building, music I hadn't heard earlier.

"No, not music," I told myself, listening a little closer. Just a voice. A woman's voice, throaty and passionate.

She was singing "Bye Bye Blackbird."

Just as quickly as I'd heard it, the song was gone, and I dismissed it as a passing car and a way-older-than-oldies radio station. At the same time, I shook away the funny little cascade of shivers that tapped along my shoulders like bubbles climbing up the side of a glass of champagne.

I had work to do, I reminded myself.

I headed to the Lilac Lounge. I might as well see what I was in for.

# CHAPTER 3

I could just wring that Muriel Sadler's neck!"

I was following the delicious aroma of coffee and I'd gotten as far as the restaurant when I heard the angry growl explode from the club kitchen. The words barely had time to register when a pot holder came winging through the doorway, headed straight for my head.

I ducked, leaned, avoided the flying object, and recovered it with as much aplomb as a woman who'd just nearly been assaulted with a pot holder could.

I marched into the kitchen, slapping the pot holder against one leg. "What's going on here?" I demanded.

Over near the stove, the face of a big guy (I mean, like Terminator big) morphed instantly from raging to embarrassed. His cheeks flushed the same color as the red bandanna that held his dark, curly hair out of his dark eyes.

"Were you . . . ?" He looked toward the doorway, where

I'd nearly been creamed. "Were you standing there? I . . . I swear, I didn't see you," he stammered.

"Or you did and that was your way of welcoming me to the club."

He didn't get the joke. In fact, he still looked as mortified as any big, muscle-bound guy could. He clenched and unclenched his hands into ham-sized fists. He held his arms close to his sides as if it were the only thing that would keep him from shooting up like a rocket and banging a hole in the ceiling and into the Lilac Lounge, directly above us. His nostrils flared and his mouth flapped.

Pot holder attack aside, I couldn't stand to see him look that ill at ease. I stuck out a hand and introduced myself.

He hung his head and looked down at his super-sized feet. That is, right before his jumbo hand swallowed mine. "Quentin Cruz. I'm the cook around here."

"You've got lousy aim, Quentin."

The laugh that bubbled out of Quentin sounded as if maybe it hurt. "Sorry." He brushed a finger under his wide, doughy nose. "It's just that sometimes, I see red. You know what I mean? And I came in here today and the grill, it isn't working, and—"

Not that I know all that much about grills, but I stepped nearer for a closer look. "And?" I asked him.

He bit his lower lip.

"He don't want to tell you on account of how he don't want to get in no trouble."

When the voice came from behind me, it was the first I realized Quentin and I were not alone there in the kitchen with its vintage appliances, its walk-in freezer, its prep counter that was as clean and as shiny as a table in an operating room. I turned and found myself face to face with a scrawny woman with stick-straight hair the color of straw.

Her face was unremarkable—pale skin, pale eyes, small features. The restaurant hostess/waitress who'd brewed a pot of tea for us the day before, when Agnes was in full I-started-the-fire meltdown.

"Geneva." I'm not psychic (whatever Aunt Rosemary might like to believe); I was just reading the nametag she had pinned to her maroon cardigan. "What kind of trouble could Quentin possibly get in because the grill isn't working? And what does it have to do with Muriel?" I glanced Quentin's way. "I did hear you threaten to wring her neck, didn't I?"

Waitress and cook exchanged looks.

Quentin clamped his mouth shut.

Geneva pretended to find something very interesting to watch on the ceiling.

It was early in the morning, and I'd just come downstairs from my rooms on the third floor. I never slept well, not the first night in a new place, and the lumpy mattress on my bed didn't help. After tossing and turning all night, I was groggy and that coffee I'd smelled earlier was brewing nearby. The aroma was heavenly and provided just the distraction I was looking for to diffuse the situation.

I slanted Quentin a look. "Can I have a cup?"

"Coffee?" He hopped to and got a cup and filled it for me. "Milk? Sugar?" he asked and when I told him both, he got that and added it too and presented the cup to me, hot and steaming.

I sniffed, sipped, and sighed. Dark roast and hearty, the best coffee I'd had in as long as I could remember. My coffee craving satisfied—at least for a moment—and the fog in my head beginning to lift, I stepped back and leaned against the prep counter, the better to see both Quentin and Geneva when I said, "Maybe we're getting off on the wrong foot."

"I wasn't actually throwing the pot holder at you," Quentin burbled, and with a wave of one hand, I told him that wasn't what I was talking about.

"We're all there is of a staff around here," I said. "And if we're going to make this work, we're going to need to be on the same page. If there are problems, I need to know about them. Especially if it means keeping you from wringing Muriel's neck."

Quentin's top lip curled. "That woman boils my blood."

I leaned forward, the better to catch his eye. "Because . . . ?"

"Because Ms. Sadler . . ." He spit the words out from between clenched teeth and I couldn't help but think of a teakettle at full boil and about to let off steam. "She just doesn't listen! I told her about the grill. Told her six weeks ago. Told her a month ago. Told her every time I've seen her since. The grill, it needs a new thermostat. I told her that."

"And Muriel said what?"

"Said she'd talk to Bill Manby about it. Only if she ever did, Bill never did anything about it, and that's not like him at all. Johnny-on-the-spot, you know? And now . . . well, now he can't fix anything around here, can he?"

"She fired him!" The words escaped Geneva on the end of a horrified gasp. "Just like that. In one swell foop." The snap of her fingers ricocheted around the kitchen. "No warning. No nothing. If she can do that to him, she can do it to any of us."

True, and not exactly something I wanted to think about, not my first morning on the job.

It was the wrong time and place to take sides, I knew that. Years of working in the hospitality industry had taught me that as easygoing as waitstaff and cooks could be, they were a tight-knit bunch. One wrong word and I'd risk the possibility of both Quentin and Geneva walking out on me. Or maybe instead, they'd decide that I couldn't be trusted, that I wasn't supportive, that I'd never see things the way they did, and they'd shut me out completely and do whatever the heck they wanted, whatever the heck way they wanted to do it.

Needless to say, neither scenario would be a good thing for me while I was not only trying to make the club run like clockwork but while I was also trying to establish myself in the hierarchy of management.

But I had to stay loyal to the club, too.

My head told me that.

So did my gut.

And like it or not, as president, Muriel *was* the club.

I drew in a long breath. I took another drink of coffee. I considered my options.

"I'm sure Muriel's been a little overwhelmed," I told them, even though I was not sure of this at all. "Without a business manager to keep things under control, I bet she's had lots of extra responsibilities. And then there's the fire, of course. That's got everyone preoccupied. There's a lot going on, what with trying to get Marigold back in shape."

"Fire!" Quentin had a wide mouth and lips so plump they'd be the envy of a runway model. When he folded his mouth in a grim line, it looked as if an artist had added a broad stroke of a fat pencil above his square chin. "She was never easy to work with. Not before the fire. Not after."

"Then I'll tell you what . . ." I finished the coffee in my cup, and nodded when Quentin stepped forward with a look on his face that told me he was offering to refill it. "From

now on, I'll run interference for you. You won't have to deal
with Muriel directly. Not about anything."

"You'd do that?" Quentin asked at the same time a smile
of what I could only call relief brightened Geneva's face.

"I'll do it." I accepted the second cup of coffee and
glanced around. "Toast?" I asked, and Quentin was only
too happy to oblige.

He managed eggs and bacon too, though he had to keep
a careful watch on the grill while they cooked so they
didn't go up in smoke, and within a couple minutes, the
three of us were sitting down at a table in the corner near
the door that led into the dining room, sharing breakfast.

Geneva sopped up egg yolk with a piece of wheat toast.
"She don't . . . She doesn't like me neither," she grumbled,
and I knew exactly who we were talking about. "Always
talking about nobles oblige, whatever that is, and she says
I've got no class."

With a snicker, I told her exactly what I thought about
that. "You got the job here, didn't you? And I bet you work
plenty hard."

"Would like to," Geneva admitted. "We ain't . . ." As if
Muriel was actually there watching and tallying her every
grammatical error, Geneva glanced over her shoulder.
"We're not all that busy. Not like we used to be. What do
we have for reservations this week? Two lunches?" She
looked Quentin's way for confirmation.

"And three last week." He chomped a slice of bacon.
"Not like the old days, that's for sure."

"You've been here long?" I asked them.

"Me," Quentin said, "six years this August and every
day's the same. That Ms. Sadler . . ." He tore into a piece of
toast with his teeth. "Woman's like a broken record. She
never gets tired of telling me to cut my hair. She even expects

me to wear one of those sissy white chef hats. Yeah, like
that's going to keep my hair out of my eyes when I'm working. I ask to have things repaired and well, you see how
she's ignored me so far when it comes to the grill. I order
food and she calls our suppliers and changes the order.
How am I supposed to plan a menu when she does crap like
that? The other day, I wrote jambalaya out on the board and
I heard a couple of the ladies, they talked about how that
sounded so good. Only when I went to start cooking it, I
found out the tomatoes I ordered never came. Ms. Sadler,
she called and canceled the order." He growled, a powerful,
throaty sound. "She drives me up a wall and one of these
days . . ."

I knew better than to ask what he had planned for one of
these days.

I also knew better than to let him carry on and just get
angrier.

I turned in my chair to look at Geneva. "And you? How
long have you been here?"

"Six months, and I don't think Ms. Sadler wants me
around neither. I got hired by Ms. Martingale, the club's last
president. Real nice lady. She said she didn't care how I talk or
nothing like that. She said after a while my rough edges, they'd
get smoothed. She said what really mattered was how hard I
worked."

"So Muriel must be new to the job as president." I don't
know how, but this was something that had escaped my
notice until that moment. I guess because I thought it wasn't
important. I still wasn't sure it was. Well, except for how
Muriel taking the club's reins affected Quentin and Geneva.

I finished the last of my bacon, pushed back my chair,
and told Quentin, "I hope you don't think I'll expect breakfast every day."

He waved one meaty hand in my direction. "Anytime. You live here, right? The way I see it, the kitchen's yours to use. Feel free to cook for yourself, anytime you want. Only check the pantry before you do to make sure you have everything you need. And keep an eye on that grill."

Point taken.

I took my dishes over to the sink and rinsed them, then set them in the dishwasher. It was the first I noticed a sign hanging high up on the wall across the room. It was a funny little sign, homemade. Yellow background. Red letters, some of them a little wobbly, a little crooked.

Even if the sign didn't read *Dodie's Dumbwaiter*, I would have known what was behind the door it hung over.

I'd seen dumbwaiters in a number of the restaurants I'd worked in. They were a type of elevator, only they weren't big enough to carry people. They were designed to deliver dishes, like from the basement where they were washed to the first-floor kitchen, and they were usually operated by hand thanks to a system of pulleys.

"Who's Dodie?" I asked.

Quentin shook his head while he grabbed his dish and Geneva's. She shrugged.

"Whoever she was, she was gone long before we ever got here," Quentin told me. "The sign, I hear it's been there forever, and it just sort of stays there. You know, like a memorial or something."

It was one of the things I liked about PPWC from the moment I found the job opening online. There was a real sense of history in the building and, thinking about it, I made a mental note to myself to find someone to fix the grill and was smiling when I went upstairs to the Lilac Lounge to get it ready for Jack. It was the first I noticed the dumbwaiter on the far wall in there. So Dodie's Dumbwaiter ran from the kitchen directly up to Lilac. Or at least it used to. Something told me a dumbwaiter carrying hot food was not exactly something needed much these days at PPWC.

I'd just finished checking out the dumbwaiter when I saw Agnes out in the hallway.

"Good morning," I called to her.

She stopped dead in her tracks. "Good morning to you. It's awfully early for you to be working."

I glanced at the mess that was the Lilac Lounge. The day before, I managed to get two small writing desks and two reading chairs out of the way to (hopefully) make room for a desk big enough for Jack to work on. Before he left the day before, he'd told me he'd also need room for things like a worktable, supply shelves, and bookcases.

"I've got my work cut out for me," I told Agnes.

"I'm sorry." From the way her lips puckered and her nose twitched, I figured another fire apology was coming and I ignored it. As far as I was concerned, the woman didn't need to spend eternity doing penance for one stupid smoking mistake. She stepped into Lilac. "If there's anything I can do to help, let me know. It's the least I can do."

"You can tell me if we have tables somewhere. Big worktables. And a desk. And I know I shouldn't ask because there's no way it's in his job description, but do you think Quentin would mind helping me move some furniture?"

"He's got a good heart. And not much else to do down in the kitchen these days. You'll find some of the stuff you're looking for up in the attic, I think. Just don't let Muriel catch wind of what you're doing. Quentin and Muriel, they don't get along."

Sure, it was only my first day on the job, but I figured

there was no time like the present to start understanding the lay of the land. "Does she get along with anyone?"

Agnes had to think about this, and she never did answer. Maybe because she figured I already knew the answer.

"You'll want to be very careful," she said instead. "You know she's just itching to find some excuse to fire you."

I sucked in a breath. "But I just got hired."

"Uh-huh." The small smile that played around Agnes's mouth told me she felt a little sorry for me being simple. She stepped nearer, glanced over her shoulder, lowered her voice. "If it was up to Muriel, you never would have been. The rest of us, we loved you from the moment we met you. We knew you were the right woman for the job. But Muriel has other plans." Another step closer. "Muriel would like to see her granddaughter manage the club. Oh yes, make no mistake. That's exactly what she's been working to do ever since she took over as president. You don't need to be afraid." Agnes patted my hand because she apparently thought that me standing there with my mouth hanging open meant I was afraid rather than just stunned. "But you do need to watch your every step."

I guess there was no time like the present to start because no sooner were the words out of her mouth than Muriel swept into the room.

"Be careful." Agnes mouthed the word before she turned to Muriel to say good morning.

Muriel didn't bother with any pleasantries. "Need you downstairs, Agnes. Victoria Oldham is coming in this afternoon with her card group and you know how Victoria gets when the cushions on the chairs in the Carnation Room aren't just right. You're the only one who knows just how to fluff them."

"Certainly, Muriel." Agnes smiled. "I'll be along in a minute."

"And if you spend another minute in here, that's one more minute Avery's going to stand there doing nothing." Muriel lifted her chin, turned on her heels, and left.

Agnes didn't have much of a choice but to follow.

Muriel was like a winter cold front. She left everyone frozen in her path. Once she was gone, I shook the ice away and darted into the hallway.

"Muriel," I called after her. "I need to talk to you. It's about the kitchen."

She was nearly at the stairs and she moved aside so that Agnes could go down, then came back in my direction. "What about the kitchen?"

"The grill isn't working right. It needs a new thermostat. And Bill Manby isn't here to fix it."

Her lips puckered. Her eyes narrowed. "So they've got you on their side, do they?"

"I'm not sure who *they* are. And I don't think this is anything to take sides about. I only know the grill's not working right and someone needs to fix it."

Muriel turned away. "There's a toolbox in the basement somewhere," she told me. "I'm sure if you look hard enough, you can find it and get to work on the grill."

# CHAPTER 4

Remember what I said about Muriel's superpower? The one she uses to freeze people solid?

Like an evil sorceress, she used it again and again and I was rooted to the spot. At least for a second. Then a rush of anger melted the ice in my veins. Was I crazy to ignore Agnes's warning about how Muriel wanted to sack me? Maybe. But sometimes outrage trumps crazy.

"Hold on there, Muriel!" I stepped forward and I guess such a bold move caught her off guard because Muriel actually stepped back. "I don't think maintenance and repairs are something I'm supposed to be doing. You're the one who fired this Manby guy. Maybe you should be down in the kitchen fixing the grill."

That morning, Muriel was a vision in pink. Pink sheath dress. Pink jacket. Pink lipstick that matched both. But even the pink blush on her cheeks couldn't hide the fact that every ounce of color drained from her face. She lifted her pointy chin.

"How dare you!"

I closed in on her and hey, being nearly six feet tall has its advantages. From my lofty height, I was able to look down on Muriel—and on her condescending attitude. "I'll tell you how I dare. I'm here to make sure this club runs smoothly and efficiently. To handle the schedule, to make business contacts. To keep this place from sinking like a brick. I can't do that if I'm fixing a thermostat on a grill. And besides that, I can't fix the thermostat on a grill. I've got a lot of talents, but electrical engineering isn't one of them." I twirled around and marched to the other side of the room, the better to put some distance between myself and Muriel.

It worked. Away from the gravitational field that surrounded her and pulled everyone and everything into her nasty orbit, I was able to think more clearly.

"I'll put an ad online today for a maintenance man," I told Muriel in no uncertain terms. "With any luck, we'll have someone new aboard by next week."

"If I approve the hiring." She had the nerve to add a tsk to the statement. "After all, the board has a final say in who works here and who doesn't. If you're smart, you won't forget it."

She made to leave, but I wasn't finished yet, and my words stopped her in her tracks. "If the board has final say, why were you the one who fired Bill Manby? Seems to me no one else had any say in it at all."

Her eyes glinted like steel in the early morning light that flowed from the windows behind me. Her patrician nose (small and straight and as delicate as a rose) lifted a tad. "No one else knows the whole story."

"Then maybe now is a good time to tell it. You said you would. After I'd officially started. Well . . ." I lifted both arms, then slapped them back down to my sides. "Here I am. On the job."

"For now," Muriel reminded me.

My smile felt stiff, but I think it was pretty convincing. Cold and calculated, just like the knife-edged grin she shot back at me. In that one moment, we understood each other, me and Muriel. We both knew neither one of us would ever budge an inch.

"Start talking," I said.

Muriel did. "It's actually a kindness that I've kept my mouth shut this long about the whole Bill Manby incident. You see, I didn't want to ruin his reputation. Bill was stealing from the club."

I pulled in a breath but stopped myself just short of apologizing. I know, immature of me. After all, stealing was a serious offense, and Muriel had done what she had to do when it came to firing Bill. I wasn't prepared to own up to the fact that I'd judged her too quickly. But that didn't mean I couldn't be a grown-up about the whole thing.

I swallowed hard.

"I didn't know. I can understand why you fired him. What did he take?"

To Muriel's great credit, she didn't look smug at winning this round. At least not too smug. She clutched her hands at her waist. "Two stained glass lamps. A porcelain ewer and bowl. White, decorated with pink roses. And an oil portrait of Hortense Dash's little Percival. Sweet child. Golden ringlets. Angel smile. As difficult as it apparently is for you to believe it, I did my homework. And my research. I thoroughly investigated. I wouldn't have gotten rid of Bill if I hadn't. No one could have removed those items from the club except him. He was . . ." She glanced away, collecting herself, and darn if I didn't have any choice but to think she was sincere. "He was a good and conscientious worker and he'd given us years of loyal service. I don't know what happened to make him change, but after I discovered what was going on, I didn't have any choice. As much as it pained me, I had to let him go."

And there I was, frozen again, feeling like a fool for challenging her when obviously she'd made a tough decision because she knew it was the right thing to do.

I actually might have admitted it if I had the chance. But just as I opened my mouth, the lights flickered off. Ten seconds later, they flashed on again.

Muriel didn't seem surprised. In fact, she didn't even comment until she sailed out of the room and was already in the hallway. "The fuse box in the basement is testy," she called back to me. "The lights go out all the time. We've got flashlights on the windowsills of every room, just in case. When you're finished fixing the grill in the kitchen, that fuse box should be the next thing on your repair list."

In that one moment, I felt Quentin Cruz's pain.

If there were a pot holder nearby, I would have thrown it.

Then again, if I did throw a pot holder, I wouldn't have hit Muriel because just that quickly, she was gone.

And I probably would have kerthunked Jack Harkness, because the next thing I knew he strode into the Lilac Lounge.

He had three rolls of wallpaper under one arm, a briefcase packed to overflowing under the other, and if he heard me muttering to myself, he ignored it. Just like he ignored it when, too agitated to keep still and wishing there was a pot holder handy, I slapped a hand against the nearest delicate writing table.

Jack juggled everything he was carrying and one of the rolls of wallpaper slipped to the floor. "No desk?" he asked.

It's the kind of question that needs to register before it's answered, and once it did, I propped my fists on my hips. "No desk. Not yet. And there won't be one if you're not willing to help me find one and move it in here."

He plopped the other two rolls of wallpaper and his briefcase on the floor before he pushed his glasses up on the bridge of his nose. "Of course. Only before you commit the club's resources and any more time or energy into this project, I think there's something you should know." He cleared his throat and steadied his shoulders and I swear, he looked like a kid who'd been asked to give a book report up in front of the class.

"I was wrong," Jack said.

Apparently this was something of a momentous announcement, at least if the tightness of his jaw and the stiffness of his shoulders meant anything.

It was enough to make me wish I'd had a third cup of coffee.

I shook my head, hoping to clear it.

It didn't help.

"Wrong about what?" I asked him.

He cleared his throat. Again. "The wallpaper in Marigold. I said it went into production in 1945. I checked my research last night and I thought it was important for you to know right up front before we went any farther with the project. The wallpaper was actually printed in 1946."

I didn't even bother to stifle my laugh. "You're kidding, right?"

He actually had to think about my reaction for a minute, and while he did, his mouth settled into a thin line and his forehead furrowed. "You mean you don't mind that I was inaccurate?"

"Look . . ." I drew in a long breath and let it out again on the end of a sigh. "I've got a kitchen grill that isn't working, a electrical system that likes to go on the fritz, a former maintenance man who is also a thief, and a club president who would like nothing better than to serve my head on a silver platter. You really think I care what year the wallpaper was printed?"

He glanced over his shoulder, out into the hallway, where only minutes before Muriel had been standing.

"Silver platter, huh? What's her problem?" he asked.

"Apparently she wants her granddaughter to get my job. And just for the record, I'm not going to let that happen. I'm stubborn like that."

He smiled and some of the Muriel-induced tension that had knotted my insides like a tightly wound rubber band eased up just like that. "Good for you. Don't let her push you around."

"I have a feeling before Marigold is back in shape, I'll be offering you the same advice."

"Muriel?" He made a face. "She doesn't scare me." He gave me a wink. "She doesn't know how to hang wallpaper, and I do."

It was something of a shock when I realized Jack Harkness had a superpower completely opposite Muriel's. She could freeze with a glance. And Jack? He had a smile and a warm sense of humor.

"So . . ." He rubbed his hands together. "Where will we find my desk?"

"Upstairs, I've been told." I pointed toward the ceiling. "In my part of the house." His blank expression meant he didn't need to ask. "I live here," I explained. "At least, I'm going to live here until I can save up enough money to buy a house of my own. I'm staying in the old servants' quarters."

"Cool." His eyes glistened, but then, I guess talking about the interesting ins and outs of old mansions is a sure way to a restorationist's heart. "Maybe . . ." He took his time gathering the words. "Maybe we can get together sometime?"

A date?

Even I was a little surprised he'd come right out and asked so quickly. But now that Jack was smiling and animated, now that he was actually engaged in conversation rather than pressing his nose to the vintage wallpaper in Marigold, it hit me that there was a lot about him that was attractive.

Great smile. No denying that.

Right thinking. He'd encouraged me not to give into Muriel's bullying.

Good taste. He had, after all, seen something in me he found appealing.

That being said, I'm grateful I never let the word— *date*—slip from my lips because the next thing out of Jack's mouth was, "I'm fascinated with light fixtures from the early twentieth century, when this house was built, and my guess is as time went on, they weren't updated in the servants' quarters like they must have been in the rest of the house. Maybe sometime I can come upstairs and have a look?"

I ignored the little spurt of disappointment that reminded me that jumping to conclusions was always a bad idea and made sure I added a smile so he'd never suspect that I'd nearly made a royal fool of myself. "That's what you meant by getting together?"

"Well, I wouldn't want to go up there without your permission."

"Whatever," I mumbled to myself and then, louder, told him, "Sure," when I headed for the door.

Jack followed me. "Great." He rolled up the sleeves of his white shirt. "Let's get to work."

Work we did, and thank goodness Quentin wasn't busy in the kitchen and was able to help. By early afternoon, we'd brought a desk, two worktables, a desk chair, a guest chair, and three bookcases into the Lilac Lounge, and we'd taken away the furniture that was in there before the transformation and carried it upstairs. I put one of the pretty little writing desks in my own rooms. The rest went into storage in the vast, drafty attic.

The unpacking and arranging, that was up to Jack, and watching him get to it, I stepped back and wiped a long cobweb from the front of my shirt. It was the first I realized that I had a smudge of dirt on my sleeve—I swiped at that, to no avail—and that my shoes were coated with dust.

"I've got a chamber of commerce meeting to head off to," I told Jack. "Looks like I'll need to change before I go. You've got everything you need?"

He'd already been down to his car for a crate of books and he was bent over it, emptying it book by book, peering at the spines, arranging them on the shelves. "I'm good," he said. "See you tomorrow."

The rest of the day passed at the speed of light. A quick shower. A change of clothes. A trip across town (I only got lost once) to the restaurant where every month, members of the Portage Path Chamber of Commerce got together to network. I was the new kid on the block, and as such, they gave me five minutes to introduce myself to the group and talk about my background. While I was at it, I reminded them all that the building that belonged to the Portage Path Women's Club was beautiful, historic—and ideal for meetings, weddings, and retirement parties. By the time I talked one on one with members over dinner and listened to a guest speaker who touted the benefits of social media for small businesses, I was whooped. But my day wasn't done. I stopped at the grocery store for basic supplies like peanut butter (in my humble opinion, the most perfect food on earth), sparkling water, canned soup, a bottle of wine, and some snacks.

It was early October, and by the time I arrived back at the club, it was dark.

No worries. The light above the main entrance went on dusk to dawn and, of course, I had a key. I went inside, rode the elevator to the second floor, then climbed the steps from there to my rooms on the third floor.

Once upon a time, the third floor had bustled with activity. When the Dennisons, the family of prestigious moguls who had built the house, were in residence, I imagined they had an army of servants, and there was room after room up there, some of them once used as sleeping quarters, others with brass plates outside their doors that said things like, *Ironing Room*, and *Linens*. According to what I'd been told when I hired on, my suite—a sitting room, a bath, a tiny bedroom, and a kitchen just big enough for a microwave and a mini fridge—had once belonged to the housekeeper, and as such, was the finest set of rooms on the floor.

At that point, fine was the last thing on my mind. I was bone tired, and I'd promised Aunt Rosemary I would call.

First I'd check in with my aunt, then I'd celebrate surviving my first day on the job with a glass of wine and some cheese and crackers.

It wasn't until I pulled out my phone that I realized it was nearly out of juice. So the cheese and crackers and wine would come first, I told myself, while the phone was on the charger. And that wasn't such a bad thing.

Smiling, I pushed open the door to my suite, touched a hand to the switch on the wall.

And stopped dead in my tracks.

My room had been trashed!

I looked around—at the suitcases I had yet had time to empty now spilled on the floor, at the books that were once a neat TBR pile and were now strewn everywhere, at my notebook computer, open and running, even though I knew I'd shut it down before I left that afternoon.

My stomach bunched. My throat soured. The front door had been locked when I arrived back at the club and the security system was activated, which meant this had happened sometime before the last member had left for the day and locked the door behind her.

But who could have done such a thing?

And why?

I'd barely had a chance to wonder when all the lights flickered.

They winked.

They blinked.

And they finally went off.

# CHAPTER 5

I counted to ten.

The lights did not come back on.

I waited longer.

Nothing.

"Don't panic. Don't panic," I reminded myself and maybe I would have actually listened to the advice if I could hear my own voice above the noise of the jackhammering inside my chest. Someone had been in my rooms. Someone had been pawing through my things. Someone who might still be lurking—somewhere—in the dark.

My first thought was to grab my phone, to call the cops then activate the flashlight app. But no juice, remember.

My second thought?

Sad to say, it was Muriel.

Well, not exactly Muriel. More like something Muriel had said to me earlier in the day.

"Flashlights!" The word bumped along on my uneven

breaths, and I carefully maneuvered my way through the dark, over my spilled suitcase and my tumbled books, toward the windows that looked out at the back of the building. "A flashlight on every windowsill. That's what Muriel said."

It wasn't on windowsill number one. It wasn't on windowsill number two. I'd pretty much convinced myself that the servants' quarters and the business manager who lived in them weren't deemed worthy of a flashlight when I groped around the sill of window number three and my hand met cold metal.

Like I was drowning and it was a life preserver, I grabbed it and held on tight, then turned on the flashlight.

Nothing happened.

People everywhere know there is only one cure for a nonworking flashlight. With the flat of my hand, I gave it a thwack.

The magic worked.

The flashlight flicked on.

The beam of light was yellow and anemic, but hey, it was light, and I followed its feeble shaft over and around the mess, and got down the stairs to the first floor. I'd never been in the basement of the club, but I knew the access door was just off the main entryway. While I stutter stepped my way there, I realized that for the first time, I was grateful for the undependable electricity in Aunt Rosemary's house, the weird flickering of lights, and the fact that they sometimes turned on or off all by themselves. Aunt Rosemary, bless her wacky little heart, attributed it all to the influence of Spirit. I knew better, and early on, I'd learned to change a fuse like a pro.

All I had to do was hope that the flashlight wouldn't poop out before I found the fuses and the fuse box and that the person who'd made a mess of my possessions wasn't waiting in the shadows to ambush me. Finally where I was supposed to be, I pulled in a breath, steadied my shoulders, and yanked open the basement door.

A current of chilly air slapped my face. The scent of mildew and history wrapped around me and made my nose twitch. I started down. The railing on my left was wobbly, so I didn't dare hold on too tight, but I glided my fingers along the surface, using it as a guide, inching my way down, my light barely strong enough to illuminate the next step in front of me.

When I stepped on something big and soft, I sucked in a breath of surprise that turned into a screech when my feet went out from under me. I made a grab for the railing, but it bowed and that threw me even more off-kilter. After that, it was impossible to keep upright. My feet tangled, my knees gave way, and then everything was a blur.

I wheeled. I tumbled. With a thud, I landed on the basement floor on my butt.

It took me a while to catch my breath. A minute, two, maybe more. At the same time my head spun, I thanked my lucky stars I hadn't landed on it. I was sore, sure, and I'd be black and blue by morning, but I was pretty sure nothing was broken.

To test the theory, I wiggled my toes and stretched my arms over my head. It was the first I registered the fact that when I'd fallen, the flashlight had jumped out of my hand. It was ten feet across the basement, spinning, spinning, its light making crazy pinwheel patterns on the paneled walls. It stopped finally (which was a good thing because I was already dizzy from the fall and the whirling light didn't help), its pallid glow illuminating a small patch of plain, unremarkable wall.

That is, until that patch glistened like moonlight on water.

My eyes were playing tricks on me. I was sure of it. I rubbed them, but that didn't change a thing. In fact, it only made the weird lights brighter. The glistening settled into a shiny smudge, the smudge came into focus around the edges. It formed a picture. A picture of a woman.

She was wearing light-colored shoes that tied with a showy satin bow at the instep and had short chunky heels. Her stockings were rolled below her knees, just inches from the hem of a dropped-waist, tube-shaped dress covered with beads.

Her dark hair was cut in a short sleek bob, and she wore a headband decorated with beads and feathers.

I tallied the details in a flash. Right before she moved and I realized she wasn't a picture at all. The surprise of seeing the woman standing there kicked me in the gut.

I was up on my feet in a flash just as she stepped closer. "Hey, sister, that was quite a tumble. Everything jake?" she asked.

I didn't know who this Jake guy was, or what he had to do with any of this; I only knew that a sudden burst of outrage overwhelmed even my fear.

"Who are you?" I demanded. "What are you doing here?"

The woman flinched. Right before she smiled. "If that ain't the cat's particulars! You mean you can see me? You can hear me?"

"Of course I can." Sure not to take my eyes off her, I sidestepped over to where the flashlight lay and made a grab for it. I wasn't sure who I was dealing with and I felt better with a weapon—a lame weapon, but a weapon nonetheless—in my hands. "What, you thought you could hide down here and no one would be any wiser? You should have known I'd find you sooner or later. What were you doing up in my rooms?"

"You're all wet!" She waved a hand in my direction and now that she was standing closer and I was able to shine the flashlight directly at her, I saw that she was younger than I first thought. Not a woman. More like a girl. Twenty if she was a day and trying her darnedest to look older thanks to bright red lipstick on Cupid's bow lips and smoky eyes outlined all around with kohl.

I watched her glance around the basement. "I ain't left here. Not for a long time."

"Oh yeah?" Not the best comeback, I admit that, but the only thing I could think to say. That is, right before logic kicked in. "The door is locked. I know because I had to unlock it when I got back this evening. If you've been here a long time, how did you get in?"

"I was invited." She had a dainty nose and she lifted it in the air. "By none other than old man Dennison himself."

"Dennison? Well, he's not a member of the club—I know that for sure, since the club is only open to women. And there's no Mrs. Dennison on the roster." Still, the name tickled a memory in the back of my mind and when it did, my mouth dropped open. "Cut the bull! Dennison? Chauncey Dennison built this house more than one hundred years ago so I'm pretty sure he's not hanging around inviting people over. You're going to need to come up with a better story than that once the cops get here and ask what you were doing in my rooms and what you took."

"Poor little bunny, you don't know the worst of it." She pursed her lips. "You got bigger things to worry about than me, don't you think?"

I tightened my grip on the flashlight and did my best to

sound braver than I felt. "I don't know what you're talking about."

"Dumb Dora," she mumbled, and she pointed to the stairs behind me.

I turned that way.

Pink.

Even in the odd half darkness, the color was unmistakable. Pink sheath dress. Pink jacket. If Muriel Sadler wasn't crumpled facedown on the stairs, I bet I would have seen her pink lipstick and blusher, too.

Even without getting closer, I knew something was terribly wrong. Muriel's body was bent into impossible angles. Her left leg was out, her right leg was tucked up under her. Her arms hung limp at her sides. When I inched nearer, I saw the back of her skull was bashed in and bloody.

Maybe to stifle a scream, maybe to keep the sourness that filled my throat from escaping, I clamped a hand over my mouth and stared for I don't know how long. At least until I told myself that was no way to handle an emergency.

With one breath for courage and another to settle the wild beating of my heart, I closed in on Muriel and when I touched her neck to check for a pulse, my hand shook.

No pulse. No movement. She was already a little cold.

My brain spun and I scrambled for something that evenly vaguely resembled a plan. It was that or give in to the terror that gripped me. First I'd tell the girl in the strange clothes to stay put and not to touch anything. That's what I'd do. Then I'd go upstairs and call the cops.

My mind made up, I spun to face her.

The girl was gone.

"You can't hide down here forever," I called and hoped she'd hear me wherever she'd scampered off to. "This is the only door in or out of the basement." I did not know this to be true, but it sure sounded good. "You stay right . . ." I skimmed my flashlight over the area. The basement steps ended in a wide hallway that dissolved into the darkness both to the left and to the right of me. From the looks of the deeper blotches pressed into the shadow to my left, there were a number of rooms down that way. One of them was probably the electrical room, where I would have found the fuse box. To my right, the hallway opened into a room big enough that it was impossible for my light to penetrate the gloom.

"You stay right where you are!" I finished the order with as much gumption as a woman scared out of her wits could and, careful not to disturb Muriel, I hopped over her body and raced up the stairs.

The front door of the club, just feet from my desk, was flanked by wide windows, and here the glow of the security lights out in the parking lot seeped in, cold and pale. I grabbed the phone on my desk, dialed 911, and told them about the emergency, about the body.

The dispatcher who answered ordered me to stay put and wait, and said the cops would be there soon and I should keep calm, but really, I wondered if she'd ever had to deal with a pitch-dark mansion, an odd intruder, and the body of a little-loved club president.

Too antsy to keep still, I paced from my desk back over to the basement door.

"I've called the cops," I yelled down into the darkness because if nothing else, it made me feel like I had control. Over something. "There's no use hiding. They're on their way."

And I knew they were. And that they'd be there soon.

But hey, they say discretion is the better part of valor. And this girl is no Dumb Dora, in spite of what some people might say.

Rather than sit there in the dark and think about Muriel and the girl who was probably a burglar and who might be a killer, I raced to the front door, unlocked it, and waited outside for the police.

I should have known it wouldn't take long. On the whole, Portage Path is a safe community, at least if what I'd heard that evening at the chamber of commerce meeting was true. The cops didn't have a lot to keep them busy and, of course, I'd used the magic words, *dead body*.

Two black-and-white patrol cars raced into the parking lot, sirens blaring and lights flashing. They were followed by an unmarked car with a pulsing blue light in the front window. The unmarked car stopped closest to the building and a young man in a raincoat jumped out.

"You the one who called?" he wanted to know. "Where's the victim?"

As anxious as I was to get out of the building, the fresh air hadn't revived me the way I'd hoped. My movements were stiff, my brain was foggy. It took some effort, but I managed to nod and point to the front door.

The guy in the raincoat stepped aside and let three of the uniformed officers go into the club ahead of him. The fourth guy—fresh-faced and looking a little worried—was ordered to stay outside and keep an eye on me.

"Where?" was all the guy in the raincoat asked.

I swallowed the sand in my throat. "Basement steps."

Naturally, the cops tried to turn on the lights inside the door and when that didn't work, they flipped on flashlights. I had never had flashlight envy before, but one look at the powerful beams and the pure white light, and I sighed.

But then, I'm pretty sure I wasn't thinking straight.

"You all right, miss?" the cop who stayed with me asked.

If only I knew the answer! And, really, it hardly seemed to matter, not right then and there. What did matter . . .

I snapped to and shook my head. "There's an intruder in the basement," I told the cop and I guess I sounded convincing enough because he radioed the other cops and told them what I'd said.

There was a pretty wooden bench nearby with an elaborately carved back, and without asking the cop's permission, I went over to it and sat down. It was that or collapse into a puddle of mush right there at the front entrance of the Portage Path Women's Club. The very thought made me wonder, "What would Muriel think about that?"

My second thought was to close my eyes and try to make the image of her, bloodied and crumpled, vanish. I lost track of time and before I knew it, there was more commotion—a crime scene team arrived; another two patrol cars showed up; the neighbors, alerted by the lights and noise, gathered around the perimeter of the parking lot; and one of the newly arrived cops was sent to keep things under control.

Eventually, the lights inside the club snapped on, and automatically I breathed a sigh of relief. At that moment, there was something about dispelling shadows that seemed to matter. It wasn't too long after that the cop in the raincoat came back outside. He sat down next to me and flashed a badge.

"Sergeant Alterman," he said. "And you are . . . ?"

Honestly, I had to think about it, and I guess that didn't make a good impression, because Alterman leaned forward, face squinched with the sort of expectant look that

said he wasn't holding his breath and waiting for my answer
so much as he was thinking I'd better hop to. He had dark
hair and dark eyes and even though he was no more than
thirty-five, he was obviously in charge. I wondered if the
older, more experienced cops resented him.

And told myself to get my act together.

I cleared my throat. "Avery Morgan. I'm the club manager."

"You're managing the club awfully late tonight, aren't
you?"

It took a couple seconds for me to get his drift. "I live
here. Up on the third floor."

"Do you know why the victim was in the building?"

*The victim.*

The words had a funny sound to them, like metal scrap-
ing metal.

"Her name is Muriel Sadler," I told him. "She is . . ." I
swallowed hard. "She was the president of the club."

"What was she doing here this evening?"

I don't suppose shrugging counts as an answer, but it
was all I could think to do. "As president, she has . . . er,
had . . . an office on the second floor. I guess she could have
been working. But I don't know, I was out," I explained. "At
a chamber of commerce meeting. I didn't get back until just
a little while ago."

"Can anyone verify that?"

It took a second for me to realize what he was getting
at. Was I a suspect? As crazy as it seemed, it was only
natural for him to wonder, and hey, the man was just doing
his job.

I weighed my words carefully. Sergeant Alterman
needed the truth and he needed it fast. Wasting his time

with me when the real killer was out there somewhere would get him nowhere. "Anyone at the chamber of commerce meeting will tell you I was there," I said. "It was a dinner. And there was a speaker. You know, the usual networking sort of thing. After I left there, I went to the grocery store and . . ." Luckily, I'd stuck the receipt for my groceries in the pocket of my jacket, and I fished it out and handed it to him. "You can see the time there. I came back here straight from the grocery store."

"And that's when you found Ms. Sadler."

I shook my head. "That's when the lights went out. It's an old building; they do that all the time. I went downstairs to replace the fuse and . . ." Just like that, the image of Muriel on the stairs came screaming back at me and I choked over my words. "That's when I found Muriel. But that was after I was upstairs and saw that my room was trashed."

This was not something Sergeant Alterman was expecting. He ran a hand through his hair and sat back. "Who did that?"

"Well, I don't know, do I? And I was all set to call the police about it, but that's when the lights went out and then I went into the basement and . . ." Another memory washed over me. "And there was a woman down there."

Alterman sat up straighter. "So I heard. Did you know her? A member of the club?"

Another shake of my head.

"Can you describe her?"

"Young," I told him. "Dressed weird. Like in a costume." I swung toward the building, ready to stand. "She's got to still be in there."

He put a hand on my arm. "We'll look."

"She could be the one who . . ." I couldn't bring myself

to say the word *murder*. It burned my lips. It cracked my heart. "Maybe she hurt Muriel."

"Maybe." Something told me it was as much of a definitive statement as I'd get out of him. "You can be sure we'll look into it. For now . . ." When a man in coveralls came out of the building, Alterman stood and stepped back. "This is Jason Starks," he said. "Jason is from our crime scene investigation unit. He's going to look you over and take some samples."

"It will only take a minute," Jason told me. He checked my hands and had me stand so he could check out my clothes. When he was all done, he told Alterman, "There's a little bit of blood on her hand."

"I checked for a pulse," I explained. "When I found Muriel, I checked to see if she was still . . ." I hiccupped over the word. "Alive."

"She could have changed after she killed Ms. Sadler." Alterman said this to Jason Starks, but the message was clearly meant for me, and it had its intended affect. My knees shook like jelly.

"She could have," Jason agreed. "And if she did, we'll find the clothes here somewhere. The victim's been dead between three and four hours."

When he walked away, I told Alterman, "You won't find bloody clothes that belong to me. I didn't kill her."

"I didn't say you did."

"But you have to check."

"Ducks in a row." He gave me a careful look. "You need some coffee or something?"

"I just bought of bottle of wine at the grocery store. That's what I really need."

He smiled as if he understood, but unfortunately, he didn't agree. He got out his wallet, handed the cop who'd been watching me earlier a wad of cash, and told him to find the nearest take-out place.

"You don't need to do that. I can make coffee." I stood. "That is, if I can use the club kitchen."

"Any chance of sandwiches?" Alterman wanted to know.

I was about to tell him that I couldn't eat a bite, not after everything I'd seen that night, when I realized he wasn't talking about sandwiches for me. He and the other cops were hard at work, and who knew how long they'd have to be there at PPWC.

"I'll check," I told him.

The same young cop who'd been told to keep an eye on me earlier—his name was Danny—accompanied me to the kitchen, and together, we rooted through the fridge and came up with enough turkey and roast beef to make up a sandwich platter. There was a loaf of pretty-fresh bread to go with the meat, and I found a jar of pickles in the pantry. When I had it all assembled and a pot of coffee brewing, Danny radioed Alterman and he came to the kitchen. He looked over the tray where I'd arranged everything and nodded with appreciation. "You going to eat?" he asked.

I looked at the roast beef, dripping with juices, and my stomach soured. "I think I'll stick to coffee. When can I get back into my room?"

He wrinkled his nose by way of telling me he had no idea, and once he left to put the food out in the dining room and to put the word out to the other cops that there were sandwiches available anytime they were ready for a break, I plunked down on the chair where only that morning, I'd had breakfast with Quentin and Geneva.

"Long night, huh?" Danny the cop had made a sandwich for himself while we were setting out the food and he brought it over to the table and sat down. "What are you going to do now?"

I knew the answer.

I just didn't want to face it.

"Now . . ." I finished the coffee in my cup for courage. "Now I have no choice. I've got to call the board."

# CHAPTER 6

The members of the board were appropriately shocked by the news.

But this was, after all, the Portage Path Women's Club, and even word of its president's death was not enough to keep these women from their duty. They'd been raised right. With plenty of money. Each of them knew in her heart of hearts that she had obligations—to country, to family, to the city of Portage Path. Most of all, they believed they had an obligation to PPWC, and far be it from any of them to shirk it.

It was the middle of the night.

They showed up at the club anyway, and in record time.

Patricia bustled in first, a little out of breath, a little disheveled, and wearing jeans and a navy-blue sweatshirt. The color matched the bruise on her cheek, which hadn't been there when I saw her earlier in the day.

Of course I asked, "What happened?"

Patricia plunked down at a table in the dining room with its dainty tables, its wallpaper of pink and white roses, and pictures of old-time Portage Path in elaborate frames on all the walls. The kitchen, this one table in the dining room, and everything else in the club was off limits to us at the moment, including my rooms. Sergeant Alterman's orders. He made sure of it by leaving us under the watchful gaze of Danny, who for the record, was now on his third sandwich and had a plate of chocolate chip cookies in front of him. At the same time I wondered where he'd found the cookies, my stomach heaved to remind me eating was a very bad idea.

"Oh, this." Patricia fingered the bruise and leaned nearer. "Don't tell the others. There's no way they'd understand not having a professional in to do the job. But some of us are more self-sufficient than others. I'm sure you understand." She gave me a conspiratorial wink. "I was installing a new J-trap in the sink in my downstairs bathroom and the screwdriver slipped."

"Do you need ice?"

She waved away my concern. "I could use a couple of those cookies, though," she said and when she leaned forward to snatch a couple cookies off Danny's dish, her sleeve rode up and I saw there was a bruise on her arm, too.

Dangerous things, screwdrivers.

Gracie came in next looking appropriately solemn in gray pants and a thundercloud-colored sweater. Agnes followed. Like the others, I was sure she'd been in bed when I called and had dressed in a hurry. That would explain why she was wearing a lovely beige suit, a string of pearls—and pink fuzzy bunny slippers.

The last person to arrive was Valentina Hanover, the one member of the board I'd never met. Valentina, the club secretary, was in Europe when I interviewed for the job, and in fact, according to what she'd told me when I called her about Muriel's passing, she'd just returned. I'd caught her at the airport just as she was picking up her luggage.

She was younger than the others, a lithe, elegant woman with wide dark eyes, inky hair, and dusky skin. Her makeup was perfect. Her jewelry was tasteful. She traveled in style—white linen suit that was as crisp and as unwrinkled as if it had just come from the cleaners, expensive handbag, stilettoes that would have made me scream in pain within three minutes of slipping them on. Looking that good and that fresh after traveling a few thousand miles should be illegal. Valentina pulled it off like a pro.

I brought a carafe of coffee and some cups to the table.

"We should be serving you." To prove it, Valentina took the carafe from me and shooed me into the nearest chair. She filled coffee cups and passed them around. "You've had a horrible shock, Avery."

"Terrible thing." Gracie's eyes welled. "Terrible, terrible thing."

I couldn't even begin to tally how much coffee I'd had since I discovered Muriel's body, but when Valentina handed me a cup I accepted it and sipped. If I was thinking straight, if I cared, I would have been worried that I wouldn't sleep for a week. The way it was, I was pretty sure it didn't matter. I wasn't going to sleep anytime soon, anyway, not with the nightmare image of Muriel's dead body stuck in my head.

I glanced around the table at the women. Their eyes were sad, their gazes were fixed on their cups, as if looking deep enough into the black liquid might provide some answers. "The police are going to want to talk to each of you," I told them.

"Talk? To us?" Gracie gulped.

"Of course," Patricia said.

"I'm afraid I won't be able to help them," Valentina cooed.

"I can't imagine why." By way of emphasizing her point, Agnes harrumphed.

"You all knew her well," I pointed out. "And the police are naturally going to want your input."

"I hope that Sergeant Alterman interviews me." Gracie had obviously met the sergeant on her way to the dining room, and now she flapped a hand on her chest, like a cartoon character showing a wildly beating heart. "He's a looker!"

Patricia rolled her eyes.

What they didn't know was that I'd talked to Sergeant Alterman too, just minutes before they arrived. I knew something I hadn't been able to tell them when I talked to each of them on the phone earlier.

I cleared my throat and did my best to force the words out from behind the lump of emotion that blocked my breath. "She was . . ." I coughed. "The police are sure Muriel was murdered."

I don't need to report how they responded, to talk about the gasps, the tears, the moans. It was Valentina who came to her senses first. She clutched her hands together on the table in front of her and looked me in the eye.

"How can they be sure?" she asked.

"They'll give you the details." I looked over my shoulder when I said this, out to the hallway, where now and again, we could see a uniformed police officer come up from the basement and head outside or a crime scene tech come in the door with an equipment case in hand. "What they told me was that it was obvious Muriel had died somewhere else, that her body had been dragged over to the basement door and . . ." It was nearly too painful to put into words. "Just tossed down."

There were more tears, more sobs, and there was nothing I could do but let them cry themselves out. When they were done, I said, "So maybe we should talk about this before the police question all of us. What do any of you know? Who would want Muriel dead?"

At that time and in that place, the last thing I expected to hear was a laugh, but laugh Patricia did. "Anyone who ever met her," she said.

Accurate or not, the comment was callous, and her fellow board members told Patricia so, but rather than be penitent, Patricia sat up straight and sent a laser look around the table from woman to woman.

"Oh, come off it, girls! Every single one of us knows what a mean, nasty person Muriel was. There's no use pretending otherwise now that she's gone. Talk about revisionist history! Agnes, all you've wanted your whole life was to be president of the club, and when Muriel got the position, well, you tried to hide it, but we all could tell how upset you were."

"Upset, maybe," Agnes admitted. "But that doesn't mean—"

"And Valentina." Patricia swung her gaze that way. "We all knew how much Muriel disliked you. She never thought you were good enough for the club. You were Bob Hanover's secretary at the bank, and if Bob hadn't divorced his first wife, and you hadn't married Bob and his millions, there's no way you would have ever been accepted as a member here."

To this, Valentina didn't say a word. She just sat, as still and as cold as an ice sculpture.

"And you, Gracie." Patricia was next to Gracie and she patted the older woman's hand, not as accusatory now as she was consoling. "It's no secret that Muriel wanted you to resign as club historian. She thought you were off your game."

"Oh come on!" Gracie snorted. "Let's not be so polite about it. She didn't think I was off my game, she thought I was off my rocker! That I was too old to know what I was doing."

Patricia nodded. "Exactly. So you see, if someone wants to know who might have killed Muriel, you all had reasons."

"Don't leave yourself off the list, Patricia," Agnes snapped.

"All right. I admit it." Like she was surrendering, Patricia threw her hands in the air. "I didn't get along with Muriel. The woman was hidebound and old-fashioned. I want to see this club grow and flourish. I don't want it to disappear. If Muriel would have just listened to me and opened the club up to be more inclusive—"

"It's never going to happen," Agnes mumbled.

"You know how she treated me because she thought I was from some lower class than she was. Just a secretary," Valentina added. "If we had more regular people here as members rather than just the Portage Path elite, she would have treated them just as badly."

"She would have gotten over it," Patricia insisted. "It is, after all, how all progress is made. This club is a dinosaur, and if we were more inclusive—"

"That's what you said yesterday." Believe me, I didn't mean to sound like I was pointing fingers, but the memory came back at me and the words just fell out of my mouth. "When you and Muriel were arguing in the lobby while we waited for Jack Harkness to arrive. Patricia, you said something about being more inclusive, and Muriel, she said—"

"Over my dead body!" The way Agnes breathed the words, her voice sounded like it came from beyond the grave.

"Oh my!" Gracie picked at the white linen tablecloth with nervous fingers.

"She said that?" Valentina gasped.

"It's not like it actually meant anything," Patricia insisted. "It's just a thing people say. And besides . . ." She tucked her hands in her lap. "Just because Muriel said what she said doesn't mean I killed her. Let's not forget, Muriel was gunning for Avery, too."

When they protested, I shushed them all with a wave of both hands. "According to Agnes," I said, "Muriel wanted her granddaughter to have my job. So . . ." I looked from woman to woman. "Why didn't she get it?"

Agnes's chin came up. "Because we didn't let her get it."

"Because you're better qualified," Patricia added.

"And a much nicer person," Gracie put in.

Agnes made a face. "Although you were the only one here after hours, Avery. The police are sure to make a note of that."

"A note of what?"

Sergeant Alterman could be stealthy. None of us had heard him come into the room. At the same time I wondered how much he'd heard, I gave him as much of a smile as I could muster. "What can we do for you?"

"You can cancel any activities you have tomorrow."

Far be it from me to tell him I'd been so busy—what with setting up the Lilac Lounge for Jack's use, and attending a chamber of commerce meeting, and finding a dead body in the basement—I had no idea what was on the calendar for the next day.

As if I did and just needed to confirm it, I walked out of the dining room and over to my desk near the front door and Sergeant Alterman trailed along.

I tapped the keyboard to make my computer come alive and clicked my way through to the right program.

The next day's schedule was completely empty.

I closed down the program before Alterman could see and realize how pathetic it was.

"I'll take care of it," I told him. "In the morning."

This was enough to satisfy him. At least for now. He leaned back against the wall and folded his arms over his chest. So much had happened since I'd found Muriel's body, I hadn't had much of a chance to check out Sergeant Alterman. Now I saw that aside from that dark hair and those dark eyes I'd noticed earlier, he had an appealing face. He wasn't exactly handsome. His nose was a little crooked and there was a bulge on the bridge of it that told me he'd had it broken a time or two. His mouth was a little big. So were his ears. He was . . . I took a moment to try and define the impression I got from the man . . . interesting. Sergeant Alterman was interesting looking. Somewhere along the way, he'd taken off his raincoat. He was wearing khaki pants and a dark golf shirt and anyone who didn't know who he was or why he was there might have thought he was just passing the time there at PPWC.

He wasn't.

He gave an eagle-eyed glance toward the dining room. "How are they taking the news?"

"As well as can be expected, I suppose," I told him. "The women here at the club have known one another for years. A lot of them grew up together, went to school together. It's not easy to lose a friend, and when one of them dies the way Muriel did . . ." A shiver raced across my shoulders. "They'll be all right. They're tougher than they look."

The expression that crossed his face wasn't quite a smile. "How about you?"

I would have stood right there and lied to the man, told him I was fine, thank you very much, if at that moment, a team from the medical examiner's office didn't walk up the basement steps carrying a stretcher with a black body bag on it.

My throat clutched and silently, side by side, Alterman and I watched them walk out the door.

"Who else has keys?" I don't think it was an accident that he saved the question for the exact moment the door closed behind the men taking the body outside. Maybe he wanted to catch me when my guard was down. Maybe he was doing his best to distract me, and if that was the case, I appreciated it.

I swung around to face him. Standing this close, it was the first I realized that I was a titch taller than him. "Well, I guess . . ." I could stand there and keep trying to sound like I knew what I was talking about, or I could level with the guy. Alterman's dark eyes were perceptive, his gaze was steady without being aggressive. From what I'd seen of him, he was straightforward and plain talking. The kind of man who appreciated the truth and didn't have time for anything else.

"Today . . ." I happened to glance at the clock on the wall. It was three thirty in the morning. "Yesterday was my first day on the job," I told him. "I don't have all the answers you need."

Again, he looked toward the dining room. "But they might."

When he went to talk to the board, I trailed along. He hadn't told me not to, and besides, I was curious to hear what the member of the board would have to say—about Muriel, about their relationships with Muriel.

"Ladies." Alterman nodded a greeting and when Gracie waved him into a chair, he declined. In spite of the time, he looked fresh and eager. "I was wondering if you could tell me who has keys. I mean, besides Ms. Morgan here. I know she lives upstairs."

"And Muriel had keys, of course," Gracie put in.

"Well, we all do," Agnes reminded Gracie and told Alterman. "All the members of the board."

"And Brittany!" With one finger, Patricia gave the table an authoritative tap. "Brittany Pleasance," she explained, both for my sake and for Alterman's. "The last business manager. I remember Muriel saying something about it just a couple days ago. She was looking for Brittany's key to the front door and couldn't find it."

Alterman took a notebook out of his pocket and wrote this down. "And when did she leave her job here?"

This, they had to think about.

"Three months?" Valentina ventured.

"More like four, I think," Agnes put in. "It must be that long. We did without a manager for a while. Muriel insisted she could handle all the details of the club herself."

"And when that didn't work," Patricia said, "that's when we ran the ad and that's when we found Avery."

"And this Ms. Pleasance, why did she leave?" Alterman wanted to know.

"Didn't want to." Gracie shook her head. "She told me as much herself the day she cleaned out her desk."

Patricia looked at Agnes, Agnes looked at Valentina.

Valentina drew in a breath. "Muriel made Brittany's life pure misery," she said. "She was demanding—"

"Rude," Gracie added.

"Accusatory," Patricia said.

"Brattish," Agnes declared.

"The poor woman finally couldn't stand it any longer." Valentina shook her head. "Brittany, well, it's sad to say she wasn't the brightest bulb in the box, but her heart was in the right place. She was eager, and she tried hard to please. It was a shame to see her go."

"She was a good worker. So why did Ms. Sadler make her life . . ." Though something told me he didn't have to, that he had a mind like a steel trap, he consulted his notes. "A pure misery?"

This time, Valentina looked at Agnes, and Agnes looked at Patricia.

Gracie was the one who spoke up. "It's not helping to pussyfoot around," she told the other ladies. "We need to lay it on the line for this young man. How else is he going to figure out what happened to Muriel?" She flattened her hands on the tabletop. "Muriel wanted her granddaughter to get the job as club manager. She thought if she bullied Brittany enough, Brittany would quit."

"Which she did."

"Yes." Gracie nodded toward the sergeant. "But the rest of us, we weren't about to give in to Muriel. The job was posted and even though Kendall Sadler applied for it just like her grandmother wanted her to, Avery was hired because Avery was the one best qualified."

Alterman turned my way. "Does that mean Ms. Sadler wanted you to quit too?"

I managed a smile. "Too soon to tell."

"And then there's Bill Manby, of course." Thinking, Agnes drummed her fingers on the table. "He was our maintenance man up until a week ago. That's when Muriel fired him. Just like that."

"Oh, he was a looker!" Gracie added. "Those wide shoulders, that curly hair! Those piercing blue eyes!"

Alterman made note of this, too. Well, probably not the part about how Bill Manby was a looker, but about how Muriel had fired him.

"What about other enemies?" the sergeant wanted to know.

Gracie looked at the ceiling.

Valentina studied her manicure.

Agnes pretended to pick a piece of lint from her skirt.

Patricia bit her lower lip.

When Alterman snapped his notebook shut, every one of us flinched. "We'll talk again," he promised. "For now, you can leave your addresses and phone numbers with the officer out in the hallway. After that, you're free to leave."

He strode into the hallway. I was right behind him.

"What about me? Can I get back up to my room?"

One corner of his mouth pulled tight. "We searched the building. There's no one here who shouldn't be here."

He hadn't come right out and said I was crazy and that imagining a woman down in the basement proved it, and for this, I was grateful.

Even if I wasn't satisfied.

"But what about the woman in the basement?" I asked him.

"If she was there—"

"What do you mean, if?" It was late, I was tired. It had been a long day. Yeah, I snapped, and I propped my fists on my hips, too. I looked him in the eye. "I know what I saw."

He rubbed a hand along the back of his neck. "And I believe you. But there's no evidence of anybody else being here."

"Then what about the mess in my room?"

He had the nerve to smile. "Maybe you're a lousy housekeeper."

"As a matter of fact, I am. But I haven't been here long enough to make a mess yet. Someone was in my rooms."

He backed up, backed away from the argument. "Look," he conceded, "I know that. But we looked around and we didn't find anyone. We dusted for fingerprints so that might help. For now, what you can do is lock your door when you go to bed, and when you have a chance, go through your things and let us know if anything is missing. For now, the ladies can leave and you can, too."

"Are you staying?"

"Here? Of course. Until we're done."

I made up my mind in an instant. I was the club manager, right? Well, it might be nearly four in the morning, but I had managing to do. "Then I'm staying too," I told Alterman. "I'll be in the dining room if you need me."

Back in there, I plunked down in a chair. "He says you can all go," I told the ladies.

"And we will." Agnes finished her coffee. "But there's something we need to talk to you about first, Avery."

"It's the club." There were tears in Gracie's eyes.

"And the prospect of things going downhill," Valentina said. "I mean even further downhill than they already are."

"If this murder isn't solved . . ." Patricia shivered. "Well, I guess we won't have to worry about getting new members once we lose all our old members."

I agreed. But if that was so . . .

"Not one of you spoke up when Alterman asked if Muriel had any enemies," I reminded them.

"We did too," Agnes insisted. "We told him about Brittany."

"And about Bill Manby," Gracie said.

"But what about all that stuff we talked about earlier? About how Valentina, you were treated badly by Muriel, and how you and Muriel fought yesterday, Patricia, and—"

Agnes stood and patted my arm. "Oh, come on, dear, we're members of the club. We can't possibly be suspects."

"But there could be others," Patricia whispered. "That's why we want you to look into things."

"Look into . . . ?"

"The murder, of course." Valentina rose and looped her way-too-expensive-for-words purse over one arm. "You have the perfect position that will make it easy for you to talk to members. You know, to see what you can find out. And once you have information that will help, you can tell Sergeant Alterman."

"You've got to help us, Avery," Patricia said. "Otherwise, the club is going to be ruined."

And just like that, they marched out and left me standing with my mouth open and my head spinning. It didn't help my brain settle down when I heard them chatting in the hallway on the way to the door and Gracie's voice float back to me. "Well, let's just hope she doesn't come back as a ghost. The last thing we need around here is Muriel haunting this place."

Ghost.

Goose bumps shot up my arms.

The woman in the basement, the one the cops couldn't find. What if she . . .

I kicked the thought aside, shook myself back to reality, and reached for another cup of coffee.

I'd been hanging around with Aunt Rosemary too long.

# CHAPTER 7

M e? Solve a murder?
   It wasn't in my nature.
Or my job description.
Still . . .
As I paced the kitchen while I waited for the cops and the crime scene technicians to leave, my brain refused to let go of one tantalizing tidbit of information.
Was it a clue?
See above. Since I didn't know how to solve a murder, I'll admit I wouldn't know a clue if it came up and bit me. But I still couldn't brush off the memory of those bruises on Patricia's arm.
Fixing a bathroom sink J-trap with a screwdriver, huh?
I will go on record right here and now and say that growing up with Aunt Rosemary provided me with many skills. One of which wasn't communicating with the dead.

But see, for all her enthusiasm about life (and death), and all her community spirit (I use that last word in all its connotations), and with all her big heart and open mind, Aunt Rosemary is a total zero when it comes to the practicalities of life. As a kid, I'd learned to take care of things around the purple Victorian monstrosity of a house we called home, things like changing electrical fuses and furnace filters. And yes, I'd once replaced the J-trap in the bathroom.

No screwdriver required.

So why had Patricia lied? And what did it mean?

The thought was still pinging through my brain by the time the sun came up. With all the coffee I'd had throughout the night, I practically sloshed when I walked. Still, Sergeant Alterman was the last one out of the building, and I knew he'd had a long night, too. It would have been rude not to offer.

"You want coffee? How about breakfast before you go?"

Like he actually had to think about it, he stopped in his tracks. While he was at it, he yawned. "I can't remember the last time I ate."

"No sandwiches?" There were only crumbs left on the platter where we'd stacked the turkey and the roast beef.

"I never eat when I'm working," Alterman told me. "Slows me down."

"You're not working now."

He stretched. "Technically I am, since I've got to do all I can in the next few hours to get this case in gear. But if you could spare a piece of toast . . ."

I led the way to the kitchen, made the toast, and put on another pot of coffee. Even though there were no events scheduled at the club that day, we had a food order due to arrive around ten and Quentin and Geneva would be in to handle it. They, unlike me, had probably not spent the last ten hours mainlining caffeine. They'd appreciate a fresh pot of coffee.

"You'll probably want to talk to them." Of course Alterman didn't know who I was talking about. I can be excused. I'd been up for just about twenty-four hours and I was a little punchy. "Our cook and our waitress," I explained.

He slid his notebook across the table to me then reached for the jar of grape jelly I'd put down along with his two pieces of toast. "Contact information," he said.

I didn't know it. Not until I went out to my computer and got Quentin's and Geneva's addresses from our employee files. I dutifully wrote it all down, and by the time I got back to the kitchen, Alterman had finished the toast and another cup of coffee.

"I can make more," I told him.

"No thanks." He shot up from his chair. "If I sit too long, I'll get tired, and if I get tired, I won't do everything I need to do today. I'll be back," he promised, and he took his notebook out of my hand and headed to the front door.

I'd locked it behind the last bunch of cops who had left, and I stepped forward to unlock the door just as Jack Harkness pulled into the parking lot.

"Early for employees," Alterman said.

"Not exactly an employee. Our restorationist. We had a fire upstairs last week."

His dark eyes flashed. "The crime scene guys said something about a mess upstairs, but none of you club people mentioned it to me."

I couldn't provide an excuse, just the truth. "With everything else that happened, it slipped my mind. There was no structural damage, but the fire was in the room where our records are kept. We've got a restorationist working to save as much as he can. He'll also take care of stuff like getting furniture cleaned or replaced, getting the wallpaper stripped and redone." I did not bother to point out that the wallpaper was printed in 1946, not 1945. Something told me Alterman wouldn't much care. "I never thought to call him and tell him not to show today. Can he work upstairs?"

"I don't see why not," Alterman said. "But make sure you tell him to stick to where he's supposed to be, nowhere else. Ms. Sadler's office and the basement are strictly off limits. Don't let any one else wander around, either."

I couldn't help myself. I had to ask. "And the mysterious woman in the basement?" I asked him.

Maybe Alterman was being kind when he didn't respond. Or maybe he just didn't know what to say.

With a sigh, I swung open the front door and stepped back just as Jack Harkness got out of his car. It was a surprisingly sleek little number, foreign. Silver and shiny. For a man who was not the least bit shiny, it wasn't what I expected.

As if to prove my assessment, that morning Jack looked pretty much like he looked the last time I saw him. A little rumpled and as shaggy as a pound dog. He juggled an armful of books while he locked his car, dropped one of the books, and bent to retrieve it.

"I said I'll be back."

Alterman's voice snapped me out of my thoughts and out of watching Jack. I yawned and smiled and yawned again. "I think last night is catching up to me. I zoned out. Sorry, Sergeant Alterman."

"You'll feel better once you've had some rest." Alterman stepped outside. "And by the way, my first name isn't Sergeant, it's Oscar. But everyone calls me Oz. And once you finally have the chance, if you're looking for someone to share that bottle of wine with . . ." A smile cracked his stony expression. "Give me a call."

Just like that, he was gone. And there I was, staring again.

Only this time, not at Jack.

In fact, I never even noticed Jack walk up to the front door until he was standing beside me.

He propped the books he was carrying beneath one arm so he could slide his glasses up his nose and, like me, he watched Oz get into his black sedan and pull out of the parking lot. "Company?"

"Company? You mean like . . ." I am not a blusher. It's not in my nature and besides, my business is my business alone and no one has the right to comment, to criticize, or to condemn. Still, I couldn't help the rush of heat that raced into my cheeks. Was it because I didn't want Jack to get the wrong impression? Or because suddenly, thinking of sharing that bottle of wine with Oz sounded so appealing?

Sleep deprivation.

That was the only thing that would account for my crazy thoughts, and I shook my head to knock them out of my brain. "No, no. Nothing like that," I told Jack. "He's a cop."

Jack looked over my shoulder and into the club. "Not another fire, I hope."

"Worse than that." I stepped back so he could walk inside and he set the books on my desk while I told him everything that had happened the night before.

When I was done, Jack shook his head. "That's terrible."

"It is. Muriel could be difficult, sure, but from everything I've heard, she was a mainstay of the club. We're all going to have to pick up a lot of the slack. She'll be missed."

"Yeah. Uh . . . sure." Jack grabbed his books. "But that's

not the terrible I'm talking about. That . . ." He darted a
look out to the parking lot and the car that had just pulled
in before he took off running for the stairs. "That's terrible."

This I couldn't say.

What I could say is that an older man and a young woman
got out of the black Lincoln SUV. He was iron haired and
distinguished looking. She was dark haired, tiny, and wearing jeans with multiple holes in them (how is that a style?)
and knee-high boots of supple leather.

I'd already locked the door behind Jack so when they
walked up to it, I peered out the window at the top of the
door and spoke up nice and loud. "We're not open today."
They never budged. Maybe they didn't hear me. I waved my
hands to emphasize my message.

The woman rapped on the window. "You've got to let
us in."

I tried again, waving for all I was worth. "We're not
open today."

She propped one fist on her hip and shot me a look I was
surprised didn't melt the glass between us. "Do you know
who we are?" She tapped the toe of one boot against the
ground and gestured toward the man. "This is Tab Sadler.
You know, Muriel's husband."

Not something I was expecting.

Not someone I was expecting.

I was caught between my duty to the club and my sympathy for Muriel's family, but it really wasn't much of a
choice. I unlocked the door, opened it, and stepped back.

"About time," the woman grumbled, and just like that, I
knew who she was. No introductions necessary. Nasty
genes run deep. This had to be Muriel's granddaughter.

It was. "Kendall Sadler." She stared at me like she was
a magician doing a mesmerism act. I'm pretty sure I was

supposed to apologize. Or grovel. When I didn't, she puckered her too-plump lips. "Grandpa needed to be here."

I couldn't imagine why.

And I didn't dare say it.

Instead, I smoothed a hand over the red snap-front cardigan and navy-blue slacks I'd worn to the chamber of commerce meeting. It felt like a long, long time ago.

"There's really nothing you can do," I told my visitors.
"Everything here is under control. If you want to see
Muriel . . ." Would they? I was inclined to think not, at least
not until someone could do something about that horrible
gash on Muriel's head. "You should call the police. They'll
help you."

"Don't you get it, girl?" Tab had a craggy face and when
he frowned, it furrowed like a 3D topographical map. He
had eyes the color of slate and there was no softness in
them. He darted a look toward the stairs. "I'm Muriel's husband. I'm the grieving widower. I need to be here. I need to
see the place my Muriel died."

"I'm afraid you can't." This I didn't know for sure, but
Alterman . . . er, Oz . . . mentioned not letting anyone roam
freely through the building, and I could only assume this
was exactly what he had in mind. "The police aren't done
processing the scene."

"Of course. Of course." Tab didn't so much walk as he
did high-step, each movement as quick and as precise as if
a marching band director had choreographed it. Shoulders
back and head high, he moved around me and toward the
stairway. "But that doesn't mean I can't at least spend a few
minutes in her office."

"That's exactly what it means," I told him.

His hand was already on the bannister, and he stopped
and shot a look at me over his shoulder. "Are you telling me

I can't be alone in Muriel's office to grieve? Then Kendall"—when he said her name, she snapped to—"you come up with me."

"You can't be in Muriel's office alone. You can't be in there with anybody else, either." I had no choice but to walk up a couple steps and stand there to block his way. "The office is cordoned off. No one is allowed up there."

"When the police said no one, they certainly weren't talking about me," Tab insisted.

But of course, they were.

I told him that, and when Kendall squinched her eyes and wrinkled her nose, all set to dispute it, I gave her as much of a smile as a woman who hadn't slept in a day could manage.

"Police orders," I said.

"Well then, I'll just . . ." Tab shook his shoulders. "If you two will excuse me, I'm going to head to the men's room. Maybe when I get back, young lady"—he looked down his patrician nose at me—"you'll have come to your senses."

Before I could decide if going to the men's room qualified as roaming around the club and what I could do if it did, he disappeared in the direction of the dining room and the restrooms beyond.

Kendall watched him go. "You'll give in eventually," she purred. "Everyone always does." She slid me a look. "My grandfather didn't get to be one of the most important men in Portage Path by letting little people tell him what to do."

I pulled myself up to my full height and looked down at her. "Good thing I'm not one of the little people."

She chuckled and sashayed past me, back toward my desk, where she skimmed one finger over the surface. "I bet the police are all over this. I mean, they're bound to be, aren't they? Considering that it was my grandmother who was killed."

"I'd like to think they'd handle any murder in town the same way." My computer was still on from when I'd looked up Quentin's and Geneva's contact information, and I turned off the monitor. "I'm sure they're working as hard as they can."

"Maybe they need a tip. You know, information about a suspect."

I remembered what the ladies of the board had asked, how they wanted me to look into the crime, to nose around, to see what I could find out.

Careful not to look too eager, I straightened a pile of papers that didn't need straightening. "You know something?" I asked Kendall. "About a suspect? Who is it?"

"You, of course."

When my head came up and my mouth fell open, Kendall laughed.

I stammered. "Why would you . . . How would you . . . You don't know anything about me. How can you possibly think I'm a suspect?"

Instead of answering, she strutted over to the front door. "You didn't know my grandmother well, did you?" she asked, then before I could say a thing, she answered for me. "Well, of course you didn't. You just started working here. Muriel Sadler was a force of nature. She wanted me to have your job."

"So I hear." I gave her a level look. "It hardly matters now, does it?"

Kendall's smile was sleek. "But it does. Don't you see? It matters more than ever. I'm going to be the business manager of the Portage Path Women's Club."

I looked out the windows to the parking lot and the expensive car she'd arrived in. I checked out her outfit (pricey), her makeup (perfect), her hair (freshly styled).

"Why do you want my job?" I asked her.

Her lips pinched. "So I can do it the right way, of course."

"Except you don't know that I can't do it the right way."

"I know the job was supposed to be mine!" Yes, she actually stomped her foot. "My grandmother said—"

"Your grandmother may have been president of the club. That doesn't mean she had final say in hiring decisions. That's a responsibility of the entire board. You want this job? Go for it. But you'll have to wait until I'm ready to leave before you get the chance at it, and just for your information"—I lifted my chin—"right now I'm thinking I'll be ready to quit right about when hell freezes over."

Her laugh was silvery. But then, she struck me as the kind of woman who had a lot of practice when it came to the silvery-laugh department. She flounced her way around my desk. "Well, I can already feel it getting colder in here. You'll leave, all right, and I'll tell you why. Because the Sadlers are important in Portage Path. We've got lots of friends in high places. And if you don't leave?" She fluttered eyelashes that were in no way real. "If you don't leave, remember what I said. I'm going to make sure to tell our important friends, and our important friends are going to tell the police. And then everyone is going to know you're the one who killed my grandmother."

If ever there was a time for a snappy comeback, this was it, and in the thousand times I replayed the scene after it happened, I had one. It was on point. Brilliant. It cut Kendall off at the knees.

Only in reality, I never had time to deliver it.

And not just because I couldn't think of anything to say.

Something upstairs clunked.

And it wasn't something in the Lilac Lounge or in Marigold, where Jack was working. Those rooms were at the back of the building, and this noise came from right above us.

Right where Muriel's office was located.

"Stay right here," I ordered Kendall, and I raced to the stairway and took the steps two at a time.

I found Tab Sadler right where I thought I'd find him: outside Muriel's office. He was a sneaky one, all right. He'd come up the back stairs and he'd bumped into a nearby table and knocked down a lamp while he was trying to shimmy through the strips of crime scene tape hung over the office doorway. He had one leg through a gap between two strips of tape, one foot in Muriel's office and one foot out.

"Mr. Sadler!" I closed in on him. "What do you think you're doing?"

"I . . . uh . . ." What he was doing was pretty darned obvious. Trouble was, he wasn't doing it very well. Tab was no spring chicken. Balanced on one foot, he swayed, he wobbled.

Unlike so many of Aunt Rosemary's cockamamie friends, I do not consider myself psychic. But I did know what was going to happen. No doubt about it.

I threw out a hand to steady him before he fell over, and when I gave him a yank he had no choice—he pulled his leg out of the office and landed on both feet back in the hallway.

"The police don't want you in there." I mean, really, I shouldn't have had to point it out; the yellow tape pretty much did that. "I told you not to wander the building."

"You did. But I . . ." Tab craned his neck, the better to check out Muriel's desk, the file cabinets on the far wall, the credenza where a wilted aspidistra stood beside a heap of papers. Like he hadn't been caught red-handed, he cleared his throat and lifted his chin.

"I am her husband, after all," he said. "Her next of kin. And there are certain family treasures Muriel kept in her office. I need to retrieve them. To us . . ." He hung his head in a way that was supposed to make me feel sorry for him. Actually, the only thing it did was make me realize that though his wife had been murdered just a few hours earlier, Tab Sadler didn't look upset at all. "Those mementoes are precious," he murmured.

"Which is exactly why Oz . . . er . . . the police . . . It's exactly why the police will make sure you get back everything that was Muriel's personal property." I wound my arm through his. He was a tall man and I could tell he'd once been broad and burly, but hey, he was getting up there in years and I had spent plenty of time waiting tables. Hauling trays and slinging dishes does wonders for the biceps. When I tugged him down the hallway, he had no choice but to follow.

We stopped at the stairway. "They'll call you, Mr. Sadler. I know they will. They'll let you know when you can come in and get what belonged to Muriel. But for now . . ."

For now, what the members of the board had said earlier in the morning came back to me. This was the victim's husband, and I had an opportunity to find out more.

"Where were you last night?" I asked Tab.

He opened his mouth to answer. At least until outrage blocked his words. His jaw worked up and down. Until he found his voice, that is.

"How dare you! Do you think . . . Can you possibly think . . . Young lady, are you insinuating that I am a suspect?"

"Not my job," I told him and oh, how I wished that was

true. Too bad the board had kicked the ball clearly into my court. "You know the cops are going to ask," I told him. "You're going to tell them, so you might as well tell me."

"Oh, I'll tell you all right. I was home, that's where I was. Home all night. I was waiting for Muriel to come home for dinner. She never showed."

And with that, Tab marched down the stairway.

I had every intention of following him and showing him to the door, and I would have done it if I didn't hear a familiar voice coming from the Lilac Lounge.

It wasn't Jack.

"Kendall Sadler," I ground the name out from between clenched teeth, peered over the bannister to make sure Tab Sadler was where he was supposed to be, and headed to the Lilac Lounge.

That's where I found Kendall perched on the desk Quentin, Jack, and I had struggled to get into the room the day before. Her arms were braced back against the desktop, she had one leg bent up under her, and the other swung back and forth as if she didn't have a care in the world.

And a recently murdered grandmother.

"What part of 'stay put' and 'don't wander the building' don't you understand?" I asked her.

She pouted and slid off the desk.

"You can't possibly think that applies to me," she said.

And at the same time, Jack blurted out, "I'm sorry. I didn't know. I thought maybe she shouldn't be here, but—"

I shot him a look. "But what?"

"Oh, come off it." Kendall stepped around me and out into the hallway, where she stopped and pursed her lips. "Bye, Jack. Don't forget dinner tomorrow."

Once she was gone, I shook my head. "Dinner? She sure moves fast. You're having dinner? With her?"

He had the good sense to look embarrassed. Jack Harkness, he of the shaggy cuteness, hung his head. "She's not all bad."

"Really?" Three of the smoke-damaged books from Marigold were on top of his desk, and though I didn't dare touch them, I could see the dates on their spines: 1941, 1942, 1943. I looked up from the books and pinned Jack with a look. "Is that why you said *terrible* when you saw her pull into the parking lot?"

Jack pushed his glasses up his nose. "Kendall, she can be a little . . ." He searched for the right word. "A little pushy sometimes."

"Like about having dinner with you." I backed away, both from Jack and from the conversation, holding up both hands as I did, a show of surrender. "Hey, it's none of my business who you have dinner with. It's just that I thought—"

His head came up. "What?"

"Well, I figured you had better taste than that. But then, like you said, I'm sure Kendall has her positive points."

He smiled. "She likes horses."

"That's a real plus."

He shrugged. "Our families have known each other a long time and—"

And whatever else he was going to say, he was interrupted by a commotion downstairs.

Sadlers sneaking through the house, and now this!

I got there as fast as I could, and downstairs I found Gracie, Agnes, Valentina, and Patricia coming in the front door just as Tab and Kendall were walking out. For women who'd been up half the night, they looked mighty chipper.

"We thought you should be the first to know," Gracie told me as soon as my feet were off the stairs.

"It is, after all, of vital importance to the club," Valentina added.

"And it means there's plenty to do." Full steam, those bruises on her arm covered by a long-sleeved emerald-green sweater, Patricia sailed past me and toward the club office in the Daisy Den, just off the main ballroom. "We've got to get busy."

Before the rest of the board had a chance to disappear along with Patricia, I raised my voice. "Someone want to tell me what's going on?"

They had the good manners to stop in their tracks and the good sense to realize they'd left me out of the loop and owed me an explanation.

"It's Agnes, of course," Gracie wrapped an arm around Agnes's waist. "We've had an emergency meeting of the executive board. And we've elected Agnes president." Gracie grinned and squeezed Agnes in a hug. "Your mother would be so proud!" she told her.

Agnes's eyes welled and she burbled, but far be it from Patricia to allow time for emotion.

"Come on, ladies!" She headed toward the office. "We've got a presidential inauguration to plan!"

# CHAPTER 8

S he looks like a flapper. You know, from the roaring
  twenties."

I can be excused from not saying a word in response to
this comment. I was pretty busy staring slack-jawed at the
face that stared back at me from the computer screen in
the Portage Path Police Department. Yes, it was the face
of the woman I'd encountered in the club basement. No
doubt about that. As for her looking like she had stepped
out of the roaring twenties, there was no doubt about that,
either. Still . . .

"She must have been going to a costume party." It was
the only logical explanation, so I grabbed it and held
on tight.

"Well, if she was, she did her homework. My wife, she
took me to one of those murder mystery dinners once, and
the theme was the Prohibition era. She did all the research
and got our costumes together, and this girl . . ." The cop

who'd run the facial composite program chuckled. He was
a middle-aged guy named Dave, and he nodded toward the
computer screen. "My wife would be so jealous. This girl's
got it all down pat, from the makeup to that feathered thing
on her head."

When he looked at the face on the screen again, I did, too.

There she was. The woman I'd been invited to head-
quarters to describe to Dave, the department's sketch artist.
He'd made her come alive, thanks to the magic of computer
programming. The same dark, sleek bobbed hair. The same
Cupid's bow lips and smoky eyeliner. The same pert nose
and those pale cheeks dotted with rouge. The same pencil-
thin eyebrows. A little cheap. A little flashy. But pretty. And
very young. Sitting there and watching her face materialize
right before my eyes was incredible.

Hearing Dave say she'd stepped out of the roaring twenties, though . . .

Well, come on, that was nothing short of preposterous.

I told myself not to forget it, even as Dave asked, "You
want me to print out a copy of the picture for you?"

I popped out of the chair next to Dave's desk to distance
myself from the very idea. "No thanks! I don't need the
reminder. There's no way I can forget what she looked
like." Unfortunately, true. After the Portage Path Women's
Club board disappeared into the club office the day before
to discuss the ceremony that would make Agnes's presidency official, I'd ducked upstairs with the hopes of getting
in a few hours of shut-eye.

It never happened.

One look at the mess that was my rooms and my stomach shimmied.

One minute of closing my eyes and I saw the face of the
mysterious woman.

Right before a picture of Muriel's battered body popped into my imagination.

"Well, if this looks enough like her"—Dave looked to me for confirmation—"I'll get the picture over to Sergeant Alterman."

At the same time I gave him a nod of approval, I told him, "Oz doesn't believe she was really there."

No doubt Dave had already talked to Oz and all the other cops who'd come to the scene. He scratched a hand behind his ear. "They searched the house."

"And didn't find her. Yes, I know." Another thing I needed no reminder about. When I did finally manage to quash those disturbing pictures that popped into my mind and drift off to sleep, I woke at every little noise. After all, the cops never found the woman. And I swear, she was there. Really there.

So how had she avoided being discovered?

Where was she hiding?

And would she come back to my rooms?

Here at the Portage Path Police Department, with autumn sunshine flowing through the windows and the combined noises of voices and clattering keyboards from the cops working at the desks crammed in all around us, it seemed like a crazy thing to worry about. But at home, all alone on the third floor and desperate for sleep, the problem pounded through my brain and sent goose bumps flashing up my arms.

"Ooh, electricity shooting through you!" I could just about hear Aunt Rosemary coo the words as she had done so many times back home. "That means the spirits are trying to get your attention. No doubt about that at all!"

I ignored the voice, thanked Dave for his help, gathered my jacket and my purse, and headed outside. Too bad it wasn't as easy to shake away the thought of Aunt Rosemary and everything she believed.

What if . . . ?

I got into the car and yeah, it was crazy, but I surrendered. Maybe I was as nuts as Aunt Rosemary. Maybe I was just too tired to try and think my way through the problem of the woman in the basement. This was a unique situation and there was one person who could help me make sense of it.

Maybe.

My finger was already poised over the call button and the photo of my aunt—resplendent in a purple caftan and hoop earrings the size of circus rings—when I told myself to get a grip. There was no use putting any more goofy ideas into Aunt Rosemary's head. For years, she'd been trying to convince me that I shared her Gift, that I could receive messages from Spirit—just like she believed she did—if only I would open myself up to the possibility. There was no use enabling her. Besides, PPWC already had enough to deal with, what with the fire and the murder. The last thing any of us needed was for Aunt Rosemary to show up at our doorstep—which I knew she would if she suspected something Otherworldly might be up—eager to commune with the ectoplasm in the flapper dress.

"Costume," I grumbled, coming to my senses. "She was going to a costume party," and I shoved my phone back into my purse.

If I hoped to get a break from the thoughts of murder and mysterious intruders when I got back to the club, they were dashed. The place was in an uproar! The board was worried that news of Muriel's death would drive members away? Oh, how wrong they were! Once word of the murder became public, club members came out of the woodwork.

When I stepped through the front door, there was a line of women (many of them with guests) waiting to be seated in the dining room for lunch, and the card room beyond (Carnation) was packed with chattering club members. There were more noises coming from upstairs. I checked the schedule on my computer. Book discussion group. According to our log, no one had registered for the program, but apparently that too had changed now that PPWC was the center of local media attention. I could hear chattering from the Geranium Room at the top of the stairs.

Murder was apparently good for business.

I told myself the thought was unworthy of me and hurried into the kitchen to make sure Quentin and Geneva had everything under control. They didn't, and who could blame them? They'd spent so much time expecting no one for lunch, there was no way they were prepared to be slammed.

For the next couple of hours, I prepped salads, bussed tables, poured ice water, and ferried lunches from the kitchen to the tables, where members had their heads together and I heard talk of "poor Muriel" and "how terrible for Muriel" and even "dear Muriel," though something told me this last comment came from a club member who really didn't know Muriel very well. By the time the crowd was gone and Quentin had the last of the pots and pans in soapy water, I dropped into a chair at the kitchen table, Geneva plopped into the one next to me, and Quentin grabbed a gallon of vanilla ice cream from the freezer. He loaded three bowls, drizzled hot fudge over the ice cream, and added whipped cream to all.

"We deserve it," he said, setting a dish of ice cream in front of me before he sat across from me. "We all deserve it."

"Amen!" I raised my spoon in salute.

"You think it's going to be like this every day now that we got a murder here?" Geneva wanted to know.

"I think it will die down eventually." Yeah, bad pun, but they either didn't notice or didn't have the energy to point it out. I swallowed down a spoonful of yummy ice cream and glanced Geneva's way. "But for now, I think we'll have to be ready. It could stay busy for a while. Is that good news? Or bad?"

Geneva reached into the pocket of the apron she had looped over her neck and fished out a wad of bills. "It's great news." She beamed. "I ain't seen this many tips in as long as I've worked here!" She counted out the money, then divided it into three piles. She slipped one pile across the table to Quentin and the second to me.

"Oh no." I sent the money back in her direction.

"But we always share tips," Quentin explained. "And you worked as hard as we did, that's for sure."

"And I get a salary, remember." When neither of them took the money, I grabbed it, counted it, and added half to Quentin's pile and half to Geneva's. "I hope this crazy busyness lasts long enough to make both of you rich."

"Here's to that." Quentin toasted me with a spoonful of whipped cream. "Only we're going to need to order more supplies. Didn't think we'd go through that much sirloin tip today for stroganoff."

My fingers ached from all the salads I'd plated. "And I'm sure we need lettuce and cukes and tomatoes."

"And pasta." There was a notepad and pencil on the table, and Geneva slid them over to Quentin and poked her spoon in his direction, urging him to make a list. "We said on the special board that tomorrow's feature is pasta. We're going to need more noodles, I bet."

"And I'd better get a move on more sauce." Quentin gave me a smile. "After I finish my sundae, that is."

"Take all the time you need." I scraped the last of the fudge out of my bowl. "I'll come in later and see if there's anything I can do to help. For now"—I pushed back my chair—"I'd better go see what's happening with the board. They're planning the ceremony. You know, for when Agnes is officially made president."

"Funny, don't you think?" Quentin finished his ice cream, dropped his spoon in his bowl, and sat back, his meaty arms crossed over his barrel chest. "After everything that happened, she ends up president anyway."

Searching for answers, I looked from Quentin to Geneva. "Everything that happened?"

"Well, you missed all that. You weren't here yet." Geneva got up and gathered our bowls and took them over to the sink. "Agnes, she ran for president. You know, in the election they had just a couple months ago."

I remembered some talk about how Agnes was disappointed when Muriel got the president's job, but I never realized there was an election, and that they both ran for the top spot. I considered what it meant. "Agnes ran for president? And Muriel won?" Yeah, I sounded a little skeptical, but I didn't need to explain. Not to Quentin and Geneva. They'd worked with Muriel long enough.

"Didn't think Muriel had a chance," Quentin said. "Couldn't find one person who ever said much nice about that woman. And Agnes, well, she's mostly nice."

"She has her moments," Geneva put in when she came back to the table. "Just like all of them. You know, she can be kind of demanding. But then, that's what they're all used to, these ladies with money. They're used to getting their own way."

"And Agnes, when she complains about something, it's usually legit," Quentin added. "Like the time Bill Manby left the garden hose running by the front entrance and everything out there got soaked. Agnes came in here and read ol' Bill the riot act. But that was okay. He deserved it."

"And what did Muriel do when she found out about the garden hose running all that time?" I wondered.

Quentin whistled softly under his breath.

Geneva rolled her eyes.

I could only imagine.

"So nobody liked Muriel much, and everyone felt pretty positive about Agnes. How did Agnes lose the election?" I asked them.

"Easy-peasy." Quentin got up and lumbered over to the pantry to unload canned tomatoes. "Agnes, she dropped out of the election."

"She decided she didn't want to be president?" I asked.

Quentin shrugged.

Geneva pursed her lips. "Got me," she said. "Nobody ever tells us much of nothing when it comes to club business. I only know one day, there was *Vote for Agnes* posters stuck on all the doors, and the next day, they were gone."

"And so Muriel was the only one left running and she won," Quentin said.

"And now Agnes is president, anyway." Geneva chuckled. "Kind of funny, don't you think? Like one of them Carmen things."

Carmen aside, I did think it was pretty odd and I wondered what it meant in terms of Muriel's death. Really, it wasn't possible Agnes would kill Muriel just to become president of the club.

Was it?

I chewed over the thought, but not for long. No one was

that desperate to be president of a failing club, I decided, and I headed to the PPWC offices. I never got that far, though, not when I heard a commotion coming from the ballroom.

Back in the days before radio, TV, and the Internet, when Chauncey Dennison built the house that would one day be the Portage Path Women's Club, fancy balls, musicales, and poetry readings were the height of fashion. People made their own entertainment and the ballroom there at the Dennison mansion was the center of activity for Portage Path society. In fact, it was one of the things I planned to tout when advertising the space for weddings and parties— the grand history of the place, the glamour, the style.

The ballroom had one wall of windows that looked out over what had once been lush gardens. These days, that had been pared down to potted plants on a stone patio, but not to worry, I had plans for jazzing it up when spring rolled around. Or at least I did when I thought we had a maintenance man who would plant tulip and daffodil bulbs. With or without flowers outside, the room itself was spectacular. The walls in there were paneled in glimmering wood, the sconces on the wall were shimmering silver, and there was a grand piano in the far corner, potted palms in another. Sometime while I'd been over at the Portage Path Police Department, the presidential inaugural committee had gathered and now, they were hard at work planning the ceremony that would take place just one week from the following Sunday. There were tables set up beneath the crystal chandelier that hung from the center of the ornate plaster ceiling, poster boards on easels next to a fireplace that was big enough to step into.

There were women gathered all around, talking and laughing, many of them with piles of papers in their hands.

Gracie was ensconced in a chair next to one of the poster boards, going through a stack of old newspapers.

"What's up?" I asked her.

"Lots to do," Gracie purred, as happy as a clam to be knee deep in the preparations. She waved a yellowed newspaper clipping at me. "Agnes's mother's picture," she said, and I took the clipping from her hand and studied it. Margaret Yarborough and Agnes were an unlikely duo. Agnes's face was smooth and ageless. Margaret's (even at the time the photo was taken, which must have been when she was younger than Agnes was now) was a map of wrinkles and lines. They had the same long graceful neck, though, and that same look of prosperity and privilege; but where Agnes's nose was short and stubby, Margaret's was long and thin. Agnes's eyes were brown; her mother's were light.

"She was president of the club, you know," Gracie told me, pointing to the picture of Margaret. "And her mother before her."

"So Agnes is following in a long tradition."

"To be sure," Gracie told me. "Margaret . . ." She tipped her head toward the clipping still in my hands. "Some of us were talking earlier and we decided it would be nice if she was our special guest at the ceremony. She's in assisted living now, the poor dear, and not in the best of health, and I know she'd get a kick out of being back here and having a fuss made over her. What do you think, Agnes?" Gracie raised her voice. Across the room, Agnes was standing in front of one of the easels and studying what looked to be a chart of some kind, a mishmash of boxes and lines. She turned around when Gracie called to her.

"We'll have your mother in for the ceremony," Gracie said. "Our special guest of honor. Nice way to uphold tradition, don't you think?"

Even from where I stood, I could tell that Agnes was moved by the suggestion. Her eyes sparkled with unshed tears.

"We can add Margaret's picture to the family tree we're preparing." Valentina swept past and plucked the newspaper clipping from my hand and took it over to where Agnes stood, and I went along to see what was up. "Right here." Valentina held the picture of Margaret Yarborough up to one of the blank boxes on the chart. "We'll have a graphic artist do the final family tree," Valentina told me. "But this will give you an idea what we're going for. Agnes's grandmother." Valentina pointed to a spot on the chart that was still blank. "Then Agnes's mother. Then a picture of Agnes right here, front and center, along with the club logo. Do you have a photo you'd like us to use?" she asked Agnes. "Or shall we arrange to have a photographer come in?"

I never did hear Agnes's response. That was because Patricia came around from the other side of me and hissed in my ear, "Snobs! Every single one of them. They're only doing this family tree thing to show everyone how superior they are."

"Oh, come off it with the egalitarianism lecture." Apparently, Patricia hadn't spoken softly enough because Agnes made a face at her. "There's a reason the Portage Path Women's Club exists, Patricia. You know that as well as anybody else."

"Don't tell me you're going to take things from where Muriel left off." Patricia rolled her eyes. "Now you're going to tell me how we really are better than the rest of the riffraff in town?"

Agnes's mouth thinned. "Not all at. You know me better than that. But I am going to remind you that we have an obligation to Portage Path. We're leaders and philanthropists.

It's our duty to help people. We help our members grow as people and then they can go out in the community and give others a helping hand."

"Like the royal princesses we are!" Patricia said this with an affected—and very bad—British accent. She tossed back her head and laughed. "So what's your first queenly proclamation going to be, Agnes? There must be something around here you've been itching to do. Something you've never been able to change. Here's your big chance."

"Don't be silly." Agnes clutched her hands at her waist. "That's not the way the presidency works."

"But it would be kind of fun, wouldn't it?" Valentina's smile was sly. "If I were president, I know what I'd change. That hideous carpet in the Rose Room. Pepto-Bismol pink!" She gave an exaggerated shiver. "My first official act would be to march up there and tear it out with my own two hands."

"And if I were president . . ." Gracie had joined us, and she looked around at the other members of the committee, who were as busy as bees all around us. She lowered her voice and leaned closer. "I'd hire back Bill Manby. He was a looker, all right!"

"I'd start serving liquor at lunch," Patricia announced, and when Valentina's mouth fell open, Patricia puckered. "Oh come on. It would liven things up around here!"

"So . . ." Valentina turned to Agnes. "Here's your chance. Come on, Agnes. You've been a member here for a long time. You must have something you've always thought about doing."

"Well . . ." Agnes's eyes lit, and when she turned and headed out of the ballroom, we followed along. Out to the hallway, through the dining room, right into the kitchen.

"Get a ladder," Agnes told Quentin, and though like the rest of us he didn't have a clue what was going on, he did as he was told. She pointed toward the far wall and Quentin set up the ladder right under that funny little sign I'd seen, the handmade one that read *Dodie's Dumbwaiter*.

Agnes turned in my direction, then pointed toward the ladder. "Well, what are you waiting for?"

I am not afraid of heights. Or at least I never was until I climbed that rickety ladder. Once I got three steps from the top, I held onto the ladder with both hands and looked down at the sea of faces gathered around me. "What do you want me to do?" I asked Agnes.

"I've always hated that tacky sign." She pointed. "Take it down!"

It was on the tip of my tongue to ask why, but no one else questioned the presidential proclamation so I did as I was told.

If the layer of dust that sprinkled down on me when I took the sign off the single nail that held it meant anything, the sign had been up there for years. I sneezed, climbed down the ladder, and once I was safely back on solid ground, handed the sign to Agnes.

"Oh no!" She clutched her hands behind her back. "You all said I could do whatever I wanted as my first official act, and I definitely do not want that cheap sign anywhere in our club. Toss it!"

The order given and her first official act of office completed, she swept out of the kitchen. Patricia and Valentina followed. Quentin and Geneva shook their heads, mystified by the workings of the club officers.

Gracie held out a hand. "Give it here," she said. "Whether Agnes likes the sign or not, it's part of club history and I'm going to squirrel it away in the archives."

I handed over the sign. "Who was Dodie anyway?" I asked Gracie.

"Dodie Hillenbrand. Best darned cook this club ever had," she said and added, "No offense meant, Quentin."

"None taken," he assured her before he went back to the stove and the pasta sauce bubbling there.

"So why did they name a dumbwaiter after a cook?" I wondered.

Gracie grinned. "It was just an honorary thing, I guess. Dodie, see, she was the cook when the Dennisons owned the house, and even though she was a very young woman, she really knew her way around a kitchen! When the club took over, she stayed on, and she used to love to tell everyone how much Mrs. Dennison enjoyed her cooking. Mrs. Dennison's bedroom, it was up in what's now the Lilac Lounge, and Dodie would send breakfast up for her, fast and hot out of the kitchen. Or sometimes on chilly nights, she'd make hot cocoa and surprise Mrs. Dennison with it. The sign, well—once Dodie was gone, everyone missed her. It was a little tribute."

"One Agnes doesn't want to continue."

Gracie shrugged. "It was a long time ago and well, things didn't end as well as they should have. There was going to be a big party, you see, an anniversary celebration for Agnes's parents. And the ballroom was filled with flowers, and the musicians arrived and . . ." Her expression soured. "No dinner."

I leaned forward. "Because . . . ?"

"Because Dodie had up and quit. Never said a word to anyone, just never showed up for work again."

With all the thinking I'd been doing about murder, I couldn't help but ask, "Was she all right? Did something happen to her?"

Gracie waved a hand. "We heard from her after. A time or two. She was living down in Florida, working at some ritzy hotel and having the time of her life. It was all good. Except Agnes, I don't think she ever forgave Dodie for ruining that anniversary."

I looked at where Gracie had the sign tucked under her arm. "Where you going to hide it?"

She chuckled. "In my car for now. I don't want Agnes to see it. Not yet. She'll come around eventually and realize it's part of club history. For now"—she gave me a wink— "we'll let her think she got her way as president." Gracie tucked the sign under her gray sweater and headed out the door to the parking lot.

I got back to the ballroom just as the women were examining another newspaper clipping they'd found.

"They're talking PowerPoint presentation," Patricia warned me. "They'll want you to throw it together."

It was something I was comfortable with, so that wasn't a problem, though if the pile of newspaper articles on the table meant anything, I'd be scanning for days. The newest picture they'd found had a headline under it, *Settling In*. It showed a young Margaret Yarborough holding infant Agnes. There was a man in uniform standing beside Margaret.

"Daddy." Agnes leaned over my shoulder and took a look at the picture. "It was 1942 and he'd been in England and had orders to head right back. He was here in Portage Path only long enough to be present when I was born."

"It's a great picture." I set it down on the pile. "I'll need your help with the PowerPoint. You'll need to explain who people in pictures are and why they're important to your presidency."

Agnes nodded. "Of course. If there are any questions you have—"

"There is one." It had been bugging me, and I figured this was the perfect opportunity, but I waited to ask it until Patricia and Valentina had drifted off. "You ran for president recently. Why did you drop out of the election?"

Agnes's lips puckered. "Does it really matter?"

"Probably not," I admitted. "But I'm curious. Everyone I've talked to thinks you'll be a great president."

At this, she clucked all the right, humble phrases.

"And I can tell you're going to enjoy holding the office."

She lifted her chin. "It's always been my obligation to serve the club."

"So why did you step back and let Muriel win?"

Agnes put a hand on my arm and tugged me toward that wall of windows, farther away from where the committee worked.

"I can't tell anyone else about this," she said, her head close to mine. "But in your position here, I feel you have the right to know. It was Muriel."

"What about Muriel?"

Agnes sighed. "I . . . Well, this isn't easy to admit, especially considering everything that's happened. But Muriel . . . well, I felt sorry for Muriel."

I couldn't imagine anyone on earth feeling sorry for Muriel Sadler. Not the Muriel I knew.

Apparently, Agnes knew this, because she smiled. "There's so much you need to learn about the Portage Path Women's Club, Avery. This is a good place to start. You see, we are ingrained with the notion of service. All of us. And not just from when we join the club, but at home, from an early age. This was especially true for me, since both my mother and my grandmother were once president here. We are also not prone to tooting our own horns, but . . ." She turned away and for a second, I thought it was all she'd say, but she lifted her shoulders and turned back to me.

"Muriel desperately wanted to be president of the club. She wanted it more than anything in the world. And when I realized I had the support of the club, I knew I would win the election, hands down."

"Isn't that the whole point of elections?" I asked her.

"It is. But so is good sportsmanship. Muriel wasn't getting any younger and, well, I don't want you to think I'm gossiping, I just want you to understand. She had a terrible home life."

I thought about steely-eyed Tab Sadler. "You mean—"

Agnes nodded. "I gave up the presidency so Muriel could have her moment in the spotlight, and I don't regret it for one minute. She deserved some happiness. Her husband . . ." A shiver skittered over Agnes's shoulders. "Tab Sadler is a monster. In fact . . ." She looked around just to be sure we were still alone. "We asked you to look into the murder, remember. Well, think about this, Avery. I wouldn't be at all surprised if Tab was the one who killed Muriel."

# CHAPTER 9

What did I know about investigating a murder?

In a word, absolutely nothing.

Okay, that's two words, but they are two words that pretty much say it all. The PPWC board had asked me to look into what happened to Muriel. And I had. Sort of. I'd talked to Tab Sadler and asked him where he was the night Muriel was killed. I'd spent hours thinking about Patricia and her bruises and her lies. I'd considered Agnes wanting the presidency, giving up the presidency, getting the presidency after all.

But really, what had I found out?

In a word—okay, two—absolutely nothing.

The thought weighed on my mind, even while I helped Quentin and Geneva get ready for the next day's lunch and what we expected would be a full house and a whole lot of pasta served. It knocked at my brain as I lent a hand when the presidential inauguration committee cleaned up the ballroom.

The thought of how I'd promised to look into the murder—and more importantly, the realization that I didn't know what I was doing—wouldn't leave me alone, not even when Jack came down the stairs, ready to leave for the day, and gave me a rundown on where he was in the restoration process.

"I've ordered more plastic runners to put down on the carpeting in Marigold." He showed me the invoice from the online site where he'd placed the order. "Those should be arriving first thing tomorrow. From what I've been able to see so far, most of the books can be saved. There's smoke damage, of course. I've got one air ionizer running in Marigold and another one running in the hallway between Marigold and Lilac. That should help get rid of the smoky smell." He took a deep breath. "You can barely detect it down here and . . ." He bent and leaned closer, the better to peer into my face. "You're not even listening, are you?"

"Is it that obvious?" I'd been standing by the front door, ready to lock it behind Jack as soon as he left, and I dragged around to the far side of my desk and dropped into the chair there. My head hurt. My spirits were down in the dumps. I'd barely slept since the night Muriel died, and the exhaustion was taking its toll. "It's the murder," I told him.

Jack set down the briefcase he carried in one hand and the piles of papers he had in the other and came to stand in front of me. He ran a hand through his hair and I can't say if that was meant to make it look any tidier, I only know that when he did, it stuck up on one side. "It's only natural," he said. "Everyone is upset."

"Yeah, but not everyone is in charge. I am, and I've got to make sure Muriel's death doesn't hurt the club."

"From what I saw today, that's not going to happen. The place was hopping."

"It was," I admitted. "But for all the wrong reasons."

"You mean—" When Jack made a face, his dark-rimmed glasses climbed up the bridge of his nose. "People were here just because . . . They wanted to be at the club because . . . They were rubbernecking?"

I'm not exactly sure it qualifies as rubbernecking when it comes to murder, but I knew what he was getting at, just as I understood the way his face paled. Jack was as baffled as I was by human nature and the fact that Muriel's death had caused a spike in club attendance. We were on the same page, me and Jack. I actually smiled.

"That's better." Jack smiled back, and some of the tension that had been coiled inside me slackened off, eased by the warmth of his expression. "Hey, look, it's not that late and . . ." He cleared his throat. "I know you're new in town and . . ." He lifted his chin and threw back his shoulders. Yeah, like a guy facing a firing squad.

"You want to have dinner?" he asked. "I mean, with . . . uh . . . me?"

A little more of that stress that had me tied in knots backed off.

At least until I came to my senses.

I stared at Jack.

He looked back at me, bewildered.

One second ticked by. Two. Three.

Finally, I took pity on him. "Dinner? Tonight?"

"Well, we could do it tomorrow, but you look so tired, I can't imagine you're going to cook for yourself. That's why I thought tonight would be better. We'll go somewhere where people can wait on you and you can order comfort food."

I gave him another chance. "Tonight?"

One corner of his mouth screwed up. "Not a good idea?"

"Not when you're having dinner with Kendall."

"Oh my gosh! Kendall!" He groaned. "I forgot all about Kendall." He pulled out his phone and checked the time, then scooped up his papers and briefcase. "I'm sorry, Avery. Rain check?"

Jack wasn't at all my kind of guy. That had always been—much to Aunt Rosemary's dismay—the pickup driving, blue-collar, country music type. But Jack was definitely cute, even if he was a little squirrelly and, let's face it, when a woman is feeling sorry for herself, cute has its charms.

"Sure," I told him.

Was it the same thing I'd told Oz when he talked about sharing a bottle of wine?

Maybe dark, policey, and not-so-tall has its charms, too.

Or maybe I was just so dazed by everything that had happened since I walked into PPWC, I wasn't thinking straight about either man.

Once he was out at his car, Jack waved and raised his voice so I could hear him where I stood just outside the front door. "Oh, and if you could tell the ladies not to touch anything in Marigold or in Lilac, that would be terrific."

"No worries," I assured him. But of course, I had plenty of worries.

I went back inside, locked the front door, checked the security program on my computer to make sure all the other doors in the building were secured, and considered my options.

I could go upstairs and fall into bed, where I wouldn't sleep a wink because I was too antsy.

I could go upstairs and make myself some dinner, which

I then would proceed not to eat because just thinking about the effort of popping something in the microwave made me too exhausted to chew.

Or I could get down to business.

Automatically, my gaze shifted over to the doorway that led into the basement. There was still yellow crime scene tape draped over it in a crazy crisscross pattern, but Oz would understand, right? The PPWC was my home, so of course if anyone was allowed access to all its rooms, it was me. And besides, I wasn't going to touch anything. I was only going to think. Only going to see if going down into the basement shook loose any memories of the night of the murder, if it would help me figure out what happened to Muriel and thus fulfill my promise to the board.

Yeah, my hands shook when I went to reach for the doorjamb so I could brace myself as I squeezed through the strips of tape. That was right before I reminded myself not to be too dramatic. Or too stupid.

I pulled the sleeves of my shirt down around my hands so I wouldn't leave any fingerprints on the doorjamb, and did what I'd seen Tab Sadler try to do in Muriel's office. I limboed my way through and around the strips of tape, got myself safely to the top step, then started down the stairs.

This time I had a distinct advantage: the lights worked.

Well, maybe that wasn't such a blessing after all, not when I saw the deep red stain on the step where I'd found Muriel crumpled and dead.

I hopped over that step, got to the bottom of the stairs, and turned around to look things over.

"Crazy thing, huh? I mean finding somebody who's been bumped off like that."

My breath caught, my heart stopped. I spun around.

And there she was, the girl in the beaded dress.

"How did you get in here?" I demanded.

She lifted one slim shoulder. "Same as always, sister."

"But I just checked the security system." I pointed back toward the steps and up to about where my desk was on the floor above us. "All the doors are locked. All the windows are alarmed. Everything's as secure as secure can be and still . . ." When my heart started up again, it was with a thump that jolted me forward. My stomach froze into a block of ice. My blood whooshed in my ears.

Yeah, I suspected, but this was the first moment I actually knew.

I swallowed down the sand in my throat. "You're a ghost."

The girl grinned. "Want me to prove it?"

Just like that, she disappeared, then popped up again a second later, right next to me.

I didn't so much gasp as I did groan.

"What?" She screwed up one side of her mouth. "You ain't gonna scream? Or faint? You ain't gonna cry?"

"You sound disappointed."

"Well . . ." Her shoulders rose and fell. "I always thought it would be more of the goat's whiskers, you know? A really big deal. Vanishing right in front of somebody." She did exactly that. There one second, gone the next. Then back to standing across from the stairs, where she'd been to begin with. "Maybe I just need to be a little more dramatic."

She levitated three feet off the ground and flapped around in a circle and those big bows on her shoes fluttered like bird wings.

As soft as a whisper, she landed, then looked at me hard. "Still nothing? No shrieks? No shudders? No shouts?"

Only deep down, soul-crushing disappointment.

"I don't want to communicate with the Other Side," I groaned.

Her eyes opened wide. "Most people . . . I mean, most living people . . . they don't even believe in the Other Side."

I sighed. "It's my aunt Rosemary's fault," I told the girl. "She lives in a place called Lily Dale, New York, and—"

"Lily Dale!" The girl's eyes lit. "I've heard of it. We talk about it over on the Other Side all the time. It's a place where people like you can talk to people like me."

It was what Aunt Rosemary had always said. What I'd never let myself believe.

Now, faced with the existence of what I'd always thought of as impossible, I felt like the world had tipped on its axis. This was a new reality. Not one I was sure I liked. It would take me a while to get used to it.

My shoulders slumped. "Aunt Rosemary always told me I shared her Gift," I admitted. "I just thought . . ."

"Yeah. I wouldn't have believed it, either. I mean, not until . . ." Her voice trailed off and for a second, she dimmed, like a picture slowly going out of focus.

Before I could stop myself, I stepped forward, one hand out toward her. "Don't leave!"

She winked back into focus. "You're telling me you want me to hang around?"

"I'm telling you I need to understand what's going on here. Why are you here?"

As if she had to think about it, she cocked her head and considered the question. Finally, her footsteps silent, she led me over to the right of the stairway, where the basement opened up into a dark room. What with her being incorporeal and all, I wasn't really sure she could operate a light switch so I saved her the embarrassment of trying and failing and flicked on the overhead lights.

The room was vast and the light was too dim to illuminate it completely. It was filled with shadows—behind the

long, narrow bar along the far wall, next to the couple tables piled in a corner, and in the space beyond a stack of
wooden chairs that looked as if they had a lifetime's worth
of dust on them. Like so many of the rooms upstairs, this
one was paneled in rich, heavy wood, and the floor, now
spotted with dirt and coated with grime, was the same parquet pattern as in the ballroom.

The heavy odor of mildew filled my nose, and yes, I
couldn't help it, I checked out each and every dark corner.
I'd already come up against one ghost. I wondered if there
were more of her kind lurking in the shadows.

Fortunately, the room was empty.

It was lonely, too.

"Used to be old man Dennison's place," the girl told me.

"Yeah, sure." I twitched away the quiet and the weight
of history that settled on my shoulders. "The whole house
was his. His family sold it to the club after Dennison's
death."

"Yeah, yeah. I'm no Dumb Kuff, I know that. But this
place . . ." She swept out on an arm. "See, this was his pri-
vate gin mill."

I'm sure my blank expression gave away my confusion
because the girl tossed her head and her dark sleek hair
glimmered in the light. "Don't you get it? It was a juice
joint! A blind pig! A speakeasy!"

My breath caught. "Chauncey Dennison, the millionaire
businessman, ran a speakeasy out of the basement of his
mansion?"

The girl laughed. "You got that right, sister. Dennison,
he was an egg, all right—a big shot, sure, but he liked to
throw back a couple every now and then, and he was no
goof. Smart, if you know what I mean."

I did. Or at least I thought I did. Back in the 1920s when

Chauncey Dennison still owned the mansion that was now the Portage Path Women's Club, Prohibition was the law of the land and it was illegal to sell liquor in the United States. That's when speakeasies popped up, secret places where patrons could dance the night away and drink to their hearts'—but maybe not their livers'—content.

"So Dennison ran this place and I bet he made a bundle selling illegal liquor here," I said while I ventured farther into the room and glanced around the empty space and wondered what it looked like at the time. If there was one person who would know, it was the girl at my side.

"What's your story?" I asked her. "And what are you doing here? Who are you?"

"Clementine Bow." She made an exaggerated curtsy, then broke into a grin. "But you can call me Clemmie. Everybody does."

"Everybody did, you mean."

Her Cupid's bow lips puckered. "You don't need to rub it in. It ain't my fault I'm dead."

That was the first moment I had an inkling of an understanding of my aunt Rosemary. I mean, here I was, talking to someone from the Other Side, and suddenly I had a million questions that demanded answers. I figured I'd start with the easiest.

"How long have you been here?" I asked Clemmie.

She wrinkled her nose. "What year is it?"

I told her and her mouth screwed up. "I'm not so good at numbers," she admitted. "But I know it's been a good long time. I came here in 1927."

Yes, it had been a while.

"And in all that time . . ." I wasn't sure exactly how to ask so I took some time getting the words straight in my head. "When we bumped into each other for the first time the other night, you were surprised I could see you. That I could hear you."

"You got that right, sister."

"Does that mean, in all the time since 1927 . . . you haven't talked? To anybody?"

She waved a hand in a way designed to make me think it was no big deal, but remember, I'd grown up with Aunt Rosemary, and like it or not, I'd heard plenty of lectures on watching body language and picking up on moods and emotions. Yeah, Aunt Rosemary said it all had to do with being an empath, but I knew better. Well, at least I'd always thought I knew better. Until I met Clemmie Bow. I knew that watching and listening and picking up on emotions was what it took to be a good listener, a good waitress, a good friend. Now I realized it had a lot to do with being a good medium, too. Sure, that little wave Clemmie gave me was meant to show me how much she didn't care, but there was a certain sadness in her eyes that made my throat clutch.

"I've talked plenty," she said. "But no one . . ." She cleared her throat with a little cough. "No one ever heard me. I've been popping up all over this basement forever and a day. You're the first one who's ever seen me, all right. It's the eel's hips, that's what it is. The eel's hips to finally have somebody I can talk to."

"Oh no!" As if it would stop her thinking what I feared she was thinking, I put out both my hands. "I told you, the last thing I want to do is communicate with the Other Side."

"Except you're already doing that."

"Well, then I don't want to do it all the time. You're not going to . . ." I hated to even speak the words in case they might put ideas into her head. "You're not going to follow me around and demand attention all the time, are you?" A thought hit, and I propped my fists on my hips. "Hey, are you the one who went through my rooms the day I moved in?"

"Bushwa!" She rolled her eyes. "You think I got nothin' better to do?"

"Do you?"

She pressed her lips together and lifted her chin.

"You don't." Since she wouldn't say the words, I saved her the trouble. "Was it you? Or do you know who it was?"

"No," she said. "No, it wasn't me. And no, I don't know who done it."

"Then what about anything else that's happened around here? If you can float around all over the place and no one knows you're there, you must have seen plenty and you must have heard plenty, too. What can you tell me? About Muriel?"

"You mean that Mrs. Grundy who came rollin' down the steps the other night?"

"Not Mrs. Grundy," I told her. "Mrs. Sadler. Muriel Sadler."

I was, apparently, a dumb Dora after all, because Clemmie shook her head. "A Mrs. Grundy," she said, "is a woman who's straightlaced. High-strung. Uppity. You know the type."

I did, and it described Muriel perfectly.

"What happened before she rolled down the steps?" I asked Clemmie.

"How should I know? One second, I'm down here all by myself, and the next, that door there . . ." She looked toward the stairs. "It opens up and that woman comes crashing down."

"Was she alive when she did?"

"What do I look like?" Clemmie asked. "A sawbones? I

can tell you she wasn't moving. And I can tell you she hurt her head somehow."

"She didn't exactly hurt her head. Muriel was murdered."

I don't suppose it's possible for a ghost to get pale. After all, there was no blood flowing through Clemmie's body, so there's no way it could drain from her face. Still, I swear she turned a little more ashen. A little more transparent.

"The women of the club have asked me to look into the murder," I told her, then added, "I'm the new manager here," because unless she'd been floating around, unseen, while I was working or when I'd had my job interview, she wouldn't know that. "I thought if you saw who threw Muriel's body down the steps—"

"No." She shook her head and backed away from me. "I didn't see a thing."

"But you must have! You just said—"

"I said I pass the time around here." All of a sudden, I could see the wall behind Clemmie through her body. "I didn't say I know anything about what happened."

"What happened was murder. And you can help. You can really help."

"No." Clemmie's eyes filled with tears. She shook her head, faster and faster, and with each shake, she faded a little more. "I . . . I can't help you. I don't know."

"But Clemmie . . ." I rushed forward but I wasn't quick enough.

Clemmie was gone.

# CHAPTER 10

I'd seen it done so many times, it should have been a piece of cake.

Eyes closed.

Deep breaths.

Mind blank, floating, open to messages from the Other Side.

And . . .

Nothing.

Nothing when I tried the routine before I went to bed the night Clemmie showed me the speakeasy, and nothing again the next morning when I gave it another go before I headed downstairs to work.

So how come the whole meditation thing always worked for Aunt Rosemary when she wanted to contact Spirit?

And when I wanted to give it a go, why was it the only thing I got was a kink in my neck from sitting still too long?

Grumbling, I slid off the brown-and-orange couch that

had once belonged to Aunt Rosemary and had been delivered to PPWC the day before I arrived, and finished getting ready for the day ahead. Little by little, I'd cleaned up the mess left by the intruder, who Clemmie insisted wasn't her. But if it wasn't her, why wouldn't she tell me who it was? After all, being able to float around—and be invisible, to boot—should have been the world's best excuse to keep tabs on everyone and everything in the place. Which was exactly why I wanted Clemmie's help solving the mystery of Muriel's murder.

The bad news was I couldn't get in touch.

The good news? Well, that was a little more practical and a whole lot less supernatural.

Thanks to elbow grease and some serious organizing, my rooms finally looked presentable. I'd always pictured the suite as a refuge and a place where I could kick back after a long day.

But then, that fantasy never involved murder.

Or the supernatural.

Or burglary, for that matter.

On the way to the bedroom for my brown flats, an electrical current of unease zipped up my spine when I glanced at the list I'd prepared to give to Oz the next time I saw him.

Datebook.

Journal.

Spiral-bound notebook where I kept a list of important addresses.

Three things—three very personal things—I hadn't been able to find when I cleaned up the mess. For the life of me, I couldn't figure out why anyone would want them, and heck, I should have been able to.

After all, like it or not, it looked like I shared Aunt Rosemary's Gift. I was supposed to know what was happening in people's heads. And in the Great Beyond.

"Some Gift," I muttered. Shoes on, I locked the door behind me and started downstairs. "Never asked for it. Can't return it. And let's face it, Avery . . ." The thought soured my stomach. "You don't have a clue how to use it."

That morning, Agnes was scheduled to lead a discussion with the Current Events interest group and after the packed house we'd had the day before, I expected the club would be hopping. When I got downstairs, though, the parking lot was empty.

"No worries," I told myself. "It will be just like yesterday. Our members, they'll come."

Only they didn't.

I unlocked the door and waited.

Nobody.

I went to the kitchen to make sure Quentin and Geneva were A-OK with everything they had to do that day.

Nobody.

Agnes's discussion was set to start at nine, so I poured myself a cup of coffee, answered the phone (and promptly hung up again with a terse, "No comment,") when someone from the media called to demand more information on the murder, and I was just checking the day's schedule when Agnes arrived.

In a trim dark suit and pearl earrings, she looked professional, in charge, and up to the task of leading the group. She had a copy of the day's newspaper tucked under her arm, and I couldn't help myself. My gaze wandered to the glaring headline—*President's Peril*—above a picture of Muriel. "Current Events? Do you think they're going to want to talk about—"

"I certainly hope not!" Agnes shivered. "I've never thought of our members as voyeuristic. Not until yesterday, anyway." She shook her head in a way that told me she'd been disappointed then and the thought still rankled. "I won't allow it in my discussion group. I've already prepared the agenda, and we're sticking to it. We're talking about trade with China and the outlook on inflation. Period." I couldn't speak for the other members of the Current Events group, but the way Agnes emphasized that *period*, I was sure I, for one, would never argue with her. "All we need . . ." She glanced back toward the empty parking lot and the starch went out of her shoulders. "Nobody?"

"It's early." I used my perky voice.

Agnes wasn't fooled. Her lips folded in on themselves. "We had six people signed up for the discussion, and I saw every single one of them here for lunch yesterday. They'll be back." She gave me a sidelong look. "Right?"

I sure hoped so. I'd spent a whole lot of time the evening before designing and ordering invitations for Agnes's inauguration. They were set to arrive later that afternoon, and I planned to get them right in the mail. Would our members attend? Would they ever walk into the club again?

I wished I could be sure. In spite of what Agnes believed, I feared our members really were just plain, old-fashioned gawkers. And now that they'd seen what they wanted to see—the scene of the grisly crime—just thinking about the murder was enough to keep them away from the club.

Permanently.

"Maybe it all comes down to what the board said. You know, the night I found Muriel." A picture of her battered body popped into my head and I got rid of it as fast as I could. "We need to find answers, and since you gave me the job of doing that . . ." I glanced her way, hoping she'd catch on to what I was getting at, that I wouldn't have to come right out and ask. When she didn't, I gritted my teeth.

"Where were you when Muriel was killed?" I asked her.

As if I'd slapped her, Agnes sucked in a sharp breath. "You can't think I could have possibly—"

"No. But the board told me I have to ask."

"Yes. Of course. You're right." She steadied her shoulders and lifted her chin. "I was home. All evening. By myself." She slid me a look. "Not much of an alibi, is it?"

"No, but your word is good enough for me."

The uncomfortable questions over, she shook herself. "For now, I think our bigger problem may be today's events." She glanced at the phone on my desk. "I'm not telling you how to do your job, Avery, but—"

Maybe I was legitimately psychic after all; I knew exactly what Agnes was thinking. I rounded the desk immediately and grabbed my phone, then checked the list of members signed up for Current Events and started dialing at the same time I told Agnes, "Maybe our members just need a little reminder."

Marcy Collins, the first woman I called, did not. In fact, her response to my call—about how the Current Events discussion group was going to be meeting soon and we looked forward to seeing her—was a clipped, "There's no way I'm stepping into a building where there's been a murder."

"But—"

Yeah, I was going to remind her that she'd been there the day before for lunch and lived to tell the tale when she hung up on me.

Diana Green, Peggy Organsky, and Lily Pratak were a little more subtle, but they made it just as clear.

The Portage Path Women's Club was off their list of places to go.

At least until the police apprehended the deranged killer.

Four calls in, I hung up the phone and gave Agnes a sour smile. "They saw what they wanted to see yesterday," I told her. "They can tell their friends they were here. They can talk about how they knew Muriel. I bet some of them even peeked down the steps in the hopes of getting a look at the bloodstains. And now—"

"I get it." Agnes heaved a sigh. "Maybe I'd feel the same way, too." She hung her head and fingered the gold PPWC pin on her lapel, the picture of despondency.

At least for a minute.

Then Agnes pulled back her shoulders and lifted her chin. "But I don't have the luxury of acting the way they're acting, do I? I'm the president of the Portage Path Women's Club, and I'm going to find a way to turn this around. Starting right here and now."

As if Fate were listening, the front door popped open and the other two women who were scheduled for the Current Events discussion stepped inside.

"See?" Agnes gave me a smile. "We'll make this work, Avery. I promise, we'll make this work." And still smiling, she greeted the ladies and led them back to the Rose Room. Three cheers for Agnes. Sure, there were only two attendees, but she treated them like they were the two most important people in the building.

Which, come to think of it, I guess they were.

I had the next few minutes to myself to check voice mails and respond to emails. Three of them were from members asking how they could get what was left of their yearly membership fee refunded because they were dropping out of the club. The rest were from reporters looking for comments about the murder, background on Muriel, or just wondering why the cops were being so closed-mouth and did that mean we knew something we weren't talking about? Fine by me. Those emails were easy to delete, delete, delete.

In fact, I'd just finished getting rid of the annoying messages when the door banged open and Patricia flew into the club.

"Late, late, late," she grumbled. "Can you believe it? I've got a clock on my phone, an alarm clock on my bedside table, and a cat that every other day of the year would have had me up at six so I could feed her. Except today, when I'm scheduled to help with Current Events." She slid me a look. "Anybody show up for it?"

"A couple."

"That's all?" Patricia's eyebrows rose. She scratched a finger under her nose, and I noticed her knuckles were raw and bruised.

Concerned, I jumped up from my desk chair and went to stand in front of her. "Are you all right?" I asked.

It took her a second to realize I'd seen the injury, and when she did, she closed her eyes as if praying for patience.

"Please don't say anything to anyone else," Patricia groaned. "It's so embarrassing and I wouldn't want anyone to worry about me."

"But what happened?"

As if that would get rid of the telltale marks and what certainly must have been a whole lot of pain, she shook her hand. "Patricia Fink meets back patio," she told me. "Stupid mistake. Tripped over my own two feet."

"If you need bandages—"

"No, no. I'll be fine. Took care of all the minor first aid last night when it happened. The scrapes aren't deep. And the way I figure it, I can keep my hand out of sight if there are people around. If I bandage it up, chances are it will just attract more attention. That's all I need, everyone thinking that I'm losing my marbles and shouldn't live alone." She examined her hand. "It only hurts when I make a fist. That shouldn't be a problem. Now that Muriel's not around, I hardly ever feel like punching out anybody's lights."

She was going for funny and I got it, really I did. But it did bring up an interesting point.

"That first day I was here, Muriel told you she'd never let you change the club. 'Over my dead body.' Those were her words."

"Well, that tells you a little something about our relationship." Patricia touched one hand gently to her raw knuckles. "In fact, it says a lot about Muriel's relationship with a whole lot of people."

"Which is why when I asked who hated her, you said—"

"Everybody."

"But when Oz . . ." I realized she might not know who I was talking about. "When the detective asked the same thing, Patricia, you kept your mouth shut."

She harrumphed. "We can't go airing our dirty laundry. There are plenty of secrets in a club like this. That doesn't mean any of us has the right to go screaming them from the rooftops. That's not how it works."

"Even if there's a chance it might help the police find out who killed Muriel?"

She seemed honestly confused. "It can't be anyone here, can it?"

"We don't know that."

"But of course we do. This is the Portage Path Women's Club, and sure, there are some petty differences. Show me any place you put a dozen women together and don't get somebody rubbing somebody else the wrong way. But a murderer? Here? It's not possible." Patricia glanced at the clock on the wall above my desk. "Got to go," she told me. "I'm in the mood for a lively current events discussion, and since there's hardly anyone else here, Agnes won't have a chance to call on someone else and shut me up."

I stopped her with a question. "Is that why you and Muriel were always at odds? Current events? She wanted things here at the club to stay the way they'd always been, and you—"

"Live in the real world?" There was no amusement in Patricia's laugh. "She was impossible."

"And you weren't willing to compromise."

"Why should I have been? Muriel acted like she owned this club. She didn't think it could be as important to anyone else as it was to her. But my great-aunts were early members. And I've belonged for more than thirty years. I have as much right, as much prestige, as much of a heritage here as Muriel ever did. But that doesn't mean I'm closed-minded and set in my ways."

"But it does mean you and Muriel didn't get along. Patricia, where were you when Muriel was killed?"

Her mouth opened and closed, but no words came out of it. At least until Patricia let out a whoop that echoed against the crystal chandelier over our heads. "Are you asking me . . ." She swallowed another guffaw. "Well, of course you are. It's what we told you to do, isn't it? Three cheers for you, Avery. You are exactly the kind of manager this club needs. You're not going to shirk your duties. Even if it means ruffling some feathers. That's what I love to see. Initiative."

I like an attagirl as much as the next person, but I wasn't going to let it distract me. "So where were you?" I asked her.

"Before I went home and had to fix the sink? Right . . ." She pointed out to the door and toward the church on the other side of PPWC's nearly empty parking lot. "Right there. There was a Kids Coats event that evening. We collect coats and hats and gloves for needy kids and distribute them at a school in the neighborhood right before Christmas."

"And the meeting took all night?"

"Of course not. Started at six thirty. Like always. Ended at eight forty-five. Like always."

"And you were there the entire time?"

"It may surprise you, Avery . . ." She winked. "Once I start talking about a project that's near and dear to my heart, it's pretty hard to stop me. Chances are a few of the committee members wished I had left early. I'll see you later." She gave me a wave and zoomed toward the Rose Room. "Gotta get to it!"

I was so busy watching Patricia hustle down the hallway, I didn't realize the door had opened again. The next thing I knew, Gracie was standing next to me, looking where I was looking.

"Think she's the perp?" Gracie asked.

I laughed because it seemed a better way to answer the question than to admit I honestly didn't know. "It could be anyone."

"Not what I asked."

I gave in with a small smile. "Patricia and Muriel didn't get along."

That day, Gracie's outfit consisted of a thundercloud-gray skirt topped with a fog-colored sweater. The colors were just right for her grim expression. "I hate to speak ill of the dead, but let's face it, no one got along with Muriel. She was a bully. Always had been."

I glanced down at Gracie. "You knew her? I mean, before you joined the club?"

"Everyone in Portage Path knew Muriel from day one. She made sure of that. I'm a little older, of course, but I remember hearing stories about her growing up. Muriel this and Muriel that. The world began and ended with Muriel. It was as simple as that." Gracie's eyes clouded with memory.

"I had cousins who went to school with her back in the day. Can't say there was any love lost there. Word was Muriel cheated Felicia Martingale out of a scholarship that should have been hers."

The name sounded familiar. "Felicia . . . ?"

"She was president here. Before Muriel. Oh yeah, there were some tense times when the two of them were in a room together. And then of course, there was the whole thing about Muriel and Tab Sadler."

I remembered what Agnes had told me, how she thought Tab might be the killer. "I hear he's not the nicest guy."

"Hah!" Gracie shuffled off. "Don't ever let Agnes hear you say that. As far as I can see, she still worships the ground Tab Sadler walks on. Once upon a time a very long time ago, Agnes and Tab were engaged. That is, until Muriel up and stole him away."

# CHAPTER 11

We had pasta sauce left over.

Boy, did we had pasta sauce left over!

In the spirit of conserving money and making the most of Quentin's sauce—a blend of plum tomatoes, basil, garlic, and sweet peppers that was as subtle as our chef was not—I waited until after the lunch hour and the rush of diners we'd hoped for that never came, and I helped ladle the sauce into containers so we could freeze it.

"I'm leaving some in the fridge for you," Quentin told me when we were almost finished. "You come down and make yourself some dinner tonight. You deserve it for how hard you've been working."

Maybe.

But I didn't relish the thought of wandering the big, empty mansion after dark. Who else besides Clemmie might be waiting in the shadows for me?

The thought caused a shiver to crawl over my shoulders, but fortunately, I didn't have a chance to dwell on it before a voice called out from the hallway. "Leaving for the day!"

I turned to find Jack laden down with two huge boxes marked *Old PPWC records*. Just as I did, he glanced at the boxes, too. "I want to check out the stuff in here and see if it needs a little more cleaning. Taking these records home so I can spread them out and give them some serious attention."

I scurried out of the kitchen and through the dining room to the hallway so I could open the door for him and he wouldn't have to juggle the load.

"Oh, and just so you know . . ." Since his hands were full and he couldn't push his glasses up, he wiggled his nose. "There was a statue in Marigold."

"Yes, Hortense Dash, the first president of the club."

"Well, that statue isn't there now. I've looked all over for it. I wondered if maybe you moved it to keep it safe while I work on the renovation."

I didn't have to think about it. The statue was marble, heavy. If I'd moved it, I would certainly remember. And yet . . .

"It was there the first time you came to check out Marigold," I told Jack. "I remember seeing it when we walked into the room to take a look around. That was obviously after the fire."

Apparently Jack remembered, too. He nodded. "And before the murder."

"You don't think . . ." My stomach did a flip-flop. "Could that statue be the murder weapon?" Automatically, my gaze traveled toward the stairway that led into the basement.

Jack's did, too. He frowned. "You should probably let the cops know. If things are missing—"

"There are things missing from up in my rooms, too,"

I said, because honestly, with everything that had happened since I started my job at PPWC, I wasn't sure I'd ever told Jack how my rooms had been trashed. "But that can't have anything to do with the murder, can it?"

He shrugged and stepped toward the door, but before he could leave, I had things I wanted to ask him.

No, I wasn't about to bring up his dinner with Kendall and ask how that went. Jack's business was his own, and I had other things on my mind.

"How much do you know about this house?"

Thinking, he pursed his lips. "Built at the beginning of the twentieth century, big deal at the time. If you like, I can show you the different kinds of wood molding I've taken note of. And the doorknobs are splendid! Glass, porcelain, brass. I'm making a list, thinking of writing a paper. I haven't been up on the third floor. What kind of doorknobs do you have up there?"

I had to admit I hadn't noticed, but I didn't give Jack much time to look disappointed at this shortcoming of mine before I asked, "Did you ever hear that there was a speakeasy in the basement?"

"Really?" Jack laughed. "I always pictured ol' Dennison as a sort of puffed-up, tuxedo-wearing stick in the mud. Knowing there was a speakeasy down there would really put a different spin on the history of the house, wouldn't it? Hmmm. . . ." He was lost in thought for a couple moments and he mumbled to himself. "*House Restoration* magazine might be interested. Or the *Journal of American Trends in Home Design and Fashion.* I haven't sent anything to them since I wrote that piece on the significance of back porches in the Midwest." He snapped to. "How do you know, Avery? I mean, about the speakeasy? If you can cite sources, that would really help me."

I couldn't exactly explain, so I shrugged. "I just heard someone talking about the speakeasy. That's all."

"One of the members?" As if that person might be near, he looked around the lobby. "I'd love to speak to her. I don't suppose you have any members old enough to actually remember the speakeasy. I mean, firsthand. A first-person recounting of visiting the speakeasy would be priceless!"

"I'll . . . uh . . . see what I can find out," I promised, even though I wasn't all that sure I could. After all, my information had come from a ghost. I wondered how he'd cite that for his article.

I twitched away the thought and scrambled to explain my interest before he could ask. "If it's true, I thought we could capitalize on the idea. You know, host a Prohibition party down there or something like that. Maybe that would help generate interest in the club."

His smile wasn't as soft as it was cynical. "There were plenty of members interested yesterday."

"And some of them . . ." I thought of the two ladies who'd shown up for Current Events. The six who'd come for lunch. The few who'd helped the planning committee work on Agnes's swearing-in ceremony. "Some of them are still interested, but it's the same core group that showed up even before the murder. The rest of them came and saw what they wanted to see yesterday, and now they've deserted us again."

"So a party in the basement might be great. Even if there never was a speakeasy there, we could always say there was."

It wasn't the sort of fudging of facts I expected from a preservationist, and I smiled. At least until I thought of what else I wanted to talk to Jack about. I edged into the topic carefully.

"You know I'm not from around here. Have you ever

heard stories about the house . . . I mean, I know it sounds crazy, but I was wondering if somehow we could use it for publicity . . . Does anybody talk about this house being haunted?"

Jack laughed. "That's a good one. An old mansion that's haunted."

"I don't mean by Muriel!" I thought we should get this straight so he didn't think I was insensitive. "I just mean . . . I was thinking . . . you know, about old ghost stories."

"Ghosts!" Jack bumped open the door and stepped outside. "I get the appeal. I understand why people like to listen to stories about hauntings. But let's face it, those stories are for kids. Anyone who actually believes in ghosts has to be totally and completely out of their mind."

Did I honestly think Jack—or any right-thinking person—would feel differently about the Hereafter?

Let's face it, before I met Clemmie, I felt the same way.

And now?

Now it would have been nice to have someone I could confide in about what was happening here at the club. Someone who didn't laugh in my face at the mere mention of the word *ghost*.

Disheartened, I was all set to lock the front door behind Jack when I realized I'd left my ring of club keys in the kitchen. Too tired to drag all the way to the back of the building, I rummaged through my top desk drawer. I had a vague memory of some talk of the keys that had once belonged to the last business manager.

Success! I found the keys and the large round ring with the initials *B.P.* etched on it. Right before I remembered that Muriel had told the board Brittany's front door key was missing.

"Going home." Quentin's voice snapped me out of my

thoughts. "Me and Geneva." I looked up just in time to see him arrive in the lobby. He was wearing a black leather jacket and had a red bandanna tied around his head, and he poked a thumb over his shoulder toward the kitchen. "We're all set to go and we'll use the back door. Just wanted you to know we're leaving and we'll see you in the morning."

I weighed the keychain in one hand. "That's fine," I told Quentin. "Only . . ." I tossed the keys and caught them in my right hand. "Do you know, are these the keys Brittany had when she worked here?"

Chewing his lower lip, he leaned closer for a better look. "Sure looks like 'em. Left real fast, that girl did. Which is why they advertised and you got the job."

"Her front door key isn't here," I told him.

Quentin might not look like the brightest bulb in the box, but in that one moment, I knew he'd never let any grass grow under his feet. His eyes lit. "You mean she kept that one key when she left? And she could have used that key to come and go? You don't think she's the one who . . ." His gaze skimmed toward the basement door.

"I don't know," I admitted. A plan had already formed in my brain, and I went to the computer and checked the employment files and when I found it, I wrote down Brittany's address. I waved the sheet of paper at Quentin. "But I intend to find out."


Portage Path, Ohio, is way bigger than Lily Dale, New York—which, for the record, is more of a hamlet than a town, a place where the streets haven't been widened since they were used for horses and buggies, and where there's a year-round population of something like 275.

I got lost trying to find Brittany's address, and by the

time I pulled up to the three-story redbrick apartment building just south of the Portage Path University campus, it was late. It was rude of me to show up on Brittany's doorstep when it was already dark. It was wrong of me not to call ahead and ask if I could stop by. I was being what Aunt Rosemary (one of those 275 stalwart souls who endure year after year of upstate New York winters) would surely call insensitive.

I did it anyway.

Brittany's apartment was on the first floor and had an outside entrance, three brick steps that led to a concrete front porch. I rang the bell and when she answered, I introduced myself and told her I was the one who now had what used to be her job at PPWC.

Brittany was a woman of forty or so. Short, round, dark hair cut short and shaggy. She had a button nose. Tiny eyes. And cheeks that were round and as red as fireplugs. I wondered if she'd just gotten in from work. Or if she was headed out somewhere. She was dressed in a flower-print skirt and a gold sweater and she was wearing lipstick.

"I'd like to talk to you for a couple minutes," I said.

Brittany shuffled her feet. She bit her lower lip. She looked over her shoulder, though what she was looking at, I couldn't imagine. The apartment was so small and I could see her entire living room and from there, into the kitchen and toward a back door. There was no one else around.

"I can't really . . ." Brittany twisted her hands together at her waist. "It's not really a good time."

"I swear, only a minute." Though I hadn't been invited, I stepped up into the tiny entryway and at that point, Brittany had no choice but to let me in. Or chuck me out on my butt.

Lucky for me, she chose the former.

Once she had the door closed behind me, I breathed in deep and smiled. The apartment was filled with the aroma of garlic and onions. She was cooking, and it smelled divine. When I told her so, some of the stiffness went out of Brittany's shoulders. While she shared her recipe for sautéed mushrooms, I had a chance to look around.

Behind her, the living room was neat and tidy. Her gray couch had two enormous pink pillows on it, and the bookcase against the far wall was chockablock with Disney character figurines.

Winnie-the-Pooh gave me a grin.

I ignored him and looked, instead, at the round table for two against the far wall. It was set with two blue dinner plates, two sets of silverware, two wineglasses, and a pink candle. Brittany was expecting company.

"I won't keep you," I promised her. "I just wanted to ask you a couple of questions."

One corner of her mouth pulled tight. "It's not about some procedure at the club, is it? Or about how to deal with a vendor or fill out paperwork or keep those old birds who support the place happy? You would have called if it was something like that. You came here to talk about Muriel Sadler."

"I'm sure you've seen the news. Her death hit us all hard."

There was no amusement in Brittany's laugh. "Really? That's funny, I knew Muriel for years, part of that time when I would take my grandmother over to the club, and the rest of it . . . well, three months of it, anyway, when I worked as club manager, and I don't feel hit hard at all. In fact, when I first saw the story about what happened to her, I did a little happy dance, right there . . ." She pointed across the room. "In front of the TV."

"You didn't like Muriel." Yeah, that was pretty much a

no-brainer, but if there was one thing I'd learned in the very short time I'd been on the case, it was that a detective (no matter how amateur) needed to get her facts straight. "Why?"

"Why? You work over at PPWC and you're asking me why I didn't like Muriel?" When Brittany shook her head, her gold beaded earrings did a hula. "But you haven't really been there very long. Muriel didn't have a chance yet to dig her claws really deep into you."

Brittany had once had my job. She'd been where I was now. Well, except for dealing with a murder. We were on the same page as far as experiences, challenges. I owed her the truth. "I only worked with Muriel for one day."

She tsked. "Lucky you. But let me guess . . ." Her look was sly. "Muriel didn't want you to have the job in the first place."

I couldn't help but feel defensive. "The majority of the board supported me."

Brittany laughed and clapped one pudgy little hand on my arm. "Yeah, me, too. All of them, including Muriel, knew I had the perfect education and background for the job. I had great references who told them I'd work hard and I could really get things done. At first, everything was peachy. Then Kendall Sadler lost her job over at the boutique where she was working as a stylist. As of that day, my qualifications, my great probationary review, my ideas, none of it mattered to Muriel."

It all sounded too familiar. Even though I didn't need Brittany to confirm what I was thinking, I said it anyway. "Muriel wanted her granddaughter to have your job."

Brittany gave me the thumbs-up. "You got that right. Muriel, she would have done anything to see that happen. She fought tooth and nail for it, even though the board supported me."

I remembered Kendall, so sure of herself. So annoying. "Is Kendall that good?" I asked.

"Kendall Sadler is . . ." There was no one in the apartment except us, but Brittany lowered her voice anyway. "Kendall Sadler might be cute and perky and as rich as all get-out, but that girl is a train wreck. She's a self-centered little—" She cleared her throat. "Well, you get my point. There was nothing Muriel wanted more in the world than to get the job for Kendall, but not because Kendall would have been any good at it. Muriel wanted Kendall to start out as club manager and then someday be president of the club, but truth be told, that kid can't keep a job. Not anywhere. She got sacked from that boutique for being on her phone and ignoring customers. Over the years, she even had a couple other jobs with companies owned by the Sadlers' bigwig friends. None of them ever worked out. Muriel would never come right out and say it, but she knew the truth. She needed to snag the job at PPWC for Kendall because Kendall couldn't find another job on her own."

"But you were hired and you were good at what you did."

Brittany pressed her lips into a tight line. "And you know what? I thought that was all I needed. I always loved that old house. I loved the idea of working there, and I had a lot of really good plans for the place. They're going down the tubes, you know."

I did.

There was no use beating a dead horse.

"You said you worked at the club for three months. What finally happened?"

When Brittany made a sour face she looked like a gnome that had bitten a lemon.

A timer went off in the kitchen, and she hurried in there to handle it but was back in a second. "Kendall lost her job and things around PPWC got ugly. I never would have given Muriel the satisfaction of firing me," Brittany said. "I quit."

"Because of Muriel." It didn't take a genius to figure that much out. "What did she do?"

Brittany snorted. "What *didn't* she do? Talked behind my back. Sabotaged a project I was working on for the History Committee. She conveniently *lost*"—she gave that last word a bitter edge—"the research I'd compiled. She'd asked to see it because she said she was interested when all she wanted to do was dump it and make me look bad. Muriel was underhanded, unreasonable, unsociable, and downright nasty."

"And you didn't like her."

Brittany harrumphed. "Who did? She would have done the same thing to you if she'd lived long enough to have the chance. Just like she did to the two women who had the job before I did. There and gone inside a year. Both of them. Conveniently, they both left just as Kendall was between jobs. When I lasted three months, I thought I was pretty special. But the longer I stayed there, the more difficult Muriel was to work with. Once upon a time, I thought it was my dream job, but I'll tell you what: By the time I tendered my resignation and walked out of there, I was the happiest person in the world. Couldn't wait to put as much distance as I could between me and the Portage Path Women's Club."

"So why did you keep the key?"

Brittany flinched. She looked away. "What key? I don't know what you're talking about."

I pulled her key ring out of my pocket and jingled it in front of her gnome nose. "Every key is here except the front door key."

She stuck out her bottom lip. "That doesn't mean I took it."

"But if you did, it does mean you could come and go from the club anytime you wanted."

As if I'd punched her, she reared back. "You mean like the night Muriel was killed?"

"Where were you?"

She sniffed. "I don't see why that's any business of yours."

"Technically, it's not," I admitted. "Except the board wants me to ask around. Here I am, asking. Where were you the night Muriel was killed?"

She lifted her chin. "Right here."

"All night?"

"Yes, all night. And all day, too. I haven't found another job yet." She backed away from me. "I still don't see why this is any of your business."

"Do you have the key?"

"No." I might have actually believed her if she didn't blink wildly when she made the statement. Her voice rang out against the Disney figurines that watched us. "I never want to step foot inside that place again."

It's one thing to think about playing detective.

It's another thing to actually do it.

I didn't have the chops to make Brittany fess up.

And I had exactly zero authority.

I had no choice but to head to the door. "I get it. I really do. I'm sorry you had such a terrible experience at the club. If you need a reference for a new job—"

She shot me a look. "I'll do fine on my own, thank you. I don't need your help."

I opened the door. "Well, good luck. If you change your mind—"

"I won't," she assured me, and I think she was going to say something else, but she never had the chance.

The back door opened and closed, and the delicious aroma of grilled steak wafted into the room just as a voice called out, "Dinner's ready, honey!"

When the man holding a plate with those steaks on them strode into the room, he took one look at me and stopped cold.

He was a tall guy with curly brown hair, wide shoulders, and piercing blue eyes, and honestly, I couldn't say if he was a looker like Gracie thought, but I did know one thing. I knew exactly who he was.

# CHAPTER 12

I nodded by way of greeting. "Bill Manby, I presume."
Bill was dressed in khakis and a green golf shirt, and
he set the steaks on the table so he could cross his arms
over his broad chest. "Who wants to know?"

"It's Avery," Brittany told him. "The one who got—"

"Your job. Yeah. I remember them talking, after they
decided to hire her." Bill narrowed his eyes, blue lasers, and
shot me a look. "What do you want?"

Before I could answer, Brittany stepped toward him.
"She's looking for the front door key to the club, the one
that used to be mine. I told her I don't have it, that I don't
know what she's talking about."

Bill snorted. "What, those rich old ladies can't afford to
make a copy of a key for you?"

"I've got a full set of my own keys," I told him. "What I
don't have is an explanation as to why Brittany would want
to keep a key after she no longer worked at the club."

"She told you she doesn't have it," Bill snapped.

"She thinks I'm lying," Brittany sputtered. "She thinks I killed Muriel."

"Then you're flat-out crazy." Bill didn't spare me another look. He flumped down on the closest chair, pulled it up to the table, and used his fork to stab one of the steaks so he could set it on his plate. "You got mushrooms to go with this, right?" he asked Brittany.

We all knew she did, and she scurried into the kitchen to get them and brought them to the table along with two baked potatoes. She sat down across from Bill.

It was rude to stand there and watch them eat. That didn't stop me. I inched nearer and waited until Bill had a mouth full. "Muriel told me she sacked you because you were stealing from the club."

He swallowed and coughed, and when he kept on coughing, Brittany popped up and hurried into the kitchen and came back with a glass of water. Bill gulped it down and pounded his chest before he frowned in my direction.

"The woman was a liar. She made up that story because she wanted to get rid of me."

"Why? Did she want Kendall to have your job, too?"

My sarcastic humor was lost on both of them, so I ignored their blank looks and decided on another tack. "Look, I'm just trying to get at the truth. If Muriel made up the story about you stealing—"

"She did." Bill had a mushroom speared on the end of his fork, and he poked it in my direction. "That woman was as nutty as a fruitcake."

"That's why she fired you? Because she was nuts?"

Bill and Brittany exchanged brief looks before Bill popped the mushroom into his mouth. "That's right," he said even while he was chewing. "Nuts. And I can prove it. She said I stole stuff from the club, right?"

I nodded. "According to Muriel, you took two stained glass lamps, a porcelain ewer, and . . ." There was something else, I only had to remember what it was. "An oil portrait!" The words popped into my head and immediately out of my mouth. "A picture of Hortense Dash's son, Percival. Sweet child, or so I've been told. Blond hair, cute smile."

Bill scowled. "Well, if that was true, if she was so worried about me stealing, how come the cops have never showed up to ask me about it?"

A legitimate question.

"It's because she never filed a police report," Bill added. "Because it never happened, and Muriel knew she could get in trouble if she filed a false report. She was just looking for an excuse to get rid of me. That woman, she was a nasty piece of work."

"Where were you the night she was killed?" I asked him.

"Nowhere near the club," he assured me. His gaze flickered to Brittany. "I was here. All night. With Brit."

"So she's your alibi? And you're hers?"

He scooped up some baked potato. "Looks that way." He chewed and swallowed before he said, "Which should pretty much prove we're telling you the truth. If we were guilty and really needed an alibi, we'd come up with something better than that, don't you think? Instead of wasting your time talking to us, why don't you ask some of those fancy-schmancy ladies what they were up to when Muriel was bumped off?"

"Why? Do you think one of them killed her?"

"I know a bunch of them had reasons," Bill grumbled.

"Like?"

Bill worked on his steak a bit more, and while he was doing that, Brittany spooned sour cream onto her baked potato. "If Agnes won the election, everything would have been fine," she grumbled. "Our troubles would have been over. Agnes was a dream to work with."

"But she didn't win." I didn't need to point it out, but I thought they should know I'd heard the story straight from the horse's mouth. "She told me she dropped out of the election because she was being nice to Muriel."

Bill snorted a laugh.

Brittany nearly gagged on her baked potato.

She recovered first. "Agnes being nice to Muriel? Never!"

I couldn't help but wonder, "Then why would she drop out of the election and let Muriel walk into the president's job?"

Thinking, Brittany tapped her fork against her plate. "I wondered the same thing," she admitted. "Told Bill as much. Didn't I, Bill? Told Bill it smelled plenty fishy to me. Muriel and Agnes, they were mortal enemies."

"You mean because Agnes was once engaged to Tab, and Muriel ended up marrying him."

"You know about that, huh?" Brittany excused herself and went into the kitchen. She came back with a bottle of wine and poured some into both hers and Bill's glasses. "Agnes is a nice woman. I'm glad she's finally president."

"Then who do you think killed Muriel?" I asked her.

Brittany stood beside the table and held the wine bottle to her chest like a shield. "We've been talking about it. Me and Bill."

"Which doesn't mean a thing," Bill insisted. "Of course we'd talk about it. Anybody who worked with somebody who's been murdered would talk about it."

"And we think . . ." Brittany skimmed a look in Bill's

direction and when he didn't object, she cleared her throat. "You know, she cut Tab off."

It took a second for me to process this piece of information. "Muriel? You mean she—"

"Cut the purse strings. Just like that." Bill put down his fork long enough to snap his fingers.

"She was the one with all the money," Brittany added. "Old family money, and there's plenty of it. And Tab, from what I've heard, he loves to spend it. Cars, vacations, clothes. Once he married Muriel, he never had to worry and he never had to work a day in his life, either. Then one day, I heard Muriel on the phone with him. Not that I was eavesdropping or anything," she added quickly. "I was just passing the president's office and it was impossible not to hear. That's how angry she was. That's how loud she was talking. She said, 'That's the last of it, Tab. No more allowance. No more meal ticket. I've had it with you.'" Brittany shrugged. "I never had the nerve to ask her about it, and now . . . well, I guess now it doesn't matter."

"Yeah," Bill added. "Because now that Muriel's dead, Tab probably gets all her money, anyway."

D id Tab inherit Muriel's fortune?

It was an interesting question, and one I'd have to dig into when I had time.

The way it was, when I got back to the club, it was late, it was dark, and after watching Bill and Brittany eat their dinner, I listened to my stomach rumble and realized I was starving.

Just as I rolled by the front of the club, I saw a movement in the shadows near the front door, just out of the circle of the glow of the security light, and when I pulled my car closer, I saw the shadow detach itself from the darker shadows around it.

I made sure my car doors were locked and reached for the phone just as the person stepped into the light. That's when I breathed a sigh of relief and put down my car window.

"Oz, what are you doing here?"

He sauntered over looking all official in the kind of beige trench coat so many cops wear in so many movies. "Looking for you, of course."

"I was . . ." How could I explain that I'd been out interviewing suspects? Rather than try, I shrugged and pointed across the parking lot to the space where I usually left my car. "I'll be right back," I told him.

Leave it to a cop not to allow a woman to walk across a dark parking lot all by herself.

By the time I got out of the car, he was right there waiting for me.

"When I realized you weren't here, I was all set to leave and I figured I'd just call you in the morning. I still can. If it's too late."

It was late. I was whooped.

"How do you feel about pasta?" I asked him.

"Depends if I'm cooking it or just eating it."

"Quentin made the sauce. I think I have the culinary skills to deal with the noodles."

He grinned. "Well, since I was pretty sure my dinner tonight would have been from the drive-through at McDonald's, that sounds perfect to me!"

Inside, I turned on the lights in the hallway and the dining room, and once we were back in the kitchen, I put a pot of water on to boil and found the container of sauce Quentin had earmarked for me, put the sauce in a pan, and set it on the stove to heat.

"You're working." Not much of a deduction, since when he slipped out of his raincoat, I saw that Oz was wearing a dark suit and a crisp white shirt. His tie had little dots on it, red against a navy background.

He stretched. "One thing they never emphasize enough at the police academy is the lousy hours."

"If they did, would you have quit and done something else?"

As if he had to think about it, he cocked his head, but he answered quickly enough. "Nah. It's in my blood. My dad was a cop. So were both his brothers. I always knew this was what I wanted to do."

"Except for the lousy hours."

He grinned. "Sometimes the company makes up for the hours."

He was talking about me. He was smiling at me.

And I suddenly felt like a high school freshman at her first dance.

Good thing I noticed the steam rising from the pasta pot. Tossing the pasta in the boiling water gave me something to do, something to think about besides Oz's warm smile.

"You stopped by to see me." Done with the pasta, I spun to face him, and yes, I sounded as totally dorky as I suddenly felt. "What did you want?"

Maybe Oz felt dorky, too. He stuffed his hands in his pockets. Took them out again. "You were going to look through your rooms. To see if anything—"

"Yes, of course." I'd tucked that list of missing items in my purse and I took it out and handed it over to him and Oz read it, then looked up with a question in his dark eyes.

"This stuff is all awfully personal," he said.

"My thoughts exactly."

"So who here would care that much about you?" He

made a face. "Sorry. That didn't come out like I meant it. What I mean is, you're new in town, right? But the list of things that were taken from your room . . ." He consulted it. "Address book, journal, datebook. A burglar wouldn't have bothered. He would have gone after a TV or jewelry or cash. But these things . . ." He tapped a finger against my list. "They sure don't sound like anything a stranger would care about. Are you sure you haven't run into anyone here who you knew back in Lily Dale?"

His words hit, along with a realization, and I froze. "You checked me out."

"Well . . ." He gave me a sort of one-shoulder shrug. "It's what I do."

"You think I'm a suspect."

Another shrug pretty much said it all. "At the beginning of an investigation, everyone is a suspect. And you were right here at the scene. You found the body. You called 911."

"Yes, but I—"

He held up a hand to stop my protest. "I know. You were at the Chamber of Commerce meeting. I verified that. And I know you went to the grocery store after, just like you said you did."

"I gave you the receipt to prove it."

"And I went to the grocery store and watched the security tapes just to make sure you were telling the truth."

I sucked in a gasp. "You really did think I might have done it!"

"Occupational hazard."

"And that's why you did a background check on me, too. That's how you know I'm from Lily Dale."

He pulled his notebook out of the pocket of his suit jacket, but something told me he really didn't need to look at what was written in it. He looked through the pages, anyway.

"Twenty-nine years old. Born in Buffalo. Raised in Lily Dale. But not by your parents."

"They died in an auto accident when I was six."

"You were raised by Rosemary . . ." This, he did need to check in his book. "Rosemary Walsh."

"My mother's sister."

"And a medium."

I gave him the same flippant answer I'd always given the kids at school when they found out where I lived and who I lived with and started making fun. "Truth be told, Aunt Rosemary is more like a large!"

He smiled politely. That is, right before he asked, "Do you suppose she could contact Ms. Sadler for us?"

His question caught me off guard.

Right before it made me laugh.

"You're not serious?"

He pursed his lips. "If there's one thing you learn on the police force, it's that there are a lot of weird things out there. Talking to the dead would just be another one of them."

"You mean . . ." I barely dared to ask. "Do you think it can be done?"

He slid me a look. "Do you?"

I balanced the idea of telling him about Clemmie against not wanting to look crazy. After all, dorky doesn't hold a candle to whacked out.

I was saved from deciding when the timer went off. The pasta was done.

I drained the noodles, filled our plates, ladled on sauce.

I remembered what he said about how he was still on the clock. "I don't suppose you can have a glass of wine?"

He sighed. "Another rain check. But go ahead, if you want to."

I didn't. It seemed mean-spirited to drink wine in front of him when he couldn't.

Oz leaned over his plate and breathed in deep. "That smells great. Your chef must be a genius. Where'd he do his training?"

I'd just twirled up a forkful of pasta and I stopped before I could put it in my mouth. "Something tells me you already know that. You must have run a background check on him, too."

"Touché!" Oz chewed, swallowed, and smiled his approval. "He's got a record, you know."

I didn't.

"All penny-ante stuff, nothing violent. And nothing lately."

"How about the rest of them?"

"You mean the ladies of the club?" He grinned around his next forkful of pasta. "Patricia Fink once threw a beer at a belligerent guy in a bar. He filed charges."

I swallowed a mouthful of spaghetti. "For a beer?"

"The guy admitted he saw the PPWC pin she was wearing and figured she had bucks. Nothing came of it. And then there's . . ." He flipped the pages of his notebook. "Gracie Grimm. She had her driver's license taken away six months ago. Ran into her neighbor's mailbox. Again."

I didn't bother to mention I knew Gracie drove to the club that morning. Some things were better left unsaid.

"How about our president, Agnes Yarborough?"

"Clean as a whistle. As is Valentina Hanover. Geneva Duran once punched her husband in the nose. He told the cops who came to the scene that he deserved it. And Bill Manby . . ."

I held my breath. If Oz knew about Bill's sticky-finger

problem, that put a whole new spin on everything Bill had told me.

"He doesn't work here, anymore," I told Oz.

"Yeah, so I found out. He did some time twenty years ago. Grand theft auto."

Which was not the same as stealing from the Portage Path Women's Club, I reminded myself.

"Sounds like everyone has secrets," I said.

"Like the mysterious woman lurking in the basement?"

I set down my fork. "Oz, what you said about my aunt Rosemary, about how she contacts the dead—"

His phone rang.

Oz took one look at the caller's number, sighed, and answered. "Alterman."

He listened for a moment before he pushed his chair away from the table. "I'm not far. I can be there in a couple minutes."

"You have to go?" I didn't have to pretend to be disappointed. I enjoyed talking to Oz. Even when we were talking about murder. And I felt sorry for a guy who didn't even have a chance to finish his pasta before he had to get back to work.

"Duty calls." He slipped into his coat. "Sorry to leave you with dishes to wash."

"Sounds like that's the least of your worries." I walked him to the door. "Come back for pasta. Anytime you want."

Oz gave me a smile. "It was good pasta. And better company." He pushed open the door and stepped outside. "And oh, Avery, there's something else you should know. I mean, about that background check I did on you. Sure, it was all part of the job, but truth is, I also did it because I'm interested."

I smiled as I watched him leave. After all, I knew he wasn't talking just about the murder.

# CHAPTER 13

The third Saturday of the month. It was written in stone. A club tradition. One that went back forty years or more. Puzzle Day.

I got downstairs early, set up six card tables in the Carnation Room so the puzzle builders would have plenty of elbow room, and went to the supply closet to retrieve six different puzzles, ranging from easy to hard, one hundred pieces to one thousand.

From what I'd heard, dissectologists (honestly, that's what people who love jigsaw puzzles are called!) can be really picky about their preferences, and the way things were going there at the club, I wanted everything to be perfect for them. When it came to puzzle pictures, I had all the bases covered— cute animals, still life, panoramic scenery, abstract design.

Ridiculously satisfied by my own efficiency, I poured myself a cup of coffee and waited for the dissectologists to arrive.

And then I waited some more.

Three women showed up. Loyal to the cause of dissectology, from what I heard, they hadn't missed a Puzzle Day in years. Gracie was one of them.

"Ooh, five hundred pieces!" She crooned over the puzzle box with a picture of a fuzzy kitten playing with six balls (all different colors) of yarn, then slid a look across the room at the two ladies already sorting edge pieces from middle pieces. "This ought to keep those old biddies busy for hours," she whispered and gave me a wink. "I'll make sure of it. That way they'll stick around for lunch."

My smile told her I appreciated it, but that smile only lasted as long as it took me to get back to my desk near the front door. From what I'd heard, Puzzle Day used to be one of the highlights of the PPWC social calendar, attracting dozens of members. Now there were just the three of them busy in Carnation, and the four other activities scheduled for the club that day—bridge, watercolors, book discussion, and mah-jongg—had no one registered at all. I couldn't help but feel down, and at that point, I should have known better than to check my phone messages. What I found were voice mails from five members expressing their outrage at belonging to a club where a murder had been committed and that a murderer might still be on the loose. Every single one of them wanted to know how to get a refund on their membership fees.

"We're doomed," I moaned to myself and I will admit to a black moment of doubt, one that included me actually thinking about getting online to start the search for another job. After all, once the club failed, a club manager wouldn't be needed, and I'd be out on the street. Did I like Portage Path enough to stick around? Or would I head back to the peace, quiet, and unearthly delights of Lily Dale?

I wallowed in my misery. At least for a few minutes. Then my common sense took over and when it did, it brought along with it a big dose of outrage and a figurative boot to the butt.

Or maybe that had something to do with the caffeine in my coffee finally kicking in.

The Portage Path Women's Club wasn't going to fail.

Not on my watch.

My mind made up, I gave my desk an affirming slap and headed upstairs. Quentin and Geneva were busy in the kitchen. Our three dissectologists were hard at work in Carnation and would be until every last little furry piece of that kitty was exactly where it should be. The presidential inaugural committee wasn't scheduled to arrive for another two hours.

I had the place to myself and I intended to make the most of every minute.

Upstairs, I stood outside Muriel's office and thought about how I'd seen Tab try to worm his way in there the day after the murder. He hadn't been so successful, but I was younger and more agile, and within a minute, I was in don't-go-there territory, on the other side of the tape.

The president's office.

Muriel's inner sanctum.

Aside from that aspidistra on the credenza—more wilted than ever—nothing there in the office had changed from the day I'd peeked inside when I ordered Tab to leave the premises. The cops had been through the place, sure, but that didn't mean they were looking for what I was looking for.

Then again, I had no idea what I was looking for.

"I'll know it when I see it," I told myself, and I got to work.

I started with Muriel's desk, a hulking antique that was probably as old as the house. I had no doubt it had been used and used proudly by every PPWC president over the years. I went through it drawer by drawer and did the same thing with the credenza, and what I found was a big ol' nothing.

At least nothing that was interesting.

And nothing all that personal, either.

The thought hit and I dropped into Muriel's desk chair and considered it.

"Tab said he wanted to gather family treasures," I reminded myself. "But there are none."

No pictures.

No mementoes.

No funny magnets stuck to the side of the filing cabinet from places like Muriel's favorite coffee shop or her dentist.

The office was all business, no nonsense. All PPWC. No warmth. Nothing personal at all.

It was as if Muriel the person never existed within these walls, only Muriel the president.

As disheartening as the thought was, I didn't let it stop me. I got to work on the filing cabinets, found the first one neat and in perfect alphabetical order, and promptly lost heart again.

At least until I tried to close the file drawer nearest to the floor and it caught on something inside.

I rolled out the drawer, jiggled it, tried it again.

Again, it stuck.

The next time I opened the drawer, I paid a little more attention, peering inside as best as I was able to see what was causing the problem. There was something at the back of the cabinet, something lying flat on the bottom of the drawer, and it was catching on the files that had been strategically arrayed above it.

I squashed file folders to the front of the drawer and stuck in my hand. What I snagged was a manila folder.

Holding on tight, I dragged it out into the light without bending it too much, and flipped it open.

Bill Manby's face stared back at me.

"Picture," I told myself, then promptly revised that statement when I shuffled through the rest of what was in the folder. "Pictures."

All of them of Bill Manby.

I am certainly no expert, but my guess was they were taken with a phone, blown up and printed at some drugstore, and I wondered if the clerks there found themselves wondering what I was wondering.

Why all the pictures of Bill?

Bill standing outside the front entrance of the club, a hoe in one hand, looking at the terra-cotta pots on either side of the front door that overflowed with a spectacular arrangement of red geraniums, yellow marigolds, and some little white flowers I couldn't name.

Bill outside the old summerhouse on the far side of the parking lot, now used for storage. He was bent over the riding mower, tinkering with the engine.

Bill, shirt off and muscles rippling, patching a pothole in the parking lot, steam rising from the asphalt in a bucket at his side.

Bill on his way out the front door, pausing for a moment to say something to Brittany, who was behind her—now my—desk.

This photo seemed the most interesting to me, though I couldn't say why, not right away. It wasn't because I knew Bill and Brittany had a thing going, though looking at the two of them, I wondered how long they'd been seeing each other and if it was before or after Brittany quit and Bill was fired. I studied the picture for a few more minutes before the reality of it hit. The angle of this particular photo was odd—not taken from the first floor, where Bill and Brittany chatted, but from the top of the stairs, like someone was looking over the bannister and down on the scene.

Like the photographer didn't want Bill and Brittany to see her.

I set that particular picture aside and looked through all the others again. In each one, Bill was busy working and, just like in the photo with Brittany, I'd bet anything he didn't have a clue someone—and it had to have been Muriel—was taking his picture.

"Interesting," I mumbled, but just as quickly, my brain provided a perfectly logical explanation. Muriel suspected Bill was stealing from the club. She was keeping an eye on him. Trying to find proof, maybe. Though how a picture of a bare-chested Bill was supposed to provide that, I couldn't say.

I set the pictures aside and wondered what other secrets were hidden in Muriel's office, though for the life of me, I couldn't imagine where. Not satisfied with looking for something and finding nothing, I had another rummage through the office, looking again through the desk and the credenza and the filing cabinets, and yes, this time I checked the bottom of each and every drawer.

Nothing.

With a sigh of surrender, I finally gave up. On my way out the door—I'd shimmy out just like I'd shimmied in—I took pity on the aspidistra. Except for the fact that Aunt Rosemary is convinced they have a consciousness of sorts and that they can feel emotions, I don't know much about plants. But I knew for sure this one needed a drink. Badly.

I grabbed the pot and stopped cold.

For a parched aspidistra in a plastic pot, it was awfully heavy.

I weighed my options, which were pretty much these— yank the plant out of the pot right then and there to find out why it felt so heavy and risk making a mess that Oz would certainly notice and undoubtedly question. Or go into the basement, where I could have a little privacy and a work-room where I could take my time and clean up any mess more easily.

I set the plant out in the hallway, climbed out of the of-fice after it, and headed for the basement.

There was no sign of Clemmie, and at that point, I hardly cared. I was burning with curiosity, dying to find out what was squirreled away at the bottom of the pot, and I went right to a room off the main basement corridor, plopped the plant and its pot on a table, and got to work.

A second later, there was dirt all over the table, a bare-rooted plant sitting at my elbow, and I was staring slack-jawed at the almost-empty pot.

"What's eating you? You act like you ain't never seen a plant before."

I didn't gasp when Clemmie showed up out of whatever nowhere it was she went when she wasn't hanging around the club. Well, at least not too much. When my heartbeat finally slowed and I was able to get the words out, I pointed to the bottom of the pot.

"Not the plant. What's in there."

She leaned closer and bent down for a better look. "A book?"

"Not just any book." I retrieved the object and shook the soil from the plastic bag it was in. "My datebook. The one that was filched from my room."

Her bottom lip protruded. "The one you thought I took."

"Sorry." I meant it, but I didn't dwell. Once the datebook was on the table, I got my journal and my address book out of the pot, too, and fists on hips, I stepped back to study the scene.

"Why would Muriel steal my stuff and hide it in a plant pot?" I asked, and I didn't expect Clemmie to answer, but she did.

"Nobody would ever look there, would they?" As if the very act of thinking was painful, she wrinkled her nose. "Except you did. Maybe you ain't such a dumb Dora after all. You really know your onions!"

This I wasn't so sure about. But I did know fishy when I smelled it.

"Why would Muriel take my things? And then hide them?"

"Well, 'cause she didn't want you to find 'em, of course."

"But why take them in the first place?"

"It's fluky, all right. Unless . . ." Clemmie chewed on her lower lip, and I had only so much patience.

"Unless what?" I asked.

"Come here." Her satin shoes silent against the stone floor, she turned and walked out of the workroom and down the hallway to the furnace room. "In there," she said.

I went where she pointed and found myself face to face with a hulking monstrosity of a furnace that chose that particular moment to kick in. It groaned and whirred.

I felt my brain doing the same thing. "What's this all about?" I asked Clemmie.

By way of telling me to be patient, she held up a hand.

After a few more minutes of contortions, the furnace throttled back, the quiet settled, and I could hear myself think again. I was just about to ask what I was supposed to be thinking about when I heard a voice.

Disembodied.

Hollow.

Like it came from beyond the grave.

"Not that one, Doris. That's got a fuzzy edge and a yarn edge. We're looking for all fuzzy."

Gracie.

I slid Clemmie a questioning look.

"It's the heating ducts. Get it?" I think she was going to give me an elbow in the ribs, but she thought better of it and I was just as glad. I didn't exactly like the thought of making contact with the disembodied. "I can be down here, and sometimes, I can hear what them dames upstairs are talking about."

"Anywhere upstairs?"

When Clemmie shrugged, the beads on her dress shimmered in the dim overhead light. "Can't say where they are when I hear them talking. I only know I pick up on something every now and then."

"And you picked up on something? About my datebook? And my journal?"

"Don't know. Not for sure. I only know that one day I heard that ol' Mrs. Grundy."

"Muriel."

"Yeah, Muriel. I heard her cooing to herself. You know, like she was really happy about something. And I heard what she said, too. About how she hoped she could use something she found. Against you."

I sucked in a breath that was more about outrage than it was about surprise. "She wanted me to quit. And she thought she could look through my personal things and find . . ." I wasn't sure what Muriel thought she'd find, I only knew the thought of her trying sent my blood pressure through the roof.

It had a chance to settle when two new voices floated down to us and I stopped to listen.

"What have you heard?" I recognized Agnes's voice. "About the old records? Has that restorationist said anything to you about what he's found and how much has been damaged?"

"Not a word. Not to me," Patricia answered her. "He says he's preparing a report and by next week at this time . . ." Her voice faded and I could only imagine that wherever Patricia and Agnes had walked to as they continued their conversation, it was farther from the heating registers and so, impossible to hear down here in the basement.

"You must pick up on all sorts of interesting stuff down here," I said. "I don't suppose you heard anything at the time of the . . ." I remembered how Clemmie had reacted the last time I mentioned murder, how she'd faded right away. "That Tuesday night. Before I found Muriel. Did you hear anything that night?"

"Not a word, sister, and believe me, I'd tell you if I did. Nothing at all. Except . . ." She pursed her lips, thinking. "Come to think of it, I did hear something. Not anybody talking. But a sound. Before the door opened and that Muriel got the ole heave-ho down the steps. I heard something like a whirring."

"Not the furnace?"

Clemmie raised those perfectly penciled eyebrows. "You just heard the furnace. I'd know for sure if that's what it was. That thing is louder than the engine of a tin lizzie. No, this was a quieter sound, smoother. It made me think of the time when I was a kid and my grandmother, she took me over to O'Rourke's. You know, the department store. It had an elevator and a man who was in charge of it. He wore a uniform and greeted you when you got on. That sound I heard, it sounded like that elevator."

"Like the elevator in the lobby?"

"Is that where it is?" When Clemmie shook her head, her feathered headband swayed. "I've heard that sound and it's different. More modern, if you know what I mean. This was hushed, old-fashioned. Almost soothing, I'd say."

"Soft and soothing." I thought about it before I slanted Clemmie a look. "Like the dumbwaiter?"

Her shrug was not exactly reassuring, but that didn't stop me.

"Come on," I told her, and headed up the stairs. "Let's check it out."

I was all the way on the second floor and in the Lilac Lounge before I realized Clemmie hadn't followed me. No matter. I threaded my way around the tables and desks and chairs where Jack had set up reference books and a station to air out the pages of some of the volumes damaged in Marigold, and made my way to the far wall.

"Dodie's dumbwaiter," I reminded myself, and I flung open the door.

Here's the thing about dumbwaiters in old houses. They aren't very big. They were never intended to hold people, just objects up and down from the kitchen thanks to a series of hand-powered pulley ropes.

It didn't take me long to look it over.

That's why I couldn't miss what was inside. The statue of Hortense Dash, covered with blood.

The doors were wide open and when Oz stepped back, he studied the system of ropes and pulleys that made the dumbwaiter move from floor to floor.

"Glad you called. But I'm not happy our guys missed this."

I don't know why, but I felt I needed to defend the members of the crime scene unit who had arrived on the night I found Muriel's body. One of them, a guy with a sheepish expression and nervous hands, watched Oz from the doorway, obviously waiting to get lambasted. "It's not exactly something anyone expects to see and nobody would even notice it when the doors are closed." I moved forward to do just that so I could show Oz that when the dumbwaiter doors were closed they blended right into the wall, but he warned me off with a sharp look.

"Sorry," I said. "I forgot. Fingerprints."

He brushed a hand through his dark hair. "I'm sure yours are already all over it."

"Sorry," I said again.

"She must have been killed up here, then the murderer tossed the statue and the body in the dumbwaiter." He slid me a look. "Where does it go?"

"The kitchen."

Oz nodded. "She was a tiny woman. It would have been pretty easy to move her from the kitchen to the basement. The way she was on the steps—"

"Like the door was opened and . . ." I remembered what Clemmie had said and my stomach soured. "Muriel was given the heave-ho down the steps."

"Well, we're closer toward figuring out what happened than we were." Oz didn't sound especially pleased by this. "Now if we can just figure out what the killer used to move Ms. Sadler—"

"Well, the plastic runners I had on the carpet in Marigold were missing."

As if we'd choreographed the move, Oz and I turned to the door just in time to see Jack arrive.

I stared at him with slack-jawed wonder.

Oz closed in. "What do you mean?"

Jack was carrying a stack of books and he set them down on the desk. "I told you, Avery." He looked my way. "I told you I had to order more plastic runners."

This time I didn't even bother to say I was sorry. I just cringed. And automatically defended myself. "You didn't say any were missing. You just said you needed more. I thought—"

"Well you should have known," Jack insisted. "There were plastic runners on the carpet in Marigold. If I said I needed more plastic runners—"

"That meant you needed more plastic runners. Not that the runners you had were missing. Why didn't you—"

"All right, you two." Oz stepped between us, his hands out in a way that made me think he must have once directed traffic. "You." He turned toward Jack. "You're telling me the runners you had on the floor in Marigold were there one day—"

"The day of the murder. Yes." Jack nodded.

"And not there the next?" Oz wanted to know. "That means the murder could have happened in Marigold, the runners kept the blood off the carpet, then the body was dragged here on the plastic runners and they were taken away."

Jack flushed a color that reminded me of the puddle of blood I'd found in the dumbwaiter. "I just thought—"

Another wave of Oz's hands and Jack's words dissolved.

"And you." He spun my way. "You're saying that when . . ." He looked over his shoulder at our shame-faced restorationist. "When Jack here told you he needed more plastic runners, you never thought anything of it."

"It's not like I've ever worked where there was a murder," I reminded him. "I just thought—"

"What?" Oz demanded.

And there was really nothing else I could say. I settled for, "Sorry."

When Oz went quiet, I was sure it was because he was counting to ten. Finally, he turned toward the crime scene technician. "Go take a look in . . ." Oz glanced my way. "Marigold, did you say? Which one is that?"

I started out of the room so I could accompany the tech.

"He'll find it on his own," Oz said. "Just say where. We don't need anyone else in there messing up the scene.

I pointed across the hall.

This time, I didn't even bother to tell him I was sorry.

# CHAPTER 14

Except for special events, Portage Path Women's Club is not open on Sundays.

Oh, how glad I was there was no special event scheduled!

My plan was to spend all of that Sunday in my jammies, going over the details of what I'd begun to think of as "my case." With the way thoughts were flying through my head, I knew it was enough to keep me busy for hours.

Muriel dead.

Muriel as the burglar who'd taken—and hidden—my things.

Bill and Brittany, Patricia and Agnes, Tab Sadler.

And then, of course, the big inauguration coming up.

Really, if I thought I could lounge around that gloomy Sunday, I thought all wrong.

My brain was too full, my nerves were drawn too taut. I was up early, changed out of those comfy jammies, and rarin' to go.

If only I could figure out where I was headed.

I started at the most logical place. The ladies of the inaugural committee had been hard at work the day before, and thanks to the visit from Oz and the crime scene guys, I hadn't had a chance to catch up on their plans. After a quick trip to the kitchen to make myself coffee and rummage through the fridge (where I found eggs, which I scrambled), I went into the ballroom and looked around in awe.

The committee had been busy.

The poster of Agnes's family tree was done, complete with photos of her mother and grandmother, both proudly wearing their PPWC pins. There was a scrapbook set out that was filled with articles old and new—the Yarboroughs at the opera, the Yarboroughs serving Thanksgiving dinner to the homeless at one of the local churches, Agnes's grandmother cutting the ribbon on the building the day its title transferred from Chauncey Dennison and it officially became the Portage Path Women's Club.

*It would be great to give the ceremony even more of a spin on history.*

This note was on the table next to the scrapbook, and I recognized the loops and swirls of Valentina's handwriting.

*Historical costumes? Recipes from the past? A tour of the building, for sure. Let's get Avery going on this.*

It was a logical request. And certainly part of my job. But as I stood there in the grand and glorious ballroom, surrounded by mementoes from the club's past, ice formed in my stomach.

I really didn't know all that much about the history of the club. Or the house, for that matter. And I didn't have much time to learn.

There was, however, someone around who might know a whole lot.

I didn't waste any time. Down in the basement, I paused at the bottom of the stairs. "Hey, Clemmie! Got a minute? I need to talk to you."

A wisp of mist gathered in front of me. It swirled, congealed, solidified.

"Do I have a minute? Are you kidding, sister? I got more than all the minutes I could ever want and nothing much to do with any of them. What's on your mind?"

"History, and the way I figure it, you know more about that than anyone around here. You've lived it." When her mouth twisted, I winced. "Sorry. What I meant is—"

"I know what you meant. That I was alive back then, and I'm dead now, only I'm still hanging around. I'm not sure how I can help."

"I thought we could start with the building itself. That we could walk around and you could tell me how things used to look. You know, like how the ballroom is different than it was in the old days. Or what the rooms upstairs might have looked like and been used for before they were converted into offices and meeting rooms." I turned and headed up the steps. "It will give me some background to work with so I can put something together for the inauguration. The ladies would like to place the emphasis on history and tradition. I get that. And—"

When I got to the top of the stairs, Clemmie wasn't behind me so I bent to peer into the basement. She was at the bottom of the steps, as still as a statue.

"What are you waiting for?" I asked her.

"I . . . er . . ." Clemmie backed away from the stairs. She blurred and faded.

"Oh no!" I raced back down. "You can't disappear. I need your help."

Her spirit, or ectoplasm, or whatever it was that made it

possible for me to see her, swirled a little more and came back into focus just in time for me to see her look past me toward the doorway at the top of the steps. Her voice was small and uncertain. "I can't."

"Can't . . ." I, too, looked toward the upstairs. "Can't walk up stairs? Then float, I've seen you do that."

Her bottom lip trembled. "It's not that, it's—"

"Tell me about it when we're walking around." I'd already grabbed her hand when I realized I didn't know what would happen if I tried to make contact with Clemmie. Would my hand go right through hers? Would she feel as cold as death?

To my surprise, she felt as real as anybody else, even if she was chilly. And just a little damp.

It wasn't an icky sort of dampness, not like an old graveyard or anything. It was more the way the air feels on a summer morning when the dew is just fading from the grass.

"Come on," I said, and I tugged her up the stairs.

We were nearly at the top of the steps when I felt a jerk and turned to see what was going on.

There was Clemmie, two steps below me.

And there I was, nearly at the door, my hand still on hers.

But between us . . .

I looked in wonder at the opaque wall that suddenly separated us.

It was blue one second, green the next. On my side of the weird wall, everything felt normal, but on the other side, where Clemmie stood, my hand still on hers, the air was as cold as death. It eddied and swirled and my fingers turned to ice. Instinctively, I pulled my hand to my side and rubbed it with my other hand. It was numb and stiff and so cold, it felt as if my skin would crack.

"What's happening?" I asked Clemmie.

Her eyes filled with tears. "I've been trying to tell you. I can't!" She blinked and a single tear slipped down her cheek. "This is what happens every time I try to go upstairs. You see, I'm not allowed."

Her feet inches above the steps, she floated back down to the basement and in a flash like a sparkler, she exploded into an effervescent ball that zipped into the speakeasy. Like a comet, she left a trail of bubbling sparks.

Once Clemmie was gone, so was that wall that had separated us. I ran after her, slapping away the remnants of the cold when it threatened to settle on my shoulders. By the time I got into the old speakeasy, she was Clemmie again, as solid looking as if she were still alive. She was curled into a ball in a dark corner, hunched and crying.

I wasn't exactly sure how to console a ghost. I thought back to everything Aunt Rosemary had ever tried to teach me, but heck, mumbo jumbo didn't seem like the appropriate response. Not to a kid whose shoulders were heaving and whose sobs echoed through the basement like the wail of a banshee.

"Hey!" I put a hand on Clemmie's shoulder. "I'm sorry. I don't know what happened, but I didn't mean to upset you."

"It's not . . ." She looked over her shoulder at me. "It's not you. It's not your fault, Avery. I just can't . . . I'm not allowed . . ."

"Not allowed to go upstairs?"

She nodded.

"Who says?"

She sniffled and stood up straight and she wiped her hands over her cheeks before she said, "Mr. Dennison, of course."

I laughed. "Chauncey Dennison's been dead for like forever." I cringed. "No offense intended. What I mean is, he doesn't have any say-so in what goes on around here. It isn't his house anymore."

"No, but when it was . . ." Clemmie turned to take in the vast room that was once a speakeasy, and her eyes misted with memory. "It was such a swell place, Avery. There were bright lights and tables with linen tablecloths. The bar was over there." She pointed toward the far wall. "And the stage was there." She pointed this out, too. "It was like nothin' I ever saw before. That first time I came here—"

"When was that?"

She blinked back to reality. "I saw an ad. In the newspaper. It said this swanky joint over on Main Street, the Casbah Club, was looking for a singer. I ain't half bad, you know."

I remembered the first day I was at the club, how I'd heard "Bye Bye Blackbird" come from what seemed a long way off. "I know you're good. I heard you."

She smiled and sniffled. "I had plans. Don't think I didn't." Her shoulders shot back. "First I'd get that job over at the Casbah. You know, so that I could make a name for myself. After that, there'd be no stopping me. I was going to New York. To be a Ziegfeld girl."

I guess my blank expression spoke wonders.

Clemmie rolled her eyes. "Don't tell me you never heard of them. Ziegfeld girls, they were famous, the showgirls who danced in the Ziegfeld Follies in New York City. Gorgeous costumes! Beautiful makeup! And men falling madly in love with you. Oodles of them." She clasped her hands together and pressed them to her heart. "Swooning over you and showering you with jewelry and furs!"

Which certainly brought up the question of how Clemmie went from dreaming of the life of a showgirl to being stuck—and dead—in a basement.

I searched for the right way to bring it up without offending her and couldn't come up with anything better than, "What happened?"

Clemmie pouted. "This place happened. See, they never really needed a singer over at the Casbah. That was just a come-on. Dennison, he was really looking for a singer for this place. Only he couldn't come right out and say that in a newspaper ad—could he?—what with it being illegal to run one of these juice joints."

"And you came here to the speakeasy?"

She nodded. "For an audition. And I'll tell you what, I wowed 'em. I did, Avery. I sang 'Bye Bye Blackbird' and every big cheese in the place sat up and listened. They told me I had the job right then and there and they were going to pay me thirty dollars a week. Thirty! I couldn't wait to get home and tell my ma, and when I did, she just about fainted right there on the floor. She never knew anybody could make that kind of money. Not for just singing, that's for sure."

"But then . . ." I looked back toward the stairs and that weird blue wall that was nowhere in sight. "Why—?"

One corner of Clemmie's mouth pulled tight. "It was after my audition. I saw one of them swells go upstairs, and I figured, how could it hurt? I just wanted a peek at the place, you know what I mean? I never saw a house like this before, and I just wanted to see how the big shots lived."

"You went upstairs?"

She shook her head. "I tried. That's when ol' man Dennison

himself stopped me. I thought he was going to fire me right then and there, before I ever even started my job. He didn't, but he told me I wasn't ever allowed to go up those steps. Not ever again. I had to come and go just like I did that day, from a door hidden in the garden. It was a secret-like door he had installed in case the cops ever raided the place. So his swell friends would never be caught leaving. He told me a girl like me, well, he said my type of girl wasn't allowed upstairs with people who were better than me."

"Creep," I grumbled.

Clemmie shrugged. "Maybe he was right. I was just a kid from the wrong side of the tracks. Maybe I didn't belong upstairs."

"Well, I've got news for you. Nobody's better than anyone else. And as of right now, what you heard from Dennison no longer counts." I grabbed her arm and piloted her back to the stairway and when we got there, I left Clemmie in the basement and hurried up the steps. At the top, I turned. "Clementine Bow," I said, "I invite you upstairs into the house."

"Bushwa!" She waved a hand. "No way it can be that easy."

"It's worth a try." I raised my voice and tried my best to sound as compelling as the mediums I'd seen work back in Lily Dale. "I invite you to join me. Please." And I bowed and made a flourishing gesture toward the door. "Welcome!"

Doubt washed over her expression, but apparently doubt doesn't get you far when you come from the wrong side of the tracks. After a second or two of hesitation, Clemmie's chin went up and her shoulders shot back. As elegant as a duchess, she started up the steps.

At least until she got to the spot where the force field had stopped her before.

She slowed down. She gulped.

"Give it a try," I said. "I'm right here to help you if you need it."

And she walked up the next step, and the next, and the next.

Nothing stopped her.

When she stepped into the lobby of the club, I was waiting for her.

"Well, will you look at that!" Clemmie threw out her arms and spun around, taking in the scenery. "I'm upstairs!"

"And you're not going down again," I told her. "Unless you want to, that is."

"What I want . . ." She raced to the front windows and looked outside. "Trees. And grass. And look at those contraptions going by out there on the street. Are those automobiles? They sure don't look like nothing I ever seen." She laughed. "Can I really stay up here?"

"I don't see why not. Nobody but me will know you're here. Unless . . ." I gave her a careful look. "You're not planning on haunting the place or scaring people, are you?"

"Kid's stuff," she assured me. "I just want to look around."

She did, racing into the ballroom, hurrying into the restaurant, the kitchen, getting up the stairs to the second floor in a flash, all the while exclaiming her amazement at the furniture, the light fixtures, the carpets.

"We never had anything like this at home," she told me when I met her on the second floor. "It's like heaven and the Ziegfeld Follies all rolled into one!"

Her happiness was contagious, and I smiled. At least until I thought about what I was going to do with Clemmie. It only took a moment to come up with the perfect solution. I led Clemmie up to the third floor.

"These are my rooms," I told her and we peeked inside. "But there are plenty of other empty rooms up here. Pick out the one you want."

She sucked in a breath. Blinked. Burbled. "You mean, a room of my own? Up here, where there's light and maybe I can hear music and see people?"

"It's not as elegant up here as it is downstairs, but—"

I guess the *but* didn't matter. Clemmie leaped forward. "Well if you ain't the duck's quack!" And she pulled me into a hug that left me feeling chilled, and just a little damp.

C lemmie decided that arriving upstairs and being able to see the birds and the trees and watch the traffic that whizzed by outside the club was enough excitement for one day, so when I invited her to come with me to the grocery store and the Laundromat, she declined. By the time I got back (arms weighed down with bags since there was no way I was going all the way back down to the parking lot a second time), I found her in the room she'd staked out as her own. It was at the far end of the third floor and it had large windows that looked out over the back of the building and the maple trees just beginning to flame into autumn colors, and a deep ledge where Clemmie sat, her legs bent and her head on her knees.

"It's beautiful," she said before I could even ask how she was finding her first glimpses of the modern world. "But everyone dresses funny."

I supposed my jeans and the purple sweatshirt I wore with them qualified, so I laughed. "You don't eat, do you?" I asked her, even though I suspected I already knew the answer. "You don't mind if I make myself some dinner?"

"Go right ahead." She slipped away from the window

and followed me to my suite, floating over the hardwood floors. "It don't bother me or nothing. It's not like I ever get hungry."

I'd bought myself a bag of salad and an already-prepared chicken breast, and I pulled out a big bowl. "It must be weird to be . . ." Even my years of living in Lily Dale, the largest Spiritualist community in the world, hadn't prepared me for the moment or taught me what to say. "What I mean is—"

"That it's strange being dead. You got that right." She wrinkled her nose. "Took me a while to get used to it."

"What do you do all day?"

"I don't think time works the same over here as it does for you," she told me. "For me, one of your days is more like just a moment."

I remembered her reaction when she got to the top of the basement steps. "But you knew it had been a lot of moments since you'd been out of the basement and in the light."

"When I was down there, it didn't feel like a long time. It just felt . . ." She brushed a finger against the counter that held my coffeemaker, a toaster, and a tiny micro-wave that I'd had since I got my first job and moved away from the familiarity—and what I'd always thought of as the weirdness—of Lily Dale. Even though there was a smudge of water on the counter, her finger left no marks. As if a shiver had skittered over her shoulders, she twitched. "It felt dark down there."

A chill scraped my insides. "Dark, for a long, long time."

Clemmie shot me a smile. "But not anymore."

"You know," I told her, "now that you're upstairs, maybe you can help out. I'm investigating, and if you could keep an eye on people, listen to what they say, watch what they do, you might help more than just by listening at the heating ducts downstairs."

She didn't say she would or she wouldn't, but she did ask, "Who do you think done it?"

"I wish I knew." I poured salad into a bowl, put the chicken on top of it, and grabbed a bottle of green goddess dressing from the fridge before I sat down. "Tab Sadler's looking like a possibility," and then added, because Clemmie wouldn't know it, "Muriel's husband."

Her expression soured. "It's always the husband."

I laughed while I poured my salad dressing. "That doesn't say much about how you feel about love."

Clemmie made a face. "How do you feel about it?"

I'd just scooped up some salad and speared a piece of chicken, and I paused with the fork nearly at my mouth. "I guess . . . well, I suppose it works out for some people."

"But never for you?"

I set down my fork. "I've met some great guys. But none of them was ever the right one. Not the forever one. I'm still hoping to find that person someday." A thought hit, and I took a bite of my dinner before I asked, "Did you have someone special in your life?"

Clemmie's smile was soft and dreamy. "Alfred Higgenhooper." She pressed her hands to her heart and sighed. "He was as handsome as Rudolph Valentino, and he played the ukulele. What more could any girl want?"

"Were you his girl?"

"Well . . ." She turned around and walked to the other side of the kitchen. When she got there, she spun to face me. "I would have been," she assured me, "if, you know, if I lived."

"But you didn't."

She raised her eyebrows by way of telling me I was being far too obvious.

"What happened?" I asked her.

Clemmie jiggled her shoulders. "You don't really want to know."

"I do. I mean, come on. After all the years you've been hanging around here, you've finally found someone who can see you and hear you. And after all the years I was convinced my aunt Rosemary and her friends were all wackos, I've found out I can communicate with the Other Side. I need to find out all I can. I want to find out all I can. What happened to you, Clemmie? Why are you still here?"

As if she were alive and breathing, her chest rose and fell. "Like I told you, I came for the audition," she said. "And I got the job. Six shows a week starting the very next night. I was so excited, I couldn't sleep that night of the audition. I got here early the next day, the day I was supposed to start, and they gave me . . ." She touched a hand to the skirt of her beaded dress. "This dress, it was the most beautiful thing I ever did see, and the most expensive thing I ever touched. And I felt like a sort of princess. I had a dressing room, and I put on this here dress and my lipstick, and Avery, I couldn't even sit still, that's how excited I was about getting out there in front of that crowd to sing. I could hear them out there."

As if she still could, she bent her head as if she were listening to the buzz of voices.

"And finally Joe, he was the manager of the place, Joe came to get me. It was time for me to go on stage!"

Her expression lit. Her eyes glowed. "I walked out there and the first thing I saw was two fellas at a table near the stage. They were bickering. You know, going back and forth at each other. I figured it was the hooch talkin' and I didn't think anything of it until—"

Just that fast, all the exhilaration drained out of Clemmie. Her mouth twisted. Her eyes filled with tears. Her words caught on a gasp.

"One of them fellas, he pulled out a gun. He fired it and—"

It was as if I could see it all happening right in front of my eyes, and in slow motion, too. Horrified, I grasped a hand to my throat. "The shot hit you!"

Clemmie hung her head. "That was it. I was a goner." When she sobbed, it was a pathetic sound from a million miles away, a hundred years before. "I never had a chance to be star."

And with that last word, Clemmie faded away.

# CHAPTER 15

C lemmie never did show back up. Not the rest of that
Sunday. I looked for her after I finished my dinner,
and I did another turn around the mansion before I went to
bed. There was no sign of her ectoplasm anywhere and I
pretty much got the message—she wanted to be left alone.

That doesn't mean I didn't think about her.

About what happened to her all those years before and
how that accidental shooting in a long-ago speakeasy had
robbed her of her dreams of stardom. And her life.

A deep sadness settled over me. At least for a little
while. But little by little, that sorrow morphed and solidified. Kind of like Clemmie did when she materialized right
in front of my eyes. By the next morning, it was firmly
implanted way down inside me and it gave me a purpose, a
mission. More than ever, I knew I had to work to bring
justice to the victims of murder. After all these years, I

couldn't do it for Clemmie, but I sure as heck didn't want to miss my chance when it came to Muriel.

With that in mind, and nothing on my agenda but making arrangements to have a booth at an upcoming bridal fair where I could extol the wonders of the Dennison mansion to dreamy-eyed brides and their overanxious mothers, I sat at my desk and looked out the window, waiting.

I knew the time was right to make my move when I saw a man in dark pants, a red sweater, and a clerical collar lock the door of the neat bungalow next door to the church just on the other side of our parking lot and head over to begin his day's work at St. John's.

I gave him a couple of minutes. After all, I didn't want to bother the man before he'd had a chance to get settled. Once I figured he was, I hightailed it out of the club.

From what I'd read, I knew St. John's had been built around the same time Chauncey Dennison was planning his mansion, and back then, the church had been the pride of the neighborhood. It was beautiful, the way so many older buildings are, constructed of blocks of gray and sand-colored stone with ivy, its leaves tinged autumn red, hugging its walls and slithering up to the slate roof. The front of the church faced the street behind the mansion and had a main entrance complete with wide oak doors and a stained-glass window that had miraculously survived the years. Here at the back of the property, the building was simpler, square, and solid, with windows that were tall and narrow and had pointed arches.

Maybe it was a lack of enthusiasm or the fact that over the years, the church's congregation had dwindled every bit as much as PPWC's membership had. These days, the slate sidewalk that led to the back door was narrowed by the grass that grew over it, and the flower beds sprouted more weeds than anything else. I stepped over a crack in the sidewalk and went inside. Directly in front of me was the door that led into the church. I went to the left, following an arrow on a sign that indicated *Offices*.

The office door was open.

"Good morning!" The minister, a young African American man with a wide smile, rose from his chair and extended a hand. "Clifford Way. How can I help you?"

I told him who I was but not why I was there. Not right away, anyway. Not until I eased into a chair and declined the cup of tea he offered.

"I'm wondering about the Kids Coats charity," I said.

His eyes sparkled. "We can always use more help. And more coats. One of your club members, Patricia Fink, she's very involved and very enthusiastic. We're grateful for her help."

"Exactly what I wanted to talk to you about." I leaned forward. "You had a meeting here last Tuesday."

"Yes, we did." Reverend Way didn't have to consult the datebook that sat open on his desk. But then these days, maybe St. John's wasn't any more bustling than PPWC. "And Patricia was here of course," he added. "You wouldn't know it by looking at her, but she's a real whirlwind, that one. She's got more energy than a whole boatload of batteries, and she's willing to work hard for causes she believes in. Last Tuesday, that was the night . . ." Briefly, his gaze skimmed in the direction of the club. "That poor woman. I didn't know her, but Patricia spoke of her often."

I couldn't control the laugh that burst out of me. "I bet she did!"

The reverend laughed, too. "You know, I get it. I really do. It's hard to change long-standing beliefs, and here in Portage Path, the families that are considered the town's elite go back a long way. They spent all of the last century thinking they were better than everyone else. That means we have a lot of years of outmoded attitudes to undo. Patricia was trying, at least with Ms. Sadler. And that's the way real change happens, one person at a time. We both hoped Ms. Sadler would come around and see the advantages of making the club more inclusive."

"So this meeting last Tuesday . . ." I inched my way toward my questions. "Can you tell me when it started?"

"Six thirty, same as always."

Exactly what Patricia had told me. "And what time did it end?" I asked.

He eyed me for a minute, his lips pursed, his expression betraying nothing, his fingers rolling a pen back and forth over the surface of his desk. "Sounds to me like you're confirming an alibi."

"That obvious, huh?" I smiled because really, what else could I do? I was sure me sticking my nose where it didn't belong sounded crazy to the reverend, but then, it sounded crazy to me, too. "It's not that I don't believe what Patricia told me about her being here, but—"

He held up a hand. "I understand. Sometimes getting answers helps us through difficult situations."

"Tell me, what is the answer? What time did the meeting end?"

"Eight forty-five. Same as always. We've got volunteers who come from all around town and we don't like to keep them out too late. And you know, if you don't have a set time to wrap things up, committee meetings can easily get out of hand. Someone's bound to go off on a tangent, and that brings up a topic totally different from what you were hoping to talk about." He waved a hand, letting me know he'd come to expect it. "Happens so often, I don't even blink an eye anymore."

"You're telling me there was nothing different about last week's meeting?"

"Not a thing! Except . . ." A thought hit and he cocked his head. "Well . . ." He peered at his calendar. "The days sometimes blend one into another. I'd totally forgotten until right now. The only thing different last week was that the meeting had to be rescheduled."

It wasn't what he said, it was the way he said it. I sat up a little straighter.

"We always meet on Wednesdays," the reverend told me. "But last week I had a conference to attend up in Cleveland on Wednesday. I knew I wouldn't be back in time, and I didn't want to miss the meeting. It's not that I don't think the volunteers can handle things on their own," he was quick to add. "They're a terrific group of people. But Mae Hunnicut, she promised to bring brownies. Mae's brownies . . ." His sigh was pure satisfaction. "Mae's brownies are a thing of beauty and no way I was going to miss them. So we met on Tuesday instead."

"And on Wednesdays? I mean usually, when the meetings are on Wednesday, Patricia is here?"

"Sure, the whole time. Just like everyone else. In fact, she usually stays late to help me get the coffee and the cookies we serve all packed up and put away."

I held back what felt like a tingle of excitement. "And so last Tuesday, that's what she did, right?"

"Well, now that you mention it." He wrinkled his nose. "Patricia wasn't too happy when I called her to say we were going to reschedule. In fact, she tried to talk me out of it."

"Did she say why?"

"Not specifically. Not that I remember, anyway. Which is kind of weird because Patricia, she's usually so straightforward. Plain talk, no beating around the bushes. If you know Patricia, you know that. But when I asked why Tuesday was bad for her, she hemmed and she hawed, and she mumbled about how Tuesdays aren't really good days for meetings." He chuckled. "Believe me, if I knew the optimum days for meetings, I'd take advantage of that!"

I was almost too much of a chicken to ask, but I had to get at the truth. "She came to the meeting, anyway, right?"

"She sure did."

So there was no way Patricia could have killed Muriel.

I'd just begun to release a sigh of relief at the news when the reverend's next word made it wedge in my throat. "But . . ."

Afraid to hear the rest, I closed my eyes and took a deep breath. I wallowed in exactly three seconds of apprehension. Then I gave myself a figurative kick in the butt. I was there for answers. Whether I wanted to hear them or not, I had to keep digging.

"But . . . ?" I asked the reverend.

"She bustled into the meeting and hardly said a word. I figured she was just mad at me, you know, for upsetting her schedule. She sat in the back and kept her mouth shut, too. That's not like Patricia at all! And then . . ." His shoulders rose and fell. "We weren't halfway through the meeting when she got up and walked out."

With plenty of time to slip back over to the club and . . .

I dashed the thought away. It was too soon to make judgments and I needed to stay on track. "Patricia left the meeting before eight forty-five?"

He nodded. "Long before eight forty-five. If that's the time she told you she left, she's getting her meetings mixed up. You do think . . ." He gave me a penetrating look. "You do think that's all it is, don't you?"

Since I couldn't say, I didn't answer. "And she never said anything about why she left early?" I asked him.

"Not to me. And naturally, I asked a couple of the other volunteers. I wanted to make sure everything was all right. You know, that Patricia wasn't sick or anything. Martin Forsam, he said Patricia mumbled something about how inconvenient the meeting was for her but how she knew she had an obligation and she had to be there. And Glenda Sythe, she told me she was coming back from the ladies, room just as Patricia was leaving. Said Patricia raced out of the building like her shoes were on fire."

"When she left"—I swallowed hard—"did she go back to the club?"

"That, I can't say. Glenda didn't mention anything about it, but then, she came right back into the meeting room, so she probably wouldn't have noticed anyway. All I know for sure is that Patricia, she's always busy with one thing or another. All of us, we just figured she had another meeting to go to."

A meeting, yeah. One I'd bet anything had nothing to do with that J-trap she claimed to be fixing after the Kids Coats meeting that evening.

Cold realization seeped through me, and what felt like betrayal soured my insides. Patricia had lied to me and of course I wondered why. Suspicion made my nerves tingle.

I had to find out why Patricia felt the need to make up an alibi.

I don't know where it came from, but an idea popped into my head. "What do you suppose would happen if you rescheduled this week's meeting?" I asked the reverend.

His eyebrows slanted. "You mean tomorrow instead of Wednesday? You think that would tell us something?"

"I have no idea!"

He nodded. "Well, if it might help you figure out what happened over at that club of yours, I'd say it's worth a try. I'll make the calls, get the word out. Let's see if we can help you get Patricia's alibi sorted out."

I thanked the reverend and left, already planning what I'd do the next evening, how I'd keep an eye on the Kids Coats meeting, and on Patricia.

Could anyone blame me for being curious?

As I walked back across the parking lot toward the club, I couldn't help but wonder why Patricia just happened to leave the meeting early that Tuesday. And if her early departure had anything to do with those bruises I'd seen on her arm, her lame explanation about the J-trap in her sink, or Muriel's murder.

I wondered about something else, too. I took a long look at the shaggy lawn around the mansion and the piles of newly fallen leaves gathering against the walls. I studied the showy flower arrangements in urns that had greeted our members and their guests all summer and saw brown and crinkly leaves, drooping flower heads, bourgeoning weeds.

It was a sad fact—PPWC looked as unkempt as St. John's, and at the same time I wondered who on earth was going to tend to all the outside chores now that Bill Manby was gone, I stopped dead in my tracks, sure of the answer.

Without Bill to do the work, it was up to me to make sure PPWC got spruced up in time for Sunday's inauguration.

I hurried inside, where I checked my phone messages (none), checked my email (none), and firmly ignored the pile of inauguration invitations marked *Return to Sender* and sitting amid the mail that had been slipped through the slot on the front door while I was gone.

I raced upstairs, and by the time I got back outside, I was wearing my rattiest jeans, a T-shirt (a going-away gift from one of Aunt Rosemary's friends) that proclaimed *Dead People Love Me in Lily Dale, New York,* and a pair of tennis shoes that had seen better days. The only question now was where to start.

Fists on hips, I stood in the middle of the parking lot and weighed my options.

The urns, I decided, would be the easiest.

I had slipped my ring of club keys in my pocket before I left the building, and now I pulled it out, tossed and caught it in one hand, and headed for the summerhouse at the very edge of the property.

Back in the day, the summerhouse had been just that, an oasis in a wooded park-like area of the Dennison estate, designed as a shady retreat from summer heat. I imagined Mrs. Dennison lounging there on sultry afternoons, dressed in white linen and waving a fan in front of her face, sipping tea brought by the inimitable Dodie. When the Dennisons sold the house, the acres surrounding it were sold off too, bit by bit, and where there were once grand gardens and tall trees, there were now homes and businesses, parking lots, a playground, a frozen custard stand. These days, that shady haven of a summerhouse was tucked between a sleek mid-century ranch house and a convenience store.

The house itself was a miniature version of the mansion, dark stone with faded white woodwork, beveled windows and, so it could be used as a place of cooling relaxation, a wide stone front porch designed to catch every errant summer breeze. The summerhouse wasn't large, and once the club bought the property, I heard there had been plenty of discussion on how it could be used. Little theater. Art gallery. Bed-and-breakfast.

None of the plans had ever come to fruition, and over the years, the summerhouse had never been used for anything except storage. Christmas decorations were kept in what used to be the living room. Extra tables and chairs for parties that never happened these days were stored in the various bedrooms. The grounds maintenance supplies were around the back, so I'd been told, in the kitchen, where the old back door had been replaced by a lift door and the back steps by a ramp.

I let myself in that way and didn't close the door behind me. For a fall afternoon, it was pleasant enough outside, but here in the unused summerhouse, the cold settled in every nook and cranny. So did the quiet.

I shook away the chill that touched my shoulders and ignored the unsettling squeak of the floorboards when I ventured farther into the old kitchen.

I wasn't there to let my imagination run wild, or to allow thought of ghosts and hauntings to distract me from what I knew I had to do. "Work gloves, a trowel, clippers," I reminded myself, and I got busy looking for what I needed.

I'd say one thing for Bill Manby: He was organized. Tools hung in orderly rows from pegboard on the wall. The clippers were wiped clean after their last use and propped against a cupboard.

Gloves, though, were harder to locate.

I looked through every drawer and cupboard, and when that didn't work, I decided to try the other rooms. I pushed through the door that led out of the kitchen and into what was once the dining room. It was dark in there, and I automatically spun around to grope for a light switch, then gasped. The first thing I saw were two big blue eyes staring back at me.

\* \* \*

I'm a lousy poker player. For one thing, I don't have a whole lot of money to toss around. Yeah, it's fun to win, but losing is another story. And bills don't pay themselves.

For another, it seems to me there's something just slightly dishonest about poker. And I'm not talking about players who cheat. I mean trying to bluff through a game. It always felt just a little shady to me, pretending the cards in my hand were better than they actually were, acting cool and calm and oh so in control when all I wanted to do was toss my cards on the table and admit surrender.

Having a poker face is not one of my strong suits.

Somehow, I managed.

I played my cards close to my chest, kept my voice even and calm, and made a phone call. I cobbled together a whopping good story about how I had some questions and how there was only one person who could possibly answer them. I said it had to be done in person.

Lo and behold, it worked.

Within forty minutes Bill Manby arrived at the club, and he brought Brittany with him, and the moment I saw them get out of the car, I congratulated myself—maybe my poker face wasn't so bad after all.

I met them out in the parking lot. "I'm glad you could get here on such short notice," I told them. "I hope I didn't interrupt anything."

They exchanged wary looks, then gave the same sort of slant-eyed, suspicious glance at the club.

"We don't understand," Brittany said. "When you called, you said you had to talk to Bill about something important, but—"

"No worries!" I swept past them and on in the direction of the summerhouse. "I just need some help with a maintenance problem and Bill is the perfect person to ask."

"You said it was important," he reminded me.

"Did I?" I stopped and turned to make sure they were following along like I wanted them to. "I guess I was being a little dramatic, but well, you know, with Agnes's inauguration coming up, the place really needs some grooming. I'm going to get right on it, but I just want to make sure I'm doing everything right. I know I've brought you out of your way. Both of you." Playing it as cool as possible for a woman who wasn't used to games, I slid a smile from one to the other. "I hope you'll join me for lunch in the restaurant after we're done. My treat. It's my way of thanking you for your help."

"Yeah, but—"

I didn't give Bill a chance to offer any more of a protest. I kept on going, across the parking lot, on toward the summerhouse. I'd closed and locked the back door when I left and I paused, the key near the lock. "If you'll just come inside with me."

"Sure." Bill shuffled his sneakers against the ramp that led to the back door. "I'll try to help, but—"

"Good." I unlocked the door and Bill swung it open and all three of us stepped inside.

"My questions have nothing to do with the equipment in here," I told them. "If we could just go into the dining room."

They walked ahead of me, never hesitating.

It was all the proof I needed and if I were the skeptical sort, even that cynicism would have been washed away when I saw Bill and Brittany flinch when they saw what I'd found earlier.

"What the—!" Instinctively, Bill stepped back.

"Percival Dash," I said, pointing to the painting that had greeted me when I walked into the dining room. "You didn't know the picture was here, did you?"

"No. I swear." Even in the dim light, I could see that Bill's face was pale. His eyes bulged. "Why would somebody put this painting—"

"It's not just the painting." Brittany's words were as jumpy as the breaths she took in and let out in little whooshes of surprise. She pointed toward the corner of the room. "There's a ewer and a basin, and two stained-glass lamps. It's the stuff—"

"The stuff Muriel said I stole from the club." Bill's voice was sharp. "Avery, you've got to know, I didn't—"

"I know," I told him. "You wouldn't have walked in here so casually if you knew that stuff was here."

"Then you believe me?"

"I do."

"Then why—"

"Sorry. I know you told me you weren't involved in stealing from the club, but I just needed to prove it to myself. So why—"

"Why did Muriel make up that stuff about me?" Bill asked.

I could have told them right then and there, but it was far easier to show them. The way I figured it, a picture is worth a thousand words.

And a whole stack of them?

Maybe that would help explain what Muriel was up to.

# CHAPTER 16

It seemed silly for all of us to limbo our way through the crime scene tape that covered the doorway of Muriel's office, so I squeezed my way in there alone and brought the photographs of Bill back out to the hallway, where he waited with Brittany.

He shuffled through them, and his cheeks got redder and redder.

"I thought Muriel was keeping an eye on you because she was trying to catch you stealing," I explained, peering over his shoulder while he looked at the picture of himself, bare chested, working in the parking lot. "Now that theory doesn't make much sense. It seems pretty clear Muriel made up the story about you stealing from the club and she stashed the supposedly stolen goods in the summerhouse to support her story. Obviously, she was looking for an excuse to fire you. Can you explain? What are these pictures all about? What was Muriel up to?"

When he tapped the photos into a pile, Bill's words wobbled. "I . . . I have no idea."

"Oh, come off it, Bill!" Brittany stripped the photos out of his hands and slapped them against her leg. "Avery might as well know the truth."

Bill hung his head. "It's embarrassing."

"Not as embarrassing as me thinking you might have killed Muriel," I reminded him.

His head came up. "But I didn't! You don't think—"

"I don't know what to think. And I won't. Not until I know the whole story."

Muriel's—soon to be Agnes's—office was at the top of the staircase that led from the first floor. Letting go a long sigh, Bill walked away from it, sidestepping the stairway. There were meeting rooms up on the second floor— Marigold, Lilac, Dahlia, Tulip—and outside of Geranium, there was a padded bench set against the paneled wall. Bill dropped onto it.

"Muriel . . ." He swallowed hard and looked away. "There's no easy way to say it, Avery."

Brittany stood to his right. I sat down next to him. "Then just say it and get it over with."

His shoulders went rigid. "Muriel had the hots for me."

I might have laughed if Bill didn't look so darned serious. And so appalled at the very thought.

Instead, I pointed out, "Muriel was way older than you."

He nodded.

"And technically, she was your boss."

Another nod.

"She was so hoity-toity."

This, we all knew, so he didn't bother to nod again.

"How did you—"

I didn't have a chance to finish the question when Brittany

sputtered, "She was a cougar!" Her voice pinged against the silver sconces on the wall above our heads. "She was after Bill from the moment he started working here."

"Really?" It wasn't that I didn't believe them. It was just . . .

I searched for the words that would help me explain what I was thinking, and would lead to the truth. "Muriel and Tab had been married for a long, long time."

Bill puffed out a laugh. "Like she cared about that! Honest, Avery, from day one when I came here to work, that woman was after me. She'd just happen"—he emphasized the word—"to show up places where I was involved in some project or another. Raking leaves or fixing something. Or . . ." When he looked at the photos still clutched in Brittany's hand, his top lip curled. "Or black-topping the parking lot. I never encouraged her," he was quick to add. "I was polite. And friendly enough. But believe me, I never said anything that would have made her think I was interested in more than passing the time of day with her. After a while, she'd just happen to stay late when I had to be here after hours. At first I told myself I was just imagining things, but then . . . well, I don't know any other way to explain it, but Muriel, she started coming on pretty strong."

I pictured Muriel, short and thin, dressed to perfection, cutter of the purse strings, devoted to the club. "She came right out and—"

"At first she just asked me if I'd go out for a drink with her after work one day," Bill explained. "And I figured sure, sure, why not. There were a couple projects I wanted to discuss with her. You know, stuff I thought needed to be done around here. But then the next week, she asked the same thing, and I couldn't do it, you know? I had something else going on. She wasn't happy about that. She told me if I couldn't meet her at a local bar, well, her husband was out of town, and why didn't I stop over at her place for dinner and a nightcap." He gave me a sidelong glance. "Made me plenty uncomfortable, I'll tell you that. That was when I knew I had to steer clear."

"And did Muriel? Steer clear of you?"

"She did not. She was always following me. Always asking questions about the dumbest little things. You know, not like she needed answers, just like she wanted to have something to say to me and get me to talk. Then when Brittany started working here . . ."

I knew what was coming, knew it deep down in my bones. "So it wasn't just that she wanted Kendall to have your job," I said with a glance at Brittany. "She saw you and Bill were interested in each other and Muriel, she was jealous. How did she find out?"

"About me and Brit?" Bill reached out and took Brittany's hand. "She'd see us talking together. And she knew that most days, we ate lunch together."

Brittany bobbed her head. "She started to demand I meet with her just when she knew Bill and I were going to take our lunch hours. Just so we couldn't get together."

"Then one evening, I walked out of Brittany's place and there was Muriel." Like he still couldn't believe it, Bill slapped his hand against his thigh. "She was standing on the sidewalk outside of Brittany's place. And she didn't say a word. Her face just got all chalky like. And her eyes looked like they were burning up with fire. Then she turned and stomped away; but after that night, working here was impossible for Brittany."

"Things just got worse and worse," Brittany said. "Everything I did was wrong. Everything I said, she second-guessed. That's when I quit."

"And even then, she didn't let up on me," Bill told me. "I figured the best thing to do was just talk to the woman, to explain I wasn't interested. But whew!" He whistled low under his breath. "That woman did not tolerate not being in charge. Of everyone and everything. After that, I tried to ignore her, but that didn't work, either. She finally came right out and told me that if I didn't agree to meet her at a motel up there near the highway, things were going to get really ugly here for me. She was going to let the club members know that I'd served some time. She was going to start a campaign to get them to band together and force me out. And I . . ." His chin came up, his mouth thinned with determination. "I told her to go right ahead. That I didn't have anything to hide. That I'd turned my life around, I wasn't the same person I was years ago, and I was proud of myself for it. That's when she made up the story about me stealing from the club." His shoulders rose and fell. "That's when she fired me."

I hadn't known Muriel for long, but long enough to realize it was not only possible but plausible.

"I'm sorry it ever happened," I said. "Sorry for both of you." I took Brittany in with a look. "No one should have to put up with that kind of treatment. Bill, there's only one way I can think of to make it right."

"It wasn't me killing Muriel," Bill was quick to put in. "I swear to you, Avery, there's no way I did that. Even though . . ." He chewed his lower lip before he reached into his pocket.

Blushing, he pulled out a key and dropped it in my hand and at the same time he said, "Brittany's key for the front door," Brittany jumped back and gasped.

"You . . ." She pointed a trembling finger in Bill's direction. "Avery asked about the key, and I told her I had no idea what happened to it because I didn't. And all this time—"

"I'm sorry, Brit." When she made to pull her hand away, he held on tighter. "I would have told you eventually. I just thought, well, I don't know what I thought," he admitted. "I suppose it was a harebrained plan from the start. I wanted to get back into the club, to look for that stuff Muriel said I took. I didn't know how many people she'd told about me stealing things, but I figured that if I proved those things she said I took were still here, that would show everyone I'm not a thief. But I swear, Avery . . ." He spun in his seat to look at me head on. "I never used that key. I was trying to get up the courage, waiting for some night you were out so I didn't frighten you. I figured I'd come and have a look around. I had to prove that I've changed my ways, that I was innocent."

"You've already done that," I assured him. "And now you can do something else for me."

"Anything," Bill said. "I need you to know how grateful I am that you had faith in me."

I gave him a careful look. "Lawn?"

The look Bill gave me in return was blank.

"Flower pots?" I added. I popped out of my seat and swept out an arm, taking in the building and the grounds. "Falling leaves? We've got an inauguration coming up and the Portage Path Women's Club needs to look its best. And then there's the thermostat on the grill in the kitchen."

Maybe he was trying to sort out what I was getting at. He shook his head. "What are you saying, Avery?"

"I'm not saying anything. I'm asking. I know I'll need the board's approval, but something tells me that won't be a problem. Bill, would you like your old job back?"

* * *

It was no more than a minute after Bill and Brittany left, hand in hand and smiling, that Clemmie popped up beside me. "That was real nice, what you did for him."

"It was real nice of him not to sue the pants off of us for Muriel's sexual harassment."

"Sexual . . . ?" Clemmie's top lip curled.

I promised I'd explain all about it later, but for now, we had other things to do. With Bill taking care of the grounds, I could concentrate on two things—my plan to keep an eye on Patricia the next day and the preparations that were needed to get ready for the inauguration.

"What do you think?" I asked Clemmie. "How can we jazz the place up?"

"Well . . ." She floated toward the stairway that led up to the third floor. "I was looking around this morning. There are some things in the attic that are really the berries!"

She was right. The attic was accessed by a stairway just down the hallway from the room Clemmie had staked out as her own, and it was packed with furniture, trunks, and knickknacks. We spent a couple of hours sorting through it all, and I found a painting of the lilac bushes outside the summerhouse that I promised myself I'd get restored and rehung in the Lilac Lounge once Jack was done in there. I also discovered a whole trunk of old hats. There were picture hats and cloches, hats a woman would wear to tea, and fancier headdresses for formal affairs. They'd make a wonderful display in the glass-fronted case in the Carnation Room, and would be a great way to connect our members with the house and history.

"And look here!" Clemmie called me over to the trunk

she was bent over. "Must have belonged to that showcase Mrs. Dennison when she lived here."

What she'd found was a dress similar to the one Clemmie wore and in remarkably good shape, too. I lifted it out of the trunk and held it at arm's length. The fabric was black. The glass beads that covered the dress were black and gold. The dress was sleeveless, had a plunging neckline, and fringe below the drop waist that no doubt shimmied like a flapper doing the Charleston with every move its wearer made.

It was the prettiest thing I'd ever seen.

"Ooh!" Clemmie gushed. "If that ain't the cat's particulars. Attagirl! Go on!" With one slightly clammy elbow, she poked me in the ribs. "Try it on."

"No." It was far too old, the sort of precious thing that was meant to be kept behind glass. Besides . . . I sighed. "I'm pretty tall. It probably wouldn't fit."

"Bushwa!" She gave me a wink. "Tall means the dress will be short, and a short skirt means you can show off your gams. Besides, you don't know from nothing until you try it on."

Tempted, I fingered the fringe that dangled from the dress's hem. "It's too delicate," I decided. "I wouldn't want to damage it."

"It's lasted this long, ain't it? What can it hurt?"

She was right. And I couldn't resist. I slipped out of my jeans and T-shirt and into the dress.

Yeah, it was a little short. But other than that, it fit like it had been made for me.

Clemmie clapped her hands together. They didn't make a sound. "Well, if you ain't togged to the bricks!"

I guess that was a good thing because she smiled when she said it. Anxious to see how I looked, I kicked off my tennis shoes and went over to the cheval mirror on an oak stand in the corner of the attic, and right after I decided the mirror would be a great addition to my bedroom, I took a gander at myself.

"Perfect." Clemmie hovered next to my shoulder. "You coulda been in the show with me down in the speakeasy. Only . . ." Checking me out, she wrinkled her nose. "You need more makeup."

"I don't. Not to work here in the club. I'm supposed to look understated. Professional."

"Understated and professional ain't never got a guy."

"I'm not here to get a guy. I'm here to do my job. Besides, who says I want a guy?"

Clemmie's lips thinned. "Who says the cute one with the shaggy hair is ever going to pay attention to you if you don't make him sit up and take notice."

"Jack?" I laughed, even though I couldn't help but feel defensive. "For your information, he's already asked me out to dinner."

"Maybe, but he went to dinner with that other one. The pushy Jane with the screechy voice."

"You mean Kendall."

She bobbed her head. "Heard them talkin'. You know, from down in the furnace room. Those two are sounding awfully cozy."

Of course I'd noticed. That didn't mean I had to admit it.

Ignoring the comment, I turned to see how the back of the dress looked, just as Clemmie said, "And then there's that copper, of course. Yeah, yeah." I spun around to face her just as she held up a hand. "I know all about that, too. He wants to share a bottle of wine with you, right?" She tsked. "Nice, but it ain't exactly a declaration of undying love."

"I hardly know the man. I'm not looking for a declaration of undying love."

"Of course you are." She dismissed my opinion with a lift of one shoulder. "It's what every dame wants. And it ain't gonna happen with you lookin' like a librarian."

Did I?

I peered at myself in the mirror. I was a practical, sensible person and I wore practical, sensible clothes.

Except for right then and there. The flapper dress was over the top and when I compared it to the kinds of clothes I usually wore, I realized that most days I looked . . .

Dull.

The realization stung, and I wrinkled my nose and pursed my lips.

"All right," I told Clemmie. "Let's try some makeup."

She followed me to my rooms. Truth is, I don't own much makeup, but I dug around in my cosmetic case and found a shade of lipstick called Candy Apple, and Clemmie claimed it was close enough to the red she was wearing to be the "bee's knees." I touched a bit of the bright red color to my lips.

"Oh honey! Come on." Clemmie made a face. "How are you ever going to attract a guy if you're that much of a shrinking violet? Put a little oomph into it, why don't you. Full lower lip."

I did as I was told.

"Now a nice bow like mine"—she pointed—"on your top lip." I did that, too.

Stunned by the image of the vamp that looked back at me, I studied myself in the mirror. "I look . . ."

"Have you always had blonde hair?"

The voice that came from the doorway surprised the heck out of me, and I shrieked and spun around.

Jack stood there, his mouth hanging open.

Hand pressed to heart, it took me a moment to recover. "Of course I've always had blonde hair."

"But you look . . ." He blinked, sucked in a breath, blinked a little more. "You look so—"

"Different?" I thought I'd help him along.

"I was going to say amazing, but if you want to settle for different, I guess that counts, too."

"Told you so!" I'd almost forgotten Clemmie was in the room. That is, until she floated out from behind Jack and hovered just above his left shoulder. The bow on her left shoe brushed his ear and Jack shivered. "You might have all the brains in the world, sister, but it takes more than that to make a guy tell you you're amazing. You're on your way!"

"I don't need to be on my way," I grumbled.

"What?" Jack asked.

I froze. Smiled. "I don't need to be on my way. Not right now. But I was just thinking of all the things I need to do today."

"Like solving that murder." The comment came from Clemmie and I did my best to shush her with a look she totally ignored. From eight feet in the air, she looked down on Jack. "This potato might be able to help."

"How?" I wondered. Yeah, out loud. Not a good move.

"How, what?" Jack asked.

"How are you doing down in Marigold?" Pretty quick recovery, huh? "Any idea how long it might be until you finish the project?"

"Well, actually, that's why I was looking for you. I hope you don't mind that I came up here. I looked all over the club, and I called out to you from the bottom of the stairway. You didn't answer, but I knew you were up here somewhere.

It sounded like you were . . ." He leaned forward, the better to look all around. "I could have sworn I heard you talking to someone."

Clemmie grinned when I told Jack, "Just myself."

"I do that, too." He made it sound like we shared some terrible secret. "I find it's often the best way to help sort through my thoughts."

Before I even had a chance to answer, Clemmie piped in, "He's got an in with that Sadler family."

"How do you know?" I asked her.

"Well, because it helps me solve problems," Jack asked. "For instance—"

"What about the problem of Muriel's murder?" I blurted out. "What I mean . . ." If I expected help from Clemmie, I was disappointed. She hung there, suspended and gossamer, her eyes wide and her expression expectant. Like Jack, she was waiting to see where I was headed. Heck, so was I.

"I've been thinking about Tab Sadler," I told Jack. "When I mention him to people, I get a few different reactions. Some people think he's a great guy. Others tell me that he and Muriel didn't get along. Somebody even mentioned that Muriel may have limited how much money he was getting. I just thought, well, you seem to know Kendall and I'm guessing that means you know the rest of the family, too. I just wondered what you thought of Tab."

As if he wasn't quite sure, he thought it over. "That stuff about the money, Kendall never mentioned it."

"And of course she'd know. She is their granddaughter."

"And she lives there. With Tab and Mu—" He blushed. "Well, just with her grandfather, now. She's been staying with them until she can find a job and get herself established."

I am reasonably certain that the eagerness in Clemmie's

eyes wasn't what gave me the idea that popped into my head. "You and Kendall are friends. If you stopped over there this evening to visit her, no one would question it, would they?"

Studying me, Jack cocked his head. "You want to come along."

It wasn't a question.

"I'd just like to have a quick look around. Tab says he was home that night, but—"

"Do you have any reason not to believe him?"

When he put it that way—like any sane person would—it made it hard not to say, "Of course not."

"But you want to make sure, anyway."

I opted for the truth. "The board asked me to look into the murder. For the sake of the club."

Jack was quiet for a minute, no doubt thinking of the best way to tell me to mind my own business. "It's Monday," he finally said. "Tab plays poker with his buddies on Mondays."

"So he won't be home. And Kendall?"

"She won't mind if I stop by. Can you be ready by six?"

I assured him I would be and Jack backed out of the room. "You're not going to wear—"

"This?" I fingered the fringe on the skirt of the beaded dress. "I promise to be more subtle."

"It's not that you don't look . . . It's just that . . ." He shook his head as if to clear it. "Kendall would ask too many questions if you just show up. We'll have to sneak you into the house . . . Fact is, I'm not used to subterfuge. If you're dressed like that . . . I . . . I can't afford to be distracted."

I was still grinning when he left, but little by little, that smile faded. I had a lot to think about, a lot to plan. If I had one chance to look around Tab Sadler's house, I needed to make the most of it.

Looking awfully pleased with herself, Clemmie floated to the floor. "Told you he'd pay attention."

"I don't need his attention. I just needed him to agree to take me to Tab's tonight."

She squealed a laugh. "You don't think he would have done that if you were your regular, boring self, do you? You got a lot to learn, sister. A little cleavage goes a long, long way."

# CHAPTER 17

The Sadlers lived in a house that looked like it came straight out of a fairy tale.

A fairy tale about rich people.

The home was a Tudor behemoth complete with elaborate brickwork decorating the outside of the first story, and stucco and half-timbering adorning the second story. The windows were tall and narrow, and when we pulled down the tree-lined street the leaded glass winked at us in the last of the evening light. There was an arched doorway up front surrounded by gorgeous flower beds that even this late in the season, were in full bloom with orange chrysanthemums, purple asters, and dazzling golden black-eyed susans.

Jack didn't park in front. "Get down," he hissed at me as soon as we approached the house and he wheeled into the circular drive and stopped the car. I did as I was told, slouching down in my seat, half on and half off the floor.

"Any sign that Tab's home?" Don't ask me why I whispered. I guess this whole sneaking-into-someone's-house thing had me a little unnerved.

"His car is gone," Jack told me. He had to glance down to throw a nervous look in my direction. "Are you sure you want to go through with this?"

It was the same question he'd asked a dozen times on the way over to the ritzy part of town, and now, like then, I gave him the same answer. "You got any other ideas?"

"As a matter of fact, I do." He steadied his shoulders. "I could excuse myself from Kendall for a while and take a look around myself. That way, I could see if there's anything that makes Tab look suspicious."

With a groan, I stopped him going any further. But then, we'd been over all this, too. "If you disappear for ten minutes, it's going to look pretty fishy," I reminded him again.

"And you sneaking into the house, there's nothing fishy about that?"

"Not if I don't get caught. Which I won't . . ." I wondered if a penetrating glare could possibly work its magic when it was delivered from the floor of the front seat of a car. "If you sit here and look like you're talking to yourself."

Jack cracked a smile. "No one would be the least bit surprised." As quickly as the grin came, it faded. He checked out the time on the dashboard. "I'll go inside and talk to Kendall. Give us ten minutes. That should be enough to get the pleasantries over with. We'll pour some wine and, since it's a nice evening, I'll suggest we sit out on the back deck. From there, there's not a chance she'll hear you when you come in the back door."

"Then what?" I wanted to know.

"I thought you had a plan."

"I do," I assured him. "Sort of."

Where else—besides nowhere—the conversation was

headed didn't matter. I heard a door open and a greeting called out, "Hi, Jack!"

Clemmie was right. Kendall did have a squeaky voice.

"Ten minutes," Jack said from between clenched teeth. "Do what you have to do and get out of there fast. Get back in the car and wait for me."

I promised I would. Get out of there fast, that is. I still wasn't sure what I had to do.

Something told me Kendall was headed over for an up-close-and-personal greeting. That would explain the speed at which Jack popped out from behind the steering wheel and hurried around the front of the car. "Good to see you!" I heard him say, then the smoochy sound of quick cheek kisses. After that, both their voices faded and the back door banged shut.

I breathed a sigh of relief—so far, so good—and dared to sit up a little straighter and take a look around.

The backyard of the Sadler house was as impressive as the front. We were parked near a four-car garage on a stone driveway bordered with more flower beds. In keeping with the season, one of them had a folksy scarecrow staked in the center of it, a fat orange pumpkin at its base.

I pulled out my phone and watched the minutes tick by in agonizing slowness, and once my clock told me ten minutes had passed, I wished I had longer to come to peace with my plan.

No time.

No dillydallying.

The only way to stop being as jumpy as a june bug was to get this over with.

I slipped out of the car and quietly closed the door behind me, then tiptoed to the back of the house. The bottom of the back door was solid, but the top of it had two panes

of leaded glass in it, so I made sure to stand to the side—
just to be sure—when I reached for the doorknob.

The door was locked.

I had already grumbled a curse when I realized that the
locked door was really a blessing. A shadow raked across the
kitchen window. A short shadow. If I'd walked into the house
right then and there, I would have bumped into Kendall.

I crouched on the stone patio.

"As soon as you called, I put a bottle of prosecco in the
fridge. That will be way more festive than wine!" Kendall
giggled. "But I don't know about the back deck." I didn't
have to see her to know she shivered. She's that kind of girl.
"It's chilly out there."

"We can sit on the porch swing together." Was that
Jack's voice? I swear, I almost stood up just so I could look
through the window and be sure. His voice was low and
husky, downright sexy. He must have been standing close
to the door because I practically felt the vibration of his
words when he added, "I'll keep you warm."

Before I had a chance to think about the miraculous
change in him, I heard the fridge open, and I knew I had
exactly as much time as it would take for Kendall to retrieve the bottle of prosecco.

I popped up and peered in the window.

Three feet away, Jack flinched at the sight of me and
motioned for me to get down.

I pointed through the window, down in the direction of
the door handle, and mouthed the word, "Locked."

He waved for all he was worth. That is, until he wiped
the panic off his face, turned to his left, and smiled.

Kendall was headed back across the room.

And there I was again, scrunched down on the patio. A
cork popped. Kendall tittered. Liquid glugged into glasses

and then those glasses clinked together in a toast and the clear sound of the crystal's ping floated outside.

"To us!" Kendall purred.

"To us!" Jack responded, then I think he must have stepped back, because I heard him say, "After you," right before I heard the lock on the doorknob turn.

In a house that size, I figured the back deck was far from the kitchen, so I gave them a minute, then slowly opened the door, looked around to make sure the coast was clear, and slipped inside.

From where I stood, I could see into a family room the size of a football field. On the far wall, it had floor-to-ceiling windows, and yes, there was a deck right outside and it had a porch swing on it. Jack and Kendall sat side by side, swinging slowly back and forth. True to his word, his arm was around her shoulders, keeping her warm.

In the best of all possible worlds, it would have been interesting to check out the house. From what I saw as I raced through the kitchen, into the dining room, and from there to a stairway that led to the second floor, the furniture was solid and expensive, the rugs were antique Orientals, and the artwork on the walls wasn't the kind of stuff sold at starving artist sales.

No matter, I reminded myself I had more important things to do. At the top of the stairway, I began my search for the master suite.

Turns out it was at the back of the house, overlooking the deck and that swing that went back and forth, back and forth even as I watched. The bedroom was a confection of gold and white French provincial furniture with pink walls, blush carpet, and gold accents.

And not one sign of a masculine presence anywhere inside its four walls.

Even if I hadn't known Muriel and Tab were on the outs, it didn't take a detective to figure out this was Muriel's room and Muriel's alone; Tab had his own bedroom.

This I found at the other end of the wide hallway. From the heavy oak furniture to the dark-green walls and plaid bedspread, the room oozed machismo. If I needed any more proof that this was Tab's inner sanctum, the sport coat he'd worn the day he visited the club still hung on the suit valet outside the walk-in closet.

I closed the bedroom door behind me and raced across the room to riffle through the jacket pockets.

A single dollar bill.

A stick of peppermint gum.

A small wad of lint.

Nothing that meant anything. Not when it came to Muriel's murder.

Too new at the espionage game to have the courage to rummage through the drawers just yet, I checked the top of the nearest dresser. Tie clip, cell phone, and a framed picture lying facedown on the dresser top. I turned it over for a quick look.

Muriel in the pink suit she was wearing when she was killed, standing outside the club.

Had Tab laid the photo on its face because he was overcome with grief when he looked at his late wife?

Did he maybe not want to be reminded of Muriel because was he miffed about the money?

Or was he the murderer, and too guilty to have the face of his victim staring back at him?

Important questions, all, but I had other fish to fry. I grabbed the phone, all set to check through Tab's recent call history. That was exactly when I heard a door downstairs slam.

"Kendall!" A man's voice rumbled its way up the stairs. "It's just me! I forgot my phone!"

Forgot—

Any second, Tab would come walking through his bedroom door, and he'd find me frozen, his phone in my hand and my heart beating a mile a minute.

Panic overwhelmed me.

Fear coated my insides with frost.

Shame and embarrassment warred within me, and I wondered what I'd say, how I'd explain, how I could ever show my face in public again. Especially when, with my pale complexion, I knew I would look lousy in an orange jumpsuit.

"Hi there, Mr. Sadler!"

Jack's voice cut through my panic. I wondered if Kendall or Tab noticed how loud he was talking. I was sure I was supposed to, and at the same time I whispered a prayer of thanksgiving for Jack's quick thinking, I bucked as if I'd been kicked and took off for the walk-in closet.

"Good to see you, Jack." Now that I was inside the closet and had the door closed behind me, Tab's voice was muffled. "You don't stop in nearly often enough."

"Been busy." Jack wasn't talking so loud anymore, and I pictured him walking up the stairs with Tab. "I've got a pretty big project to complete over at the club. Oh, I'm sorry." Jack didn't sound all that sorry. He did sound like he was right outside the bedroom door. "Maybe I shouldn't have mentioned the club."

"No problem!" A slap. Tab giving Jack a manly whack on the shoulder. "The club was always important to Muriel. Nothing's going to change that. Nothing's going to dull the memories, either. You'll find that out for yourself someday. After you and Kendall are married."

Married?

The word knocked me out of my stupor. Good thing, too, or I wouldn't have realized I was still holding on to Tab's phone.

I zipped out of the closet, set the phone down where I'd found it, and made it back to my hiding place just as the bedroom door opened. "I won't be here long enough to bother you two kids," I heard Tab say. "Realized halfway to the card game that I couldn't find my phone."

"Cards?" Jack cleared his throat. "Do you think that's a good idea at a time like this?"

"The best idea," Tab responded. His voice was louder, nearer. "I've suffered quite a shock, as you can imagine, and I need to be with friends. Not sure I'll play my best game, but the other fellas, they'll probably be glad for that. Ah, here's my phone!" He was just inches away from the closet now, and instinctively, I melted further into the darkness. I slipped behind a raincoat. I slithered in back of what felt like a silk smoking jacket. I pressed myself all the way to the back of the closet, behind a corduroy jacket, holding my breath, afraid to move a muscle.

"Well, now that you've got your phone, you'll probably be on your way again," Jack said. I wondered if Tab realized what I did, how nonchalant he was trying to sound.

"Not to worry." Tab must have turned back to the door. His voice was muted again. "I'll leave you two kids alone. I know how important it is to have a romantic evening now and again."

Romantic, huh? Another kick to the gut made me suck in a breath, and when I did, I nearly gagged. The corduroy jacket smelled funny. Like grease.

Not like car grease. I sniffed again. And not anything fine and delicious like olive oil, either. This was cheap and clingy, the kind of odor that soaked into clothes and held on fast.

"Good to see you again, Mr. Sadler!" Jack was back in the hallway. I wondered if he was doing what I pictured him doing, standing at the top of the stairway, making sure Tab was gone before he checked the bedroom. "See you in a few hours."

A second later, his rough whisper scraped the air. "Avery? Are you in here?"

I emerged from my hidey-hole, corduroy jacket in hand. "What's this about you and Kendall getting married?"

Jack's cheeks flushed the same red color as his hair. "Well, it's just that—"

"Jack! You up there?"

He spun toward the door. "Coming right down!" he told Kendall, then gave me one last look. "Hurry up!" When he left, he closed the bedroom door behind him, and being sure to keep out of sight, I went to the window and watched Tab pull away from the house.

Once he was gone, I released a breath I didn't even realize I was holding and set the jacket on the bed so I could go through the pockets.

Nothing in the right pocket.

And in the left—

I pulled out a piece of heavy cardstock.

It was a movie ticket.

Of course! That greasy smell was movie theater popcorn.

Tab had been to see . . .

I peered down at the ticket. A special showing, the sixtieth anniversary of the film *Psycho*.

I took another look at the ticket, at the date and the time stamp, and my heart bumped to a stop.

As if Tab was still there, I slanted a look at the door. "Home waiting for the missus to arrive for dinner, huh?"

On the night Muriel died, the night Tab assured me he was home, what he was really doing was going out to the movies and eating greasy popcorn.

F ind anything?"

We were out of the driveway and down the street before Jack dared to ask the question. I pried myself off the floor and hauled myself on the passenger seat.

"I found out your future grandfather-in-law lied about his alibi."

I wasn't sure if the sour look he gave me had something to do with Tab's lie or the fact that it looked like he was going to be part of the Sadler family.

Jack sighed. "Our families have known each other for years," he told me. "Mine and Kendall's."

"Uh-huh."

"And there's always been this unspoken sort of expectation. You know what I mean? My parents and Kendall's parents, they just always thought—"

"Wait a minute!" I sat up a little straighter, the murder investigation pushed from my brain thanks to more pressing questions. "Does this mean you're rich?"

He had to process the question for a moment before he answered with a, "Huh?"

"I mean, rich people usually hang with rich people. And rich people don't usually hang with people who aren't in their same social class, and if they do, they don't just naturally expect their daughters and sons to marry. So you must be rich."

"A little," he said.

If he wasn't so busy making a left-hand turn, he would have seen the way my mouth screwed up. "I don't think you can be a little rich."

"All right then, just rich."

"All right then."

"Why do you care?"

"I don't," I admitted. "Not really. I'm just trying to understand. And I don't really care that you and Kendall are getting married, either."

"We're not exactly getting married. We're just engaged."

I spared him another sour look. After all, he was driving.

"Usually when you're engaged to someone, it means you're getting married."

"Well, yes, but—"

"But it really doesn't matter. I mean, not to me." I felt it was important to point this out. After all, I barely knew Jack, and I certainly had no claim on him. Still, I couldn't help but feel a little disappointed that a guy as intelligent as him had hitched his wagon (metaphorically speaking) to a woman as shallow as Kendall. "It's fine with me if you're getting married," I told him.

"Then why are you being so prickly about it?"

I crossed my arms over my chest. "I'm not being prickly."

"You are, you're being—"

"I'm being upset that you have an intimate connection to the victim's family and you never bothered to mention it."

"You never bothered to tell me you were going to burglarize their home until today."

"It wasn't exactly a burglary." Well, except for the movie ticket that I took out of the pocket of Tab's corduroy jacket and slipped into mine, but Jack didn't need to know about that.

"And I don't consider myself exactly engaged."

"I bet Kendall would beg to differ."

"No doubt." Jack kept his hands at two and ten on the wheel. "So what are you going to do?"

"About you and Kendall getting married? I'll send something nice like a fruit basket."

He didn't even try to hide an eye roll. "About Tab. You said you found something that disproves his alibi."

"I did," I assured Jack. "He told me he was home, but he wasn't. Now all we have to figure out is why he lied."

# CHAPTER 18

"Funny, I never figured you for a hood."

I'd been busy on the computer near the front door of the club when Clemmie popped up beside me, and hearing her smart-aleck comment, I groaned. The night before, when I got back to the club, I never should have told her about my visit to the Sadlers.

"I am not a hoodlum," I told her in no uncertain terms.

"Yeah. Just a cat burglar. You know, a porch climber."

Since she was grinning when she said this, I didn't hold it against her. "As a matter of fact, I got in through the back door."

"Yeah, thanks to that Jack. He likes you. He must, or he wouldn't have helped you out like that. What a sheik!"

"An engaged sheik." I'd told her all about that the night before, too.

"Ishkabibble!" She puckered her lips. "He sure can't care about her much if he asked you to dinner."

"Chances are he was just hungry."

"He sure is a funny bird," Clemmie declared. "Maybe he just doesn't know what he wants."

I might have had a chance to agree except that Agnes wheeled around the corner from the ballroom and into the lobby at that moment. She stopped short, squinted, and looked all around.

"I thought I heard you talking to someone."

Instead of addressing the comment, I gave her a smile even as I watched Clemmie fade away over Agnes's left shoulder. "Been working on this project for so long, my brain is fried."

"Anything I can help with?" She came around the desk to stand beside me and checked my computer screen. "One of those find-your-ancestors sites? What are you up to, Avery? Oh." She read the name up in the search box at the corner of the screen and stepped back like she'd been zapped by lightning.

"You don't think it's a good idea?" I asked her.

"Well, I think . . ." She smoothed a hand over the tailored navy blue pants she wore with a green sweater. Her smile came and went. "Of course I don't know if it's a good idea or not. I don't know what you have planned." She slanted me a look. "What do you have planned?"

"It might not matter." I stretched, and since I was getting nowhere fast with my research, I closed the website I'd been reading and sat back. "I've been trying to do some Internet research ever since I found out about the inauguration. But I can't find one trace of Dodie Hillenbrand. Not in Ohio. Not anywhere."

"Why are you looking for her?"

"Oh, it has nothing to do with that sign you took down," I assured her. I didn't want her to think I was second-guessing her first presidential decree. "It's just that Gracie told me Dodie worked here in the house before the house was the club."

"Yes, that's what I've heard."

"So I was thinking that she's really got a kind of connection no one else does. And if we could find her—"

"It was a very long time ago," Agnes reminded me.

"And she's ancient by now." I grabbed a pencil from my desktop and tap, tap, tapped out my frustration near my keyboard. "For all I know, she's probably dead."

"Probably." The very thought seemed to cheer Agnes. She beamed me a smile. "And if she's not, she certainly would be too old to come here for the inauguration. That is . . ." She gulped. "If that's what you were thinking."

"It was," I admitted. "I thought Dodie would be a great connection to the history of the house. She worked for the Dennisons. She was the cook here for a number of years after the club took over. But then, I thought about it, and I knew it would be asking too much to expect her to join us on Sunday. It's too short notice. So I gave up on the idea completely. Until this morning, that is, that's when I thought that if I could locate her, I might be able to FaceTime an interview with her, or at least talk to her on the phone. I'd like to hear some of her stories, find out what things were like here. You know, when the club bought the property."

"Oh, that would be interesting."

Which didn't explain why Agnes's top lip curled.

"You'd rather I didn't."

"It isn't that. Not at all." Agnes's smile was as soft as a kitten's belly fur. "It's just that, well, it seems like an awful lot of trouble for you to go through. Especially since we don't even know if the woman is still alive. It's Tuesday. The inauguration is Sunday. Far be it from me to tell you your job, Avery. That was best left to Muriel." She smiled at her own catty remark. "I'm just saying, with the florist to deal with, and the woman who will be playing the harp during the cocktail hour, and with making sure Quentin and Geneva can handle things in the kitchen . . ."

"You're absolutely right." To prove I wouldn't let myself be distracted by the rabbit hole that was Internet research, I popped out of my chair. "I have to measure the mantel in the ballroom and let the florist know how long the flower spray there will need to be. And Quentin's making samples of the hors d'oeuvres he's thinking about making. If you'd like to help us decide which ones we'll serve, stop into the kitchen later."

"Oh, I'd like that." Agnes bustled away, then stopped and swung back around. "There will be desserts, too, I hope."

"Crème brûlée in individual ramekins. Cake pops. Four different flavors. And pavlova. Quentin says it's your favorite."

"Quentin is a genius." A smile on her face as wide as that mantel I had to measure, Agnes returned to the ball-room.

"You ain't actually going to give up on that Dodie, are you?"

I might have known Clemmie would be back. She perched on the edge of my desk, her legs crossed and her arms braced behind her on nothing at all.

"It looks like I might have to. I'm not finding out much of anything, anyway. Except . . ." A thought struck. "You were here when Dodie was around. You must have been."

She nodded. "I remember hearing the name. You know, when I was listening from down in the furnace room. I re-member some other stuff, too." She gave me a broad wink.

"Like . . . ?"

"Like the fact that some evenings, Dodie would tell

everyone here she was going home, only she wouldn't.
She'd wait around until everyone else was gone, and then
she'd sometimes meet somebody."

"Somebody who?"

Clemmie shrugged.

"How do you know?"

"Hey, I might be a ghost, but I know the sound of
barney-mugging when I hear it."

I did not need her to elaborate. Times change. So do
words. But I had a feeling I knew exactly what Dodie was
up to when she was barney-mugging.

"With who?" I asked.

"Whom." Clemmie wiggled her shoulders and corrected
me, then squealed a laugh. "That's what those swells used
to say. You know, when they were all being oh-so correct
and trying like the dickens to impress each other even when
they were down there in the gin joint breaking every law on
the books."

"So who . . . whom . . . no, it's who this time. Who was
Dodie meeting?"

"Can't say. Don't know. A big-timer, if I had to guess."

"Was it old man Dennison himself? Or was it after his
time. I hope it was after he'd sold that house. That would be
awful, wouldn't it, if it was Dodie and Mr. Dennison? Mrs.
Dennison adored Dodie's cooking. If Chauncey cheated on
her with Dodie . . ." I could only imagine the hurt and betrayal, and it made my stomach sour.

"Wish I could help. But like I told you, my days just sort
of flow, one into the other, so I can't tell you when it was.
And I never did hear much from him. Just some mumbling.
You know, like sweet nothings." She sighed. "And that
Dodie, she'd giggle and flirt. And it's funny, because now
and again, she'd go into the basement for something or

other, and I'd get a look at her. She wasn't the giggle-and-flirt type, if you know what I mean. Hardworking. Down-to-earth. But then, love does strange things to a woman. It can make some of them really goofy."

True enough.

Other things could make a woman goofy, too, and if I needed the reminder, it came when Patricia zoomed into the club.

It was Tuesday, and I had plans for later in the day. Goofy plans that included keeping a very close eye on Patricia.

I busied myself sorting through a stack of mail that I'd already gone through earlier that morning.

"Good morning!" Didn't it figure, the one morning I didn't want to talk to Patricia for fear of looking too guilty about spying on her, she was dead set on visiting. She planted herself in front of my desk. "How are the plans going?"

As if I had to think about it rather than school my expression so it didn't give me away as a spy, I finished with the mail, tapped it into a pile, and set it down. "You mean the inauguration?"

Patricia laughed. "Of course that's what I mean! We're good?"

"So far," I reassured her. "Food sampling later this afternoon. I hope you have time to stop by. I ran into Reverend Way this morning." I didn't have time to wonder if a lie about a clergyman counted as extra big. "He told me he's rescheduled tomorrow's Kids Coats meeting for tonight."

Patricia's dark brows dropped low over her eyes. "Yes. I wish he'd quit doing that. It's hard to change plans in midstream."

"You had something else planned for tonight?" What, like I hoped she'd say no, that she'd admit the only Tuesday she'd had other plans was the Tuesday she killed Muriel?

"Nah, nothing like that at all." Patricia waved away the question—and my crazy idea about how easy it might be to get her to confess. "Just the Kids Coats meeting." She started toward the ballroom, then stopped so fast, the sneakers she wore with dark brown pants and a blue sweater squeaked. "I keep forgetting to tell you, Avery." Patricia spun back around and came to stand near my desk. "I didn't think you'd mind. I asked Jack Harkness for a little help with the inauguration."

Like what, escorting his fiancée to the cocktail party?

It was small-minded of me to even think it. I banished the thought with a figurative whack to the forehead.

"He's doing some research. You know, in the old books. Since we're not allowed to touch any of them until he's completely finished with Marigold, I thought it wouldn't hurt to ask him to take a peek."

"What's he looking for?"

Patricia's shrug was quick and broad. "Just thought he might find some interesting tidbits. Let me know if he comes up with anything."

I assured her I would. And reminded her there would be cake pops available later.

Before the Kids Coats meeting.

And my surveillance.


It was fall and by six forty-five, the sky had already darkened to a deep indigo edged in the west by flaming clouds in shades of pink and orange.

"Red sky at night," I mumbled to myself from the spot I'd staked out near the window closest to my desk. "Let's hope what results is delight."

"You mean like you finding out that Patricia is really the killer."

I knew Clemmie was looking over my shoulder. Even though I couldn't see her reflection next to mine in the window, I could feel the cool breath of her presence. Together, we watched the sunset for a few more minutes, until the sky was navy blue and dotted with silver stars.

"As much as I want to find the killer, I don't want it to be Patricia," I finally said. "I like Patricia."

"I bet somebody, somewhere, liked the goon who shot me, too."

It was an interesting thought, and a grim reminder that murder leaves a wake of ache and despair, on both the killer's and the victim's friends, family, and acquaintances.

I turned to face Clemmie. It was better than trying to address the nothing that looked back at me from the window.

"Do you know who it was?" I asked her.

"Who shot me?" As if she'd never even considered the question, she wrinkled her nose. "Like I told you, it was that tough. He was an ugly pug wearing a dark suit. And he was the one who was jawing with the other tough at the table near the stage."

"But don't you wonder who he was? What his name was? What happened to him?"

"It never seemed nearly as important as what happened to me," she said, but she didn't have time to say more. She pointed over my shoulder and hopped up and down again, her shoes silently hitting the parquet floor. "Isn't that her? That Patricia you're watching? She's out of that meeting, Avery. She's headed for her car."

Clemmie was right. Patricia crossed the parking lot, heading for her car. Like she had the Tuesday before, she'd left her meeting early. I was ready. I grabbed my car keys from the top of my desk and ducked away from the window so there was no chance Patricia would see me. As soon as she pulled out of her parking space, I was out the door and in my car.

I reminded myself not to be too eager, not to drive too close, not to get too nervous. Tell that to the drumbeat of anticipation that pounded through my veins.

But then, maybe this was actually good news.

The thought hit just as I stopped three car lengths behind Patricia at a red light.

If Patricia really did have someplace else to go this Tuesday night, maybe it meant she had someplace else to go the Tuesday Muriel had been killed, too. Is it possible that when she left the Kids Coats meeting that night, she hadn't gone back to the club? That she wasn't a murderer?

I hoped so. Oh, how I hoped so, and that drumbeat of worry shifted rhythms ever so slightly. Now my heart pounded out hope.

I was still unfamiliar enough with Portage Path to not know where we were headed, but I faithfully followed Patricia's fuel-efficient hybrid car farther into the heart of town. She turned down a street that had a tire repair shop on one corner, a long-closed gas station on the other, and all around me, I saw remnants of Portage Path's industrial past. A retail establishment with boarded-up windows here. A long-closed factory there. The street curved and sloped down to the meandering Portage Path River (which, from what I'd seen of it, was really more of a stream) and at the bottom of the hill, Patricia drove past the broken bottles and piles of litter than pocked the street and toward a metal building that looked a whole lot like a barn. There was a rusted metal fence around the parking lot, where weeds cracked the pavement and garbage dotted the ground.

There were other cars there, too, but I wasn't taking any chances. I hung back and let Patricia park her car. When she got out, she was carrying a duffel bag and had something big and misshapen flung over her shoulder. I waited until she was inside the building to find a parking place in a corner away from the one blinking light that was someone's idea of security.

When another car pulled into the lot, I sank back in my seat and watched. This was another woman, about Patricia's age, and she, too, had a duffel bag, and when she opened the door of the building, a stream of anemic light hit the pavement and a muffled cheer washed outside.

More curious than ever, I slipped out of my car and over to the door just as another car pulled in. I melted into the shadows next to the building but apparently not quickly enough. When a woman approached, she nodded a greeting.

"It's not the night for trials," she said.

"No. I . . . uh . . . I knew that."

She looked me up and down. "You're too young, anyway. And too scrawny from the looks of it."

I couldn't tell if this was meant to be a compliment or the ultimate of insults.

She turned away and grabbed the door handle.

"But I can still go in, can't I?" I asked her.

She looked me over her shoulder. "You got ten bucks?"

I assured her I did.

"Then come on in." She yanked the door open further, stepped back to hold it open, and waved me inside.

She cursed, too, when I stopped just inside the door, surprise freezing me in place.

"Get a move on, skinny chick!" The woman edged around me and hurried down a hallway behind the nearest tier of bleachers.

Ahead of me, the floor sloped down and on either side of it, there were bleacher seats where those spectators I'd heard from outside huddled in groups of threes and fours. Before I took another step, I heard a cough from over on the left and turned to find a woman seated on a metal folding chair with a lopsided tray table in front of it. She barely looked up from the screen of the phone on the tray, just held out a hand.

I grabbed ten dollars out of my purse and set it down on the tray, and the woman scooped it up and stuffed it in an old cigar box. Since she didn't acknowledge me or tell me where to sit, I decided I had free run of the place. I walked the aisle between the bleachers and on toward the center of the building and the oval, light-colored floor painted with orange concentric circles.

"Hi!" I gave a little wave to a man in a red T-shirt and a fuzzy red wig who was sitting nearest to the aisleway. "Can you tell me—"

"Not now, honey!" He shushed me by frantically waving his hands. "It's about to start."

I wasn't sure what it was. I had no idea what was going on.

At least not until I heard a voice from behind me, close to my ear.

"You can't stand there looking like a deer in headlights, Avery. They're going to know you don't belong."

# CHAPTER 19

I almost didn't recognize Oz. But then, the other times I'd
seen him, he was working, and though he wasn't a flashy
dresser, he'd always looked neat and professional. Suit. Tie.
Nicely pressed shirt.

Now . . .

Not sure if my eyes were playing tricks on me, I shook
my head, squinted, and looked him over.

All the way from the jeans and the purple T-shirt to the
purple glitter in his hair.

He was munching a bag of popcorn and he held it out,
offering me some.

I declined. I was way too busy sputtering to eat.
"You're . . ." Since my brain refused to process what I was
seeing, my mouth wouldn't work. "Why are you . . . What
are you . . . What's going on here?"

The crowd roared and Oz put a hand on my shoulder and
turned me to face the center of the building just as two

groups of older-than-middle-aged women roller-skated onto the rink. Half of them were wearing red T-shirts and white helmets with red stars on them. The other half was in purple—T-shirts, helmets, short shorts.

"Portage Path Pirates versus the Cleveland Eerie Rovers. Senior women's roller derby," he said.

"But I don't . . . It can't . . . Why is—"

"Ooh!" As if he were the one out there on the rink who just got blindsided by a short woman in purple with a skull and crossbones tattooed on her right upper forearm, he oofed. "Did you see that?"

"I didn't. I don't know where to look." The action moved fast and the more I watched it, the more my brain scrambled. Bewildered, I looked over the scrum of women vying for . . . whatever. "Oz." Because he was paying more attention to the action than he was to me, I tugged at the sleeve of his purple shirt. "What are you doing here?"

Because that same woman with the skull tattoo did something that was apparently good, the crowd roared and Oz had to raise his voice. "The same thing you're doing here."

"Can we . . ." I leaned close so I could yell in his ear. "Can we go someplace else to talk?"

"Talk? Sure." He watched a few more seconds of the action before we walked up the shallow steps between the bleachers. A couple times, he looked over his shoulder so he could see what was going on in the match.

"We're going out," I told the woman behind the tray table. "We might be coming back in. You're not going to charge us again, are you?"

Since she never looked up from her phone, I figured not.

I pushed through the door and out to the blessed quiet of the parking lot.

"What the heck . . ." I pulled in a stumbling breath and

ran a hand through my hair. Yeah, like that might help order my thoughts. "Oz, explain."

"The rules? Well, it's like this. There are two periods in the game and they're played for thirty minutes each. Each team has one jammer, who has to overlap as many of the opposing players as she can, and—"

"Not the rules of roller derby!" Yes, I may have screeched. Well, just a little. But the fact that I was being lectured on the finer points of roller derby in a dark parking lot by a man with purple glitter in his hair had a way of unnerving me. "I mean, explain," I said, holding my arms close to my sides as if that might keep me from going up like a Roman candle. "Why are you dressed like that?"

Oz grinned. "I didn't want to be conspicuous."

"I've got news for you: Purple glitter is plenty conspicuous."

"Not around here." As if to prove the point, a woman whose face was dabbed with purple paint came around the corner and entered the building. She was followed by another woman, old and as skinny as a rail, who was dolled up in a red ruffled skirt, a red boa, and had her hair spray-painted fire-engine red. "I had to look like a fan," Oz said, his gaze following the purple and red ladies as they went into the building. "I didn't want Patricia to notice me."

"Patricia?" I'm not sure how I hoped it would help, but my gaze shot to the now-closed door. "I know she's here. I saw her go inside. She's some sort of roller derby groupie?"

"Better than that. She's the Finkinator." Oz somehow managed to say this like it was the most natural thing in the world, and in that moment, I realized there were depths to him that I had no clue about. "Patricia Fink is the jammer. For the Pirates."

My heart stopped, then started up with a bang that shot

me backward. "The woman with the skull and crossbones tattooed on her arm? That can't be—"

"The Finkinator. Sure. All the skaters have nicknames, see. There's the Pretty Pirate, who, for the record, isn't all that pretty. The Purple Monster. Violet Vengeance. That's my favorite. You have to admit, it is a pretty awesome nickname."

It was all starting to sink in, but I still wasn't clear on the details. "You're a fan?"

"Not until tonight." He grinned and when he moved a little closer, the watery light twinkled against the glitter in his hair. "I did my homework before I came. You know, so I could understand what was going on."

"Because . . . ?" As if it might actually urge him toward some explanation that came even close to making sense, I leaned closer.

"Because I wanted to confirm Patricia's alibi, of course."

"But her alibi was that she was at a Kids Coats meeting."

The way he cocked his head spoke volumes. "You know that was a lie, and I know that was a lie. Something tells me we both talked to Reverend Way."

"I did. You did. Of course you did. And you knew—"

"That Patricia left the meeting early the night Ms. Sadler was killed. That it was plenty suspicious since she's a dedicated volunteer and never leaves early when the meetings are on Wednesdays. So I did some digging. And some following. It's in my job description, you know. It's what I do."

I was almost afraid to ask. "What did you find out?"

"That she comes here every Friday night for practice. I took a look around then. And every Tuesday, the Pirates have a match against an opposing team."

"Which means Patricia's story about the Kids Coats meeting was a lie."

"Well, there was a meeting. But like Reverend Way told

me . . . um, us . . . like he told both of us, Patricia left early the night of the murder. She had to leave early or she'd miss the match, and from what I've heard, Patricia has been on the team for years and hasn't missed one single time. She has an alibi. I came here tonight to confirm it and there was only one way to do that. I had to fit in." As if I hadn't noticed the purple shirt or that darned glitter, he lifted his arms and spun all around to give me a good look at his getup. "Fans talk to other fans, and I got here plenty early enough to make a few new friends. They all assured me that the night Muriel died, the Finkinator was right out there on the rink, skating her little heart out."

"Well, that explains the bruises," I grumbled.

Oz's eyes lit with appreciation. "You saw them, too."

"And wondered. Especially when Patricia said they came from a screwdriver slip when she was fixing a J-trap."

The appreciation morphed into wonder and his wonder transformed right before my eyes into admiration of the kind that made my heat skip a beat and my toes tingle.

"You know plumbing?" Okay, so it wasn't the most romantic thing a guy ever said to me, but the way Oz's eyes burned with devotion, I couldn't help but smile.

"Plumbing, electricity, a smattering of carpentry."

He wound his arm through mine, and together we walked back into the building.

"Avery," he said, "I think this is the start of a beautiful friendship."


Oz insisted on staying until the end of the match and as it turned out, I was glad we did because the Pirates won and the Finkinator proved that in addition to being an accomplished skater, she had crazy skills in ramming, whacking, pounding, and crashing that gave a whole new meaning to guts and determination. I was glad Patricia had an alibi for the night of the murder. She was my new hero.

Oz and I finished that bag of popcorn together, and after the match, we met over at a late-night burger spot. Yeah, the purple glitter caused him to get a couple weird looks from people, but Oz didn't pay them any attention. I was a kid who grew up with mediums, and let me just say this, they get plenty of weird looks, too. Just like them, Oz rose above the pettiness.

He was my new hero, too.

"So . . ." He'd just taken a big bite of his Swiss cheese and mushroom burger, and he chewed and swallowed and waited until I did the same with my cheddar cheese and bacon burger. "You know what I'm going to say, right? I mean, I have to. That's in my job description, too."

I knew it would come to this eventually, and I swallowed my burger along with my pride. "You're going to tell me I shouldn't have followed Patricia. You're going to remind me to mind my own business."

"Smart and pretty." He took another bite of burger.

"The board asked for my help," I explained.

"That's what I'm here for. To help. In fact, I get paid for it."

"To help the board?"

"To find the truth."

"The truth doesn't belong to just one person."

"Nor does trouble." He set down his burger, the better to point a finger at me in a way that told me I needed to pay special attention to his next words. "There's a murderer out there."

"Yes, but—"

"And murderers don't like to get caught."

"Yes, of course, but—"

"And people who poke their noses where they don't be-long often find themselves in a whole lot of trouble."

He expected me to agree with him again. I hated to dis-appoint him.

"I haven't gotten into any trouble," I told him, firmly ignoring the memory of hiding out in Tab Sadler's closet. "In fact, I've found out a couple of interesting things."

I could tell he was itching to know more. Just like I could tell he didn't want to ask. He munched a french fry. He called over our waitress and got a refill on his coffee. He finished his burger before he said, "What?"

Since we both knew what he was talking about, I didn't ask him to elaborate. "Bill Manby was telling the truth. He's not a thief. And he was with Brittany Pleasance the night Muriel died, so he's not a murderer, either."

Oz nodded. But then, I suppose he knew all this, too. In fact, he probably knew it before I did. "And then there's Tab Sadler. You know Muriel cut him out of the family money."

Oz's dark eyebrows rose.

This was news!

The realization gave me courage. Maybe I could help out with the investigation after all.

"I don't know what he told you, but Tab told me he was home the night of the murder."

"Exactly what he told me."

"Well, it's not true. He wasn't home. He was at the movies."

"How do you know?"

Did a shrug explain it all? Apparently not, because even when I shrugged, Oz continued to stare at me, waiting for an answer.

"I found his movie ticket," I confessed.

"Should I ask?"

"Jack Harkness took me to the Sadler house. He's

engaged to Kendall Sadler, you know." All true so I didn't feel guilty leaving out the part about sneaking into the house, hiding in the closet, and leaving the property on the floor of Jack's car. "Tab's jacket was hanging right there. I just happened to look through the pockets."

As if praying for strength, Oz closed his eyes for a moment. When he opened them again, he said, "A movie is an alibi."

"Then why did he lie about it?"

This, Oz did not have an answer for. He dragged his last french fry through the splotch of ketchup on his dish.

"Did he say who he was with at the movie?" he wanted to know.

"I didn't exactly have a chance to ask." True again. "But you've got to wonder why he felt he needed to lie."

"Maybe because like you said, Muriel cut the purse strings. That gives him a solid motive. Maybe he thought if we found out he wasn't home, it would only make things look worse."

"Does it?" I wanted to know.

"The movie doesn't. The lying does."

"Will you look into it?"

"Will you?" he asked.

He wanted me to swear I'd stay far away from the investigation, and I couldn't blame him. As Oz had said, he was doing his job. I was being a busybody.

I didn't have the heart to let him down. Not when that silly purple glitter flashed in his dark hair.

Instead, I tucked my hands under the table, the better to cross my fingers.

"Like you said, it's what you get paid to do," I said. "You're the professional. I'm the amateur. I'll steer clear. I promise."

# CHAPTER 20

Crossed fingers aside, I was trying my best to be honest when I promised Oz I'd let him do his job and keep out of his way. At least semi-honest. After all, I knew he was right. I wasn't a professional. He was. I didn't have the training or the chops to handle a murder investigation. He did. But the next day, the Wednesday before Agnes's inauguration, three things happened that made me realize minding my own business wasn't going to be all that easy.

First, Jack showed up at the club with a load of books under his arm.

"I need to talk to you," he said.

I was behind my desk, tallying up the last batch of inauguration RSVPs we'd received. Thirty coming. Not bad for a club with a reputation for doom, gloom, and murder.

"So talk," I told him, checking off the names of our guests on the list I'd printed out.

"Not here," he said, and I looked up from my work in time to see him glance over his shoulder. "In Lilac."

It wasn't like him to be secretive—well, except when it came to the fact that he was engaged to Kendall, that he had money, and that he wasn't above a little subterfuge when it came to trying to pin a murder on Tab, which made me think he had suspicions about Tab, too—so naturally, I was intrigued. I followed him upstairs and when we got to Lilac, he shut the door behind us and set down those books.

"Patricia asked me to look through the old records," he said.

It was hard to line up the idea of Patricia and old records with the Finkinator I'd seen out on the rink the night before. I hid my smile at the same time I said, "She's the one introducing Agnes on Sunday." No use. Try as I might, I couldn't help but picture Patricia skating into the ballroom wearing her short purple shorts, with her arms bare and that skull and crossbones tattoo out in the open for all to see. I swallowed a giggle. "She's hoping to add some colorful stories to her opening remarks."

"Well, I think I found one." He flipped open one of the books and pointed to a page he had marked with an index card. "Minutes of the meeting on May 16, 1960, Margaret Yarborough presiding."

I nodded. "Agnes's mother."

"Exactly. And according to what I read, the meeting where the membership approved new applications. You know, for women who wanted to join the club."

I wasn't sure where he was headed with this. "OK, so what are you getting at?"

"Agnes's application was one of the ones read at that meeting."

"Makes sense." I leaned against the desk where Jack

worked. "She would have been about eighteen the time so she'd be eligible to join the club. She practically grew up here. Her grandmother was once president. And her mom was, too. You know all that. I'm sure they had big plans for Agnes."

"Then why did her mother vote against her membership?" I stood up straight. "There must be some mistake."

"I read it over carefully," he assured me. "Three times in fact."

"But that doesn't make any sense. Agnes's mother wouldn't—"

He picked up the book and cleared his throat before he began reading from the minutes of the day's meeting. "Votes in favor of Agnes Yarborough joining the Portage Path Women's Club: twenty-five. Votes against: one, cast by Margaret Yarborough."

It wasn't like I didn't believe him; I just couldn't make the words line up with my thinking. I crossed the room and took the book out of Jack's hands. "Votes in favor of Agnes Yarborough . . ." I read the words quickly and under my breath. "Votes against . . . Margaret Yarborough." I looked up at Jack. "That doesn't seem possible."

"But it sure is interesting."

"Yeah." Thinking it through, I closed the book and set it down on the table. "What do you suppose it means?"

Jack made a face. "I guess there could be any number of reasons for the two of them to be at odds. Mother and daughter had a fight. Over a boy. Over Agnes wearing too much makeup. Or maybe they disagreed about some club rule. Heck, it was 1960; maybe Agnes was ahead of her time and wanted to buy a bikini. Who knows what girls and their mothers fight about!"

"One person does." I marched out of Lilac. "And I'm going to find her and get some answers."

\* \* \*

Agnes was nowhere to be found, and as it turned out, that was a good thing. It led me to the second thing that made me realize I couldn't easily back away from the investigation. Oh, not right away. That didn't happen until after I went into the ballroom and saw Agnes wasn't there. Then I ducked into the kitchen, where Quentin and Geneva assured me they hadn't seen hide nor hair of her since we taste-tested appetizers and desserts the day before.

The president's office wasn't officially hers yet, but I knew Oz had given Agnes the go-ahead, and that little by little she was moving things in there and making it her own. That was the next place I looked, the next place I didn't find her.

Honestly, I wasn't as baffled as I was just curious. As we'd nibbled Quentin's amazing pavlova in the kitchen the day before, Agnes had mentioned that she had tons to do before she took over the official reins of the club. She told me she'd be in early that day, that she knew she'd have to stay late.

And yet she was a no-show.

My curiosity writhed and bent and knotted into worry.

I called Agnes and while I was still listening to the incessant ring on the other end of the phone, I strolled into her office. No more crime scene tape draped over the doorway. When she didn't answer, I ended the call and looked around. That dead aspidistra was gone. No surprise there, I'd removed it and found my missing diary and journal tucked in the pot. The piles of papers I'd seen on the credenza the last time I was there were gone, too. That wasn't a surprise, either. I knew Agnes had been through all the papers Muriel left behind, sorting and piling, determining what was important and needed to be kept in light of current club business and what she'd hand over to Gracie for the archives.

That wasn't the last of the changes there in the office. There was a magenta-colored African violet on the windowsill, and it brought life to the room as did the poster stuck to the filing cabinet with cheery magnets, a cat, its claws caught on the edges of a tree branch. *Hang in there!* it advised. A good reminder, I would think, for a president who had wanted the job, given it up, and ended up with it dumped in her lap along with the mess that was Muriel's murder.

There was nothing on the desktop but the nameplate that had once graced Agnes's vice president's desk down in Daisy. The wastepaper basket was empty and there was nothing—

I'd already skimmed over the single scrap of paper lying on the floor before I realized how out of place it was. I bent down and retrieved it.

It was stained and crumpled. Like it had been held close in a hand that was sweaty, and even before I flattened it out so I could take a better look, I knew exactly what it was.

After all, I'd seen one just like it before.

A ticket to the sixtieth anniversary showing of *Psycho* on the night Muriel was killed.


I was still wondering what to make of the bedraggled movie ticket when I heard a thud from down the hallway. Something fell. Something big. Something heavy.

My heartbeat echoed the sound.

We had a missing soon-to-be president.

A dead president.

An unsolved murder.

It's not like anyone could blame me when my imagination ran away with me and I took off with it.

I raced down the hallway. Jack was in Lilac, exactly where I'd left him, nose deep in a book and so lost in thought, he was totally unaware of the fact that something close by had thudded.

Left to my own devices, I ducked into Marigold and pulled myself up short.

"Good morning, Agnes," I said, my words stuttering over my ragged breaths. "I wondered where you were."

She was bent over, that's where she was, picking up a large volume of club records that had obviously slipped out of her hands and landed on the floor.

"Oh, Avery!" When she stood up, Agnes's cheeks were flushed. But then, she was no spring chicken, and at her age, picking up a heavy book counts as aerobic exercise. She held the book close to her chest. "I didn't know you were looking for me."

"We need to talk," I said.

There was another book pulled half in and half out of its place on the shelf, and with one finger, she pushed it back where it belonged then returned the other book to the shelf, too. Her hands empty, she smoothed them over her dark skirt and offered me a weak smile.

"Lots to do before Sunday," she said.

"Is your mother coming to the inauguration?" Three cheers for me, I made this sound like the most natural question in the world. "I know she's not well, but I can't help but think how much she'd enjoy being back here at the club. And my goodness . . ." I turned and walked to the far wall. Some of the wallpaper there was missing, stripped off by Jack, who wanted to make sure the vintage wallpaper he was hoping to buy was printed with marigolds of the exact right shade. Stalling for time, I studied the mottled plaster where the paper had been, then I turned to face Agnes again. "She must be so proud of you!"

Another skim of her hands over her skirt. Another thin smile. "Of course she is."

"You certainly have proven yourself over all the years you've been a member of the club." This went without saying, but I said it, anyway. After all, I hoped to get Agnes to relax and open up—about her mother and the truth of their relationship. "She must know you're the perfect woman for this job."

"That's exactly what she told me when I visited her the other day," Agnes assured me. "She's the one . . ." She glanced at the books she'd just put on the shelf. "Mother asked me to take a look through some of the old books. To gather some of the old stories. She said she'd so like hearing about them the next time I stop in."

"Except you really don't need to bother. Patricia's already asked Jack to do that." Wondering how Agnes might react, I let the news sink in, and when she didn't do anything at all except stand there, I added, "And no one's supposed to be in here messing with the books. Not until Jack gives us the go-ahead."

"That certainly doesn't apply to the president of the club," she said. "Besides, I've been very careful. Just looking. Just skimming. Just remembering the good old days."

"Like the day your mother voted against you joining PPWC?"

"Well, I . . ." Now her hands fluttered. Over her chest. Up to her hair. Back down to her waist.

"Or maybe you're thinking of some newer history that's not in the books at all. Like the night Muriel was killed and you said you were home. Only you weren't, were you?"

Her chin came up. "It's really none of your business."

"Actually, you made it my business. You and the other board members."

"Really, Avery!" She harrumphed and glided past me and out to the hallway, and I followed along, all the way to her office. When she got there, Agnes plumped into the chair behind her desk, twined her fingers together on the desktop, and sat up as straight as if there was a metal rod in her spine. "You're overstepping your authority."

I skimmed a finger along the top of the credenza before I stationed myself in front of her on the other side of the desk. "Oz wouldn't be if he asked the same questions."

"Oz." She had to think about it. "You mean that detective? You've been talking to him?"

"Not about this." I flashed the movie ticket her way. "But then, I just found it."

"You had no business going through my office."

"It was on the floor," I said, and I didn't bother to say which floor, where. Obviously Agnes had dropped the ticket. I let her think that might have been out in the hallway, where anyone could find it. "Naturally, I didn't want litter on the floor here at the club, so I just—"

"Poked your nose where it doesn't belong," she grumbled.

"Did my part to keep the club clean." I smiled and kept on smiling, even when I said, "The night Muriel was killed, you were at the movies. With Tab Sadler."

She sputtered what might have been a denial. That is, before her shoulders rose and fell and she let go a stumbling breath. "What difference would that make? We might have both been at the movie, but we weren't at the movie together," she was quick to add. "I was there. He was there.

We ran into each other at the concession stand, but that doesn't mean a thing, does it? I saw him. He saw me. We exchanged pleasantries and went our separate ways. Now you know I have an alibi. And so does Tab. We can vouch for each other."

True.

Maybe.

If Tab corroborated the story.

That line of inquiry was best left to Oz. I had other things to worry about, things more pertinent to the club.

I pinned Agnes with a look. "And your mother?"

Agnes shook her head. "It hardly matters. It happened years ago. Mother and I had a little spat right before the membership vote. It skewed her thinking, that's all. Believe me, she had a change of heart as soon as she saw what an asset I was to the club. Otherwise, she wouldn't be so excited about me being president, would she? She wouldn't have agreed to come to the inauguration. It would be best . . ." She gave me a look that wasn't as sly as it was conspiratorial. "It would be best if the membership didn't find out about Mother's vote all those years ago. It would undermine my authority."

"Did Muriel know?"

She jerked back as if I'd slapped her. "You think I killed her? Because of something as silly as my mother's long-ago mood swing?"

"I think you didn't want this secret getting out. If Muriel knew, if she threatened to tell . . ."

"Muriel liked to play tough. But she was weak and ineffective, the worst president this club has ever had. Why else do you think she felt she had to browbeat everyone? She was covering up for her own personal shortcomings."

"So she did know."

"She may have. But if she did, she never said anything about it to me. You're way off base, Avery. So far off base, you're not even in the ballpark. Let it go."

I wasn't sure if it was a plea or a threat.

I did know I couldn't afford to cave to either.

# CHAPTER 21

Truth be told, if Agnes hadn't dropped that tantalizing line about the ballpark and being off base, I would have bought her story, hook, line, and sinker. The way it was, I couldn't help but be curious. In spite of reminding Agnes to stay out of there, I waited patiently (well, semi-patiently) for her to head downstairs and get busy in the ballroom, and I made a beeline for Marigold. I was in luck; Jack was in there, peering and poking at the wallpaper.

As soon as I was through the doorway, I blurted out, "When did you find that book?"

He turned, pushed his glasses up the bridge of his nose, and gave me a blank stare.

"The minutes that show Margaret Yarborough voted against Agnes. When did you find it? Because I think she was just in here looking for it so she could keep it a secret."

One corner of his mouth pulled tight. "So?"

"So . . ." I'd been filled with zeal, on fire with excitement, about to burst because of the exhilaration of it all, and . . .

As if I were a balloon and pricked by a pin, all that exhilaration whooshed out of me. "I dunno." It was as hard to admit to him as it was to admit it to myself. My cheeks flamed. "I guess I thought that if Agnes had a secret she wanted to keep, and Muriel knew it, she might have killed Muriel." My spirits deflated a little more. "But she had an alibi. I guess I really am off base. Just like she told me."

"Probably." His confidence didn't exactly inspire me. "But Agnes is the one who started the fire in Marigold."

Since the fire, Jack had spent more time in Marigold than anyone else. "You think it wasn't an accident?"

"The fine folks from the fire department say it was."

"And we have absolutely no reason not to believe them. Besides, the minutes of the meeting were never secret, so it's not like no one ever knew how Margaret tried to pull the rug out from under Agnes. There are probably still some members around who were here that day. They know Agnes's mother voted against her."

My theory about Agnes being the killer—however half-baked that theory was—went up in smoke. "You're right," I told Jack. "I'm going nowhere with this." And I reminded myself not to forget it.

We were busy all that Wednesday and Thursday and Friday, things got even crazier. The (small but powerful) inauguration committee spent the day decorating the ballroom. I spent hours and hours on a PowerPoint presentation that included old photos, a history of the Yarborough family (no mention of Margaret's opposition to Agnes's membership), and a brief but—if I did say so myself—

interesting and informative history of the club. When I gave the presentation a final once-over, Clemmie watched from over my shoulder and declared it the eel's eyebrows.

By Friday evening, I was whooped and obviously not thinking clearly, so when Gracie whizzed across the lobby and toward the front door, car keys in her hand, all I managed to say was, "Have a good evening."

Until I came to my senses and popped out of my chair. "Uh, Gracie . . ." I remembered what Oz had told me about the background checks he'd done on our club members—and on me—and gave the keys in her hand a pointed look, hoping that would say everything I didn't want to put into words. When it didn't, I took the proverbial bull by the horns. Gently, of course. This was Gracie.

"Are you driving home?" I asked her.

"Of course. Same as always."

Another knowing look. She ignored that one, too.

"Are you supposed to be driving home?" I asked.

She gave me a vacant, old-lady stare that I knew was an act. "My mind isn't what it used to be. Have I forgotten that I have somewhere else to go?"

I put my fists on my hips. "Not what I'm talking about, and you know it."

She pressed her lips together. "Who told you?"

"Does it matter?"

"Well, Avery, how do they expect me to live my life if I can't drive?" Gracie's voice was shrill with frustration. "Those people over at the DMV, they don't know beans about what it's like to get old. If they take away my driving privileges, they might as well dig a hole and shove me in."

"Except they've already taken away your driving privileges. There might be some sort of appeal you could undertake, but—"

She flashed me a smile. "Never say the word *undertake* to a woman as old as me!"

I smiled, too, even as I reached over and slipped the keys out of her hand. "I'll drive you home," I told her.

"And tomorrow?"

"Tomorrow, I'll come pick you up."

She made a grab for the keys. She was fast, but I was faster. I tucked my hand—and the keys—behind my back. "That's too much to ask," she insisted.

"Not when it comes to the oldest member of the club."

She gave me a begrudging smile. "Older than dirt."

"Which is why on the ride home, you can tell me all about Agnes and her mother."

I t was never a secret," Gracie insisted. "Everyone at the club knew Margaret didn't care two figs about Agnes."

To a kid who had grown up without parents but with an aunt who was dotty but doted on her, it was incomprehensible. "But why?"

Gracie was wearing a gray raincoat, and when she shrugged, it wrapped around her like a cocoon. "Margaret wasn't the easiest woman in the world to know. Demanding. If you know what I mean. Particular."

"Sounds like she should have been Muriel's mother."

Gracie puffed out a laugh. "Same sort of personality, that's for sure. She was a wonderful club president, no one ever said she wasn't, but she never had much time for little Agnes."

"Which makes me think she should have been even happier to have her as a member of the club. That way, they could see each other more."

"Margaret was always more interested in Margaret than

in anyone else." The thought did not sit well with Gracie. That would explain why she pursed her lips and clasped her hands together on her lap. "Why, even old Hank Yarborough . . ." She glanced my way. "That's Agnes's father. Seems to me once upon a very long time ago, Margaret and Hank were as happy as clams together. He was always at the club helping out with things. Then once Agnes came along . . . well, I suppose there's no telling how people are going to react to parenthood. It's not an easy job."

This, I couldn't say, so I didn't say anything. Instead, I concentrated on the road and on Gracie's directions to her house. She lived in a well-tended, upscale neighborhood but not in a grand mansion like the Sadlers did. In fact, Gracie's house reminded me of the classic witch's cottage in a fairy-tale picture book. It had a low-slung slate roof, a brick walk that skirted beds of purple chrysanthemums the size of baseballs, and vining roses all around the front door.

A front door that was wide open.

"Oh!" Gracie saw what I saw exactly when I saw it, and her mouth fell open and her exclamation came out at the end of a gasp. "I didn't leave the door open, Avery. I may be forgetful now and again, but I'd never do that. What do you suppose is going on?"

By this time, I'd already slammed on the brakes, and we sat side by side, looking at the dark house, wondering.

It wasn't until Gracie made a move to open the car door, all set to hop out and have a look around, that I snapped back to reality. I grabbed onto her with one hand and used the other to pull out my phone.

# CHAPTER 22

I can't say he was there in a flash, but I can say whatever he'd been up to, he'd obviously set it aside, and fast. Oz arrived, the knot of his tie loose and his shirt unbuttoned at the neck. When he jumped out of the car, his raincoat flapped around him.

"You haven't been inside, have you?"

I think he was honestly surprised when I told him no. He nodded, signaled to the two uniformed cops who'd followed his unmarked car in their patrol car and said, "Don't move. And I mean it, Avery. Lock the car doors and stay here with Ms. Grimm."

If not for Gracie, I might have ignored his command. I was itching to see what was going on inside the house, especially when I watched the cops go inside and sat, helpless, as they turned on the lights, room by room as they did a walk-through. What were they looking for? What had they found?

I told myself it wasn't nearly as important as comforting the woman at my side. Gracie's face was as gray as her raincoat. Her hands shook. Her breaths came in quick, shallow gasps.

I reached over and covered her hands with mine. "It's going to be all right," I said. "Oz will take care of everything."

"He sure is a looker!" The tears on her cheeks belied Gracie's attempt at being upbeat. Her bottom lip trembled. "Why would anyone want to break into my house, Avery?"

I couldn't imagine. No doubt, Gracie was just as well-off as the other ladies in the club, but she certainly didn't flaunt her status or her money, and though her house was neat and cozy and downright cute, there was nothing from the outside to indicate that there might any anything of special value within.

Did Gracie have a treasure trove of family jewels?

A stamp collection of renown?

A fortune in gold doubloons hidden under the floorboards?

When I saw Oz come to the front door and motion for us to come inside, I hoped I'd find out.

I jumped out of the car and went around to the passenger side to help Gracie out, and side by side, with Gracie's tiny body shaking with every step, we went into the house.

Everything I could see from the front hallway was as neat as a pin.

"What happened?" I asked Oz.

He scratched a hand through his hair. "Not sure yet. But why don't you . . ." He handed Gracie off to the nearest uniformed officer, and once they went into the living room and the officer settled Gracie on the couch, Oz tipped his head to indicate that I should follow him.

We walked down a hallway where the walls were lined

with old family pictures and into a room that must have been Gracie's study.

That is, before it was a total and complete mess.

Three of the room's walls were lined with bookshelves, and each and every one of those shelves had been emptied. There were books on the floor, books on the desk in the far corner of the room. The books were neatly piled in some places, tossed randomly in others, their covers open, their pages fluttering in the breeze of a ceiling fan.

"Someone's looking for something." I'm pretty sure I didn't have to tell Oz this. He was a smart guy and when it came to crime, he knew his stuff. Still, the realization settled deep inside me, and I looked around at the chaos and shook my head. "What?"

The fact that he didn't answer did little to cheer me. I bent to retrieve a book.

"Don't touch anything." Oz's voice was sharp and he must have realized it, because when I stood up, he gave me a quick smile of apology. "There's a photographer coming. We can't move anything until after she's finished."

I backed away from the books, backed out of the room. By the time I got to the living room, that uniformed cop was sitting next to Gracie on the couch. She had a cup of tea in her hands.

"How bad is it?" she wanted to know.

"Nothing that can't be cleaned up." I sat in a wing chair across from the couch, all set to talk to her when Oz walked in.

"What do you keep in your study?" he asked Gracie. "Money?"

She slapped a hand to her heart. "Good heavens! No! I might be old, but I'm no fool."

"Would anyone think there was money there?"

She shook her head. "Of course not. If they wanted cash, all they had to do is look in the cookie jar in the kitchen."

With a look, Oz instructed the cop to go and check on said cash. He sat down in the spot the young officer vacated. "Why else would anyone want to look through your library?"

Gracie's shoulders sagged. "The library? Oh no, not my books." She would have popped out of her seat and gone to check on the damage herself if Oz hadn't stopped her. "Are any of them destroyed?"

"It doesn't look that way."

"Then why—"

"That's what we need to find out." I leaned forward in my seat. "Gracie, did you by any chance have any books here from the club?"

"Well, I do sometimes," she told us. "I bring the old records home. You know, so I can scan them. I started the project long before the fire in Marigold, but after that, I realized how vital it is to get it done as soon as possible. That way we'll have a backup of all our information in case another knucklehead like Agnes goes and lights a cigarette in Marigold again."

"And everyone knows about it?"

"Anyone who takes a look at the minutes of the club's meetings. It was talked about a number of times before the board gave me the go-ahead. It was mentioned in our newsletter, too. We haven't had a newsletter, lately," she added almost as an afterthought. "Brittany did the last one, and there was a story in it. About me. About how I'm digitizing the records."

There was a cherry coffee table between the couch and the chair where I sat, and I looked across it to Oz. "What you're saying is that anyone could know you might have club records here at any time."

"Well I suppose so," Gracie admitted. "But why would they care?"

Oz wasn't up to date with the latest, so I told him the story of Agnes's mother and how the minutes of that particular meeting showed her opposition to Agnes's membership in PPWC.

"No one would care about that," Gracie insisted with the wave of one hand.

"Then what else could they be looking for?" I wondered.

"And more importantly, was there a book here that was taken?" Oz put in.

"There are no club books here. At least . . ." Like two fuzzy gray mice, Gracie's brows settled low over her eyes. "At least, I don't think so. I was looking to do some work last night, you see, looking to scan some pages, but I couldn't find the books I thought I brought home. Sometimes, well, sometimes I think I've done something, then I find out I only ever thought about doing it. You'll see. When you get older, the same thing will happen to you. I think I must have thought I brought the books home. But I didn't. I'm sure they're still in Marigold."

"Could you have brought them home and someone took them before tonight?" Oz wanted to know.

Her eyes clouded with confusion. "I don't think so. No one's been in the house."

"And if they were taken earlier, why would someone get their hands on the books then bother to return tonight?" I was feeling more confused than ever and, as if it might actually help, I got up and did a turn around the room. I was right. It didn't help.

"Well, whatever they're looking for, it's not those minutes from the membership meeting." Gracie was sure of this. Her shoulders were steady, she held her head high. "It might have created some gossip around the club back in the day, but now it's nothing but old news."

I had no doubt she was right. But if she was, what was the burglar looking for?

Since none of us knew the answer, I didn't bother to ask the question out loud. I did have another thought though, and it jolted me toward the front door.

"Oz!" I didn't have to tell him to come along; he sensed something was up and was right behind me. "Jack sometimes takes books home from the club, too. If someone's looking for something in those books—"

We were in Oz's car and on our way to Jack's before I had a chance to say any more.

L ights and sirens, and Oz drove fast. I still had enough time to envision all sorts of horrible things. Jack's house ransacked. Jack unconscious—or worse—on the floor.

When we wheeled into his drive outside a sturdy brick colonial with (no doubt) period-appropriate shutters in historically accurate colors and I saw Jack standing outside next to his car, relief flooded through me.

Oz was out of the car even before I was, so he walked up to Jack first. I was just in time to see him hold up his phone. "I haven't even had a chance to call the police yet. How did you know and come so fast?"

"Know what?" My question overlapped with Oz's.

But really, I don't need to point out who was really in charge. Oz stepped closer to Jack. "What's going on?"

"You don't know?" Jack glanced from me to Oz. "But then, how—"

"Just explain, Mr. Harkness." The snap of Oz's official voice somehow didn't fit his personality nearly as much as purple glitter did, but I didn't question it. He was doing his job. "What happened?"

"Well, I just got home. A couple of minutes ago. I pulled in and that's when I saw him. There was a person standing right outside my back door. As soon as he saw the car, he took off running."

"Which way?" Oz asked at the same time he pulled out his phone and called for backup. He relayed Jack's information to the person on the other end of the phone. "I'll have some officers look around," he told Jack once he ended the call. "But chances are, the guy's long gone. Can you describe him?"

"It's dark." Jack didn't really need to point this out, but believe me, I understood. I remembered trying to line up the facts inside my head after I found Muriel on the basement steps. "I didn't see his face. He was shorter than me. Shorter than you, Detective. Kind of bulky, but then . . ." Jack shivered and wrapped his arms around himself. "He could have been wearing a coat."

"Not much to go on," Oz mumbled even as he wrote everything down. "But we'll try. Have you been into the house yet?"

Even in the dim light, I could see Jack's face pale. "You mean he could have been coming out? Not going in?"

"We don't know that yet," Oz said and because he didn't tell either one of us to stay put, both Jack and I walked along with him to the back door.

It was locked.

Jack breathed a sigh of relief, unlocked the door, then keyed his security code into the pad on a nearby wall. "If he had gotten in, my security service would have been alerted."

"Might have been better. Then we might have had a chance to catch him." Oz glanced all around, taking in the state-of-the-art kitchen with its sleek white granite countertop, the stainless appliances, the wine cooler than hummed in one corner. "There usually aren't problems in this neighborhood."

"But there might be problems because of the books," I dared to put in. "Jack, have you brought any books home from the club?"

"Yes, of course. You know that. A few over the last week. There were some that sustained too much smoke damage to—"

"Are they still here?" I wanted to know.

Jack caught the note of urgency in my voice. He led the way. Upstairs in a room that had a fireplace on one wall and the others crammed with bookshelves, everything was neat and orderly. There was a door next to one of the bookshelves, and Jack opened it and showed us into a workroom as clean and spare as an operating room. There were stainless shelves along the walls where boxes and bottles of chemicals sat alongside things like brushes and rags.

"I had books from the club. In here. I was airing them out from the smoke damage. Those were the books I took back to the club and talked about to you today, Avery." He skimmed a glance at Oz and decided I'd probably already filled Oz in. "Old club minutes are hardly worth stealing."

"And Gracie says everyone at the club at the time knew Margaret dissed Agnes. It was no secret. Still . . ." I looked over the sterile workroom and pictured it full of the club's old ledgers. "Someone's looking for something, and the only thing that connects what's happening is what's in Marigold."

# CHAPTER 23

By the end of the evening, we were exhausted from the useless effort of our brains going around in circles. We left Jack at home and Oz took me back to Gracie's, where I got my car and headed home to the club. He returned to the station to fill out what he described as mounds of reports.

It was late. I was tired. Not to mention confused.

What was someone looking for? And how was it connected to Muriel's murder?

I was too tired to drag myself up the steps to my room right away, and when I stopped to think about it, I realized I was also starving. I went into the kitchen and rooted around in the fridge for something that might possibly pass as dinner. By now, I just about expected Clemmie to pop in and out, so I wasn't surprised when I turned and saw her sitting on top of the grill.

"Move it," I told her, and poked a thumb away from the grill. "Making myself a sandwich."

She looked at the supplies in my hands. "Bread, butter, cheese. Doesn't sound half bad."

"Not sure I've even got the energy to eat it." I slathered the bread with butter, tossed on a couple piece of thick-cut cheddar, topped off the lid of the sandwich with more butter, and flicked on the grill.

I'd already turned to say something to Clemmie when her mouth dropped open. That was right before she screamed and pointed behind me. "Fire! Fire!"

E very fire is dangerous. But let's face it, I'd worked in kitchens and restaurants for years. This wasn't my first rodeo.

As cool and as calm as I could be, considering the back of my neck prickled from the heat and my eyes already stung from the smoke, I did what I'd been trained to do. I raced to where we kept the fire extinguisher.

It wasn't there.

"Avery, do something!" Yes, yes, I know—Clemmie was impervious to the flames and to the clouds of smoke that were already puffing around the grill. That didn't keep her from pointing a frantic finger toward the fire and jumping up and down. "You've got to put it out now, or you'll end up here on the Other Side with me."

It wasn't that serious.

Was it?

I looked at the grill and the tongues of fire that shot above it, the light of the orange and red flames flicking against the wall. I sucked in a breath—and regretted it immediately. I coughed and sputtered, but I knew better than to throw open a window. At least just yet. Oxygen would feed the flames, and I needed to get rid of them, not provide them more fuel.

My brain did a frantic inventory. There was a fire extinguisher at the top of the steps near Agnes's office, but upstairs was too far away. There was one in my bedroom, but that was even farther. Daisy Den—on the other side of the building. Summerhouse—out of the question. Ballroom!

As fast as my trembling legs could carry me, I hotfooted it there. What with the excitement and with the rush of adrenalin that made my heart pound and my blood race, maybe I just wasn't thinking right. I swear, the fire extinguisher was kept to the left of the mahogany fireplace mantel.

There was no sign of it and at the same time my heart squeezed and skipped over a dozen erratic beats, I saw Clemmie whoosh into the room, her ectoplasm leaving a trail as effervescent as a comet's tail. She zipped from corner to corner, from floor to ceiling, from the grand piano near the windows to the potted palms that were bunched in a corner now, the ones we'd place on either side of the doorway for inauguration day.

"Here! Here!" Clemmie called out and I went running. I grabbed the red extinguisher from behind a potted palm and made it to the kitchen in record time. By the time I got back, my breaths were labored and the fire was larger, hotter. It licked the ceiling above the grill. Its raging heat slapped my cheeks.

Clemmie eyed the extinguisher with distrust. "You know what to do with that thing?"

"Watch me!"

I did exactly as I'd been trained—pulled the pin, aimed, squeezed the handle, swept the fire, bottom to top. It felt like a lifetime, but just a couple of seconds later, the kitchen was filled with the cold fumes from the extinguisher and my hair was in my eyes. I brushed it away before I zipped over to throw open every window in the kitchen and the dining room. That done, I went to the sink and splashed my face and hands with water and rinsed out my eyes.

"You sure are one smart tomato." Clemmie stood at my side, watching my every move. "Grace under pressure, that's what you got."

Fists on hips, I assessed the damage. The grill was a mess, but that was to be expected. My grilled cheese sandwich . . . well, it was grilled, all right. Grilled to a crisp. There were black smudges of smoke on the ceiling, and the place would need a major scrubbing.

"The chemical will clear up in a couple minutes," I promised Clemmie, then realized it really didn't matter to her. She looked as fresh and as unrumpled as I was sure I didn't. I gave the grill a glare. "I guess I should have had Bill fix this thing before I had him work outside. Good thing he's coming in tomorrow. I bet he can have it done in a flash and I'll get Geneva and Quentin in early so we can start cleaning."

"Good thing you got until Sunday until the big shindig."

It wasn't like Clemmie needed to remind me. I knew I was in big trouble—we had less than forty-eight hours before the inauguration, and another disaster on our hands.


Needless to say, I didn't have much time for sleuthing on Saturday. The flowers arrived, our beverage distributor showed up with a couple of cases of champagne, and between Bill in there fixing the grill and Quentin and

Geneva trying to clean up around him, the kitchen was hopping. Me, I tried to help as much as I could.

Which would have been considerably easier if Clemmie wasn't in the kitchen, too, offering advice that no one but me could hear.

"You missed a spot," she told me and pointed to a tiny smudge of soot between the grill hood and the ceiling and clicked her tongue, grinning as she did. "Fallin' down on the job."

"At least I'm doing a job," I shot back, then when Bill glared at me from where he knelt in front of the grill fighting with some mechanical part, I gave him a quick smile.

He grunted in reply and got back to work.

I scrubbed the spot to Clemmie's satisfaction and got down from the stepladder I'd been using just as Bill stood up. He was holding up a blackened piece of metal with wires sticking out of the back of it, and he shook his head.

"Weird," he said.

"Can it be fixed?"

"Sure. Of course. I can fix anything. But this . . ." As if I hadn't seen it, he held the part out to me. "This is weird. It's the reason the grill hasn't been working, all right, but there's no way this is what caused the grill to catch fire."

I remembered the flames, the heat, the panic that built in my chest as I frantically searched for a fire extinguisher and wondered if I'd get back to the kitchen before the club went up in flames.

"So what did cause the fire?" I asked Bill.

"That's the weird part." He motioned me closer to the grill, and while he was at it, he called Quentin over, too. "When was the last time you cleaned the grill hood?" he asked our chef.

Quentin crossed his arms over his massive chest. "Are you saying I didn't?"

"I'm saying somebody didn't." Bill pointed up at the grill. "Grease. That's what started this fire. The entire inside of the hood was coated with grease."

"Hey, hey! You know me better than that." I wasn't sure if Quentin was talking to me or to Bill. He backed away from the grill and shot defiant looks at both of us. "I clean regular. And even if I didn't, we haven't cooked enough food in this kitchen lately for grease to build up anywhere."

"Maybe it didn't." I stepped closer to the grill. "You don't suppose someone could have—"

"Spread the grease up there? On purpose?" Yeah, I thought it was just as incomprehensible as Bill did. That would explain why I wasn't surprised by the disbelief in his voice.

"Di mi!" Across the room, Clemmie slapped a hand to her heart and dared to say what no one else—no one else living, that is—did. "That means somebody did this on purpose. Just like that same somebody hid the fire extinguishers. They were trying to burn down the building." Clemmie's spirit shivered and quaked. She flashed out of sight, then back again. "Or Avery . . ." She gulped. "Maybe someone doesn't like it that you know your onions when it comes to looking into this murder thing. Maybe that someone was trying to knock you off. You know, deep-six you. Blot you out. Bump you off. Snuff you—"

"All right! I get it!" Bill, Quentin, and Geneva might not have looked at me like I had two heads if I didn't screech into what they assumed was thin air. Then again, maybe they would have thought I was even crazier if they knew I was talking to a ghost.

One who just made me realize what I hadn't been able to admit to myself—somebody had tried to kill me.

I didn't get much sleep that night, what with the worry and the thinking and the wondering. And did I mention the worry?

I didn't exactly feel chipper the next morning.

It wasn't like I had a lot of choice—it was Sunday, inauguration day, and I had a job to do.

I was out of bed early, dressed, and downstairs just as Patricia and Gracie came in the front door.

"Terrible what happened at Gracie's." Rage sparked in Patricia's eyes and I couldn't help but think of her as the Finkinator, ready to skate to the center of the action and take her revenge. "I spent all day there yesterday helping her clean up. How could anyone be so cruel? And here . . ." Her sharp gaze darted down the hallway toward the dining room and the kitchen beyond. "I heard about the fire, of course. Heard from Agnes. The kitchen's back in shape?"

"Thanks to Bill, Quentin, and Geneva."

"And you, no doubt. The board won't forget this," she promised. "You're a miracle worker for making it happen and getting everything ready for the festivities today."

"Not much of a miracle worker when I haven't figured out what's going on around here."

"You think the fire was started intentionally." Patricia scowled. She hadn't thought of this before. "You could have been hurt."

"I wasn't." I managed to sound chipper. Not bad for a woman who hadn't gotten a wink of sleep.

"You could have been killed."

"No worries. I'm alive and well."

"The club could have burned to ground. Again!"

"Yeah." The single syllable left me along with a sigh. "It looks like our arsonist took a cue from Agnes."

Patricia's mouth thinned. "Well, if he ever tries it again . . ." When she made a fist, I pictured that skull and crossbones tattoo on her upper arm (hidden that day beneath a tasteful suit jacket in an autumny shade of gold), bulging and angry. "Well . . ." She shook away the moment and the rage. "Let's hope it never happens."

"If we could get to the bottom of Muriel's murder, maybe it never would. There's so much I still don't understand."

"You mean about the books." Gracie had been silent to this point. Now, she nodded sagely. "I think you're onto something there, Avery. If we had more time before the ceremony—"

"Time?" Agnes whooshed through the door, her cheeks bright with high color. "No time for much of anything. Not today. Our guests will start arriving . . ." She checked her watch. "In less than two hours. So what do you say?" She clapped her hands together. "Let's get crackin', ladies!"

Crack, we did. While Gracie, Patricia, and Agnes went into the ballroom to make sure every last detail in there was perfect, I met Quentin and Geneva in the kitchen and we went over the lists we'd made earlier in the week—what foods needed to go into the oven first, which appetizer would be served when, how Geneva would be in charge of making sure our extra bartenders and waitstaff (hired just for the day) stayed on task.

"You're sure you want me to do this?" That day, Geneva was dressed in black pants and a crisp white shirt. She had a white apron looped over her neck and an expression on her face that teetered between abject terror and out-and-out uncertainty. "I ain't never supervised nobody."

I put a hand of support on her shoulder. "You'll do great. Just remember—"

"Keep them moving. Nobody standing around doing nothing. Make sure they pass those horse doovers and clean up used glasses and dishes and that they're polite and considerate and . . ." She bit her lower lip. "Am I forgetting anything?"

"You're going to be amazing."

"Amazing." Geneva's shoulders inched back and a tiny smile tickled her lips. "Yeah, I think you're right. Today I'm going to be amazing."

Before I left the kitchen, Quentin gave me a thumbs-up.

Everything was under control in the ballroom. The dining room, with vases of fresh flowers on every table, looked perfect. Bill had arrived early and had already strung a welcome banner above the front entrance. I'm not sure how he talked her into it, considering her history with the club, but Brittany was there, too, and she pinched a brown leaf off one of the freshly planted mums in the containers near the door. The lawn had been cut and was perfect, the leaves had been raked.

For this moment, all was right with the world.

Good thing, too, because our guests started to arrive not long after, and once that happened, the rest of the time was a whirl. Our waitstaff passed champagne and appetizers. Our harpist played in the corner of the ballroom near the piano. Agnes beamed with happiness, especially when her mother, Margaret, was escorted into the ballroom by a caregiver from the home where she lived. I introduced myself and made sure Margaret got a seat in the first row of chairs we'd set up in front of the podium, where Agnes would be sworn in as president of PPWC.

I made the rounds, greeting our members and their guests. We'd included Jack in the invitations, and he'd shown up with both Kendall and Tab, and I thanked Tab for coming. It didn't hurt to show our members that the transition between Muriel and Agnes as president had his full support. I chatted with Reverend Way and the members of his congregation we'd invited to drop by after Sunday-morning services. I hoped to chat with Oz, who walked in and was immediately buttonholed by Gracie. Which didn't mean I missed it when he glanced at Patricia, then gave me a wink.

I was just about to let down my guard a tad and have one of the cucumber and salmon appetizers being passed by one of our waitresses when I saw Gracie up front near the podium. Yeah, she was dressed in gray pants and a gray jacket. But her face was absolutely green.

I raced up front and made sure I stayed far away from the microphone on the podium when I asked her, "What's wrong?"

Gracie's bottom lip trembled. "It's the club charter," she said.

I knew Agnes, like all the other PPWC presidents before her, would place her hand on the charter when she was sworn in and I knew the leather portfolio that held the charter was supposed to have been removed from Marigold (yes, we had Jack's permission) and tucked on the shelf below the podium. I looked that way. The charter wasn't there.

"Where is it?" Yeah, like my question made any sense. If Gracie knew where the charter was, she wouldn't look like she was going to keel over. I signaled the nearest waiter for water, piloted Gracie over to a chair, and sat her down. "Who was supposed to bring the charter down?" I asked her.

"Well, me. I think." Her eyes clouded with worry. "I'm

the historian, and it's part of my duties. And I thought I did, Avery. I swore I did. But it's not there, is it?" As if to make sure, she looked at the podium one more time.

We had fifteen minutes until the official start of the program. Fifteen minutes until Agnes was expected to lay her hand on the charter and repeat the words of the presidential oath. Still, I somehow managed to smile. "I'll just zip up to Marigold and get it," I told her, and I did just that.

The last person I expected to find in there was Agnes.

"Oh." When I stepped into the room, she spun away from the bookshelves. "I was just . . ." She drew in a long breath. "Just calming myself. Just reminding myself of the history of this wonderful place and all that it means to me."

I got it. I did. And I didn't want to worry her, but . . .

"Gracie left the charter up here," I told Agnes.

"I don't know about that. It's always kept right here." She pointed at an empty spot on the shelf. "She hasn't gone and lost the charter, has she?" Agnes's voice was high and tight. "How am I going to get sworn in?"

"I'll find it," I promised, even though I didn't have a clue where I was even supposed to begin looking. "For now . . ." I drew in what I hoped would be a calming breath. It wasn't. I didn't dare let Agnes know how worried I was, so I smiled and wound an arm through hers and escorted her out of the room. "For now, the best thing you can do is go downstairs and mingle. We might need to start a couple of minutes late. You can cover for me."

As soon as she started down the stairs, I rasped out, "Clemmie!"

She popped up beside me.

"You heard what we were talking about. Can you help me look?"

"Sure!" And while Clemmie did a complete sweep of

the upstairs, I went down to check the Daisy Den, the Carnation Room, and even the kitchen.

Gracie met me in the hallway. "I was thinking, Avery. What if I took the charter home? To scan it like I scan all the other old documents."

My stomach went cold. "Do you think it might have been stolen the other night?"

"Well, I don't know. We didn't see it when Patricia and I were putting things back in order yesterday. But we didn't have time to finish the cleanup. There's always a chance it's still there in the mess." She leaned far enough back to glance into the ballroom. "I can go home and look. A little more champagne and they won't even realize how late we're getting started."

A stall tactic seemed too obvious. "No. Let's get going with the PowerPoint presentation. We can do that and have a bit of a question-and-answer session after that."

At that moment, Clemmie popped up on the bannister halfway between the first and second floors. She didn't say a word. She didn't have to. The way she shook her head, I knew she'd had no luck locating the charter.

"Take your time with the PowerPoint," I told Gracie. "Ask questions as you go through it, get the audience to participate. I'll go over to your place and see if I can find the charter." My car keys were in my desk drawer and I got them out.

"The way Annette Mitchell parked . . ." Gracie made a face. "You'll never get your car out. You could take my car." Doing her best to look sheepish (it didn't work), Gracie handed me her keys.

I propped my fists on my hips. "I thought Patricia drove you this morning! You're not supposed to—"

"No time for a lecture now, Avery." Gracie turned and

marched into the ballroom. "We've got a president to inaugurate."

Gracie was right. I'd save my no-driving lecture for later. I had more important things to do.

I zipped out to the parking lot, but I guess I wasn't as subtle as I hoped. In just a couple seconds, there was Oz walking right beside me. I explained what was going on, and if he was planning on slapping the cuffs on Gracie for violating her no-driving order, he didn't say anything about it. That didn't stop him from putting a hand on my arm to stop me when we got near Gracie's car and saw the trunk was partially opened.

"Not a crisis," I assured Oz. Tell that to a man who has the blue blood of a cop running through his veins and suspicion oozing from every pore. I did my best to convince him. "I bet Gracie popped the trunk to get something, then forgot as soon as she was out of the car." I gave him a sidelong look. "There's only one way to find out."

"And I'm the one who's going to do it."

He went to the car and opened the trunk.

I was right behind him and I looked over his shoulder and sucked in a breath.

"The charter! Thank goodness!" I made a grab for the leather portfolio. "Gracie probably took it home to scan like the other club records. She forgot it was in her trunk." There were leather-bound books beneath the charter, and I counted. "And three volumes of club records. The books Gracie thought she'd brought into the house to scan and couldn't find."

"The books someone might have been looking for when they rummaged through Gracie's house."

"And when that person didn't find them at Gracie's, he tried to break into Jack's."

We exchanged looks and Oz said exactly what I was thinking. "So whatever someone was looking for—"

"It could be right here." I set the leather portfolio down on the pavement, the better to scrape my suddenly damp palms on the leg of my black pants, and asked Oz, "You want to do the honors?"

We heard music swell from inside the ballroom. It was followed by a smattering of applause. My PowerPoint presentation had ended and apparently, there weren't many questions. In just a second, Patricia would launch into the opening remarks.

"You should get back inside," Oz told me.

I knew he was right.

That didn't stop me from reaching for the first book and paging through it. "You think I'm going to miss out on this?" I asked him, but I wasn't sure he was listening. He already had another book open and was looking through it, page after page.

We didn't have any luck with book number one or book number two, and I'd already given up hope when we grabbed book number three and started through it together.

That was when a single piece of paper fluttered to the ground.

Oz picked it up, looked it over, and whistled low under his breath before he handed it to me.

I scanned it. "There was a secret she wanted to keep!"

Oz grabbed my hand and together we started back to the club. "Yeah," he grumbled, "and if you ask me, around here, a secret like that is the perfect motive for murder."

We walked into the ballroom just as Agnes stepped up to the microphone.

"You go ahead and do it." Oz elbowed me in the ribs. "Be a distraction."

It wasn't exactly how I'd pictured spending my first inauguration day.

I swallowed hard, pulled back my shoulders, and strode through the aisleway between the chairs where our guests were seated. "Excuse me! I hate to interrupt, but our new president can't be sworn in unless she places her hand on the club charter, and I'm afraid to say it was misplaced." A few of the members gasped, including Agnes, who stepped back, one hand slapped to her heart.

"No problem," I told them, and I made sure I glanced at Gracie and saw her smile. I looked at Agnes, too, who behind the podium, stood as still as that statue of Hortense Dash that had been used to conk Muriel. I held up the leather portfolio. "I found it. We've got the charter. And we can go ahead with the ceremony." The sound of tense breaths being released filled the ballroom. I was at the front of the room now, and I turned to face the crowd.

"Except," I said, "I think we'd better clear a few things up before we go ahead with the inauguration."

"Don't be silly." Agnes twittered. "We can take care of details later. For now—"

"For now there's a lot we need to talk about. Including the murder of Muriel Sadler."

"Don't be ridiculous." Tab was seated nearby, and he spat out the words. "This isn't the time or the place to talk about—"

"Going to the movies?" I asked him, and yes, it froze him right in place. While he stared, I kept going with my explanation. "I found your ticket, Mr. Sadler. The sixtieth anniversary showing of the film *Psycho*."

"Which doesn't mean a darned thing." Tab crossed his arms over his chest.

Far be it from me to disagree with him.

"It truly doesn't," I told Tab and everyone else gathered there in the ballroom. "Except if it didn't—if it didn't mean anything—then why would you lie about it? And you did lie." I swung my gaze back to Tab. "When the police questioned you, when I asked you, you said you were home the night Muriel was killed. And if all you'd really done is go to a movie, if you had that alibi, then it would have been just as easy to tell the police the truth, don't you think?"

I didn't give him time to answer. I turned to look at Agnes. "You said the same thing, Agnes. Home. That's where you told us you were. But I found out you were lying, too. You were at the movie, too. And I bet you were there with Tab Sadler."

It wasn't like some earthshattering revelation, but hey, we were an old-fashioned club with old-fashioned values. A few of our members gasped. And maybe they had every reason.

"Tab and Agnes," I told no one in particular and everyone in the room, "were once engaged, and you know what, I think they're seeing each other again."

Agnes's mouth fell open. Tab blubbered incoherent words.

"Naturally, they were trying to hide their affair from Muriel, the woman who controlled the money in the Sadler household. Can't blame them."

Tab was out of his seat in a heartbeat, and when he raced up to me, I thought Oz was going to shoot up the aisle and tackle him. One hand out, I let Oz know I was fine. But then, I was anxious to see what Tab had to say for himself.

"Just because we went to the movie together," he sputtered, "that doesn't mean I killed Muriel. Not that I wouldn't have liked to," he admitted with a grunt. "The woman was impossible. She'd always been impossible." His teeth clenched, he shot a laser look around the ballroom. "Yeah, like any of you could say anything else about her. Anything nice. You know what an awful person she was. How'd you like to live with her? No. Nobody." He emphasized the word with a slash of one hand. "Nobody could blame me for seeing Agnes here on the side. I always knew . . ." His voice choked over his words. "I always knew Agnes was the girl for me. Should have listened to my heart way back when, instead of to my family. Should have married Agnes like I wanted to. So yes!" He pulled back his shoulders and stood as straight and as tall as a soldier. "We were at the movies together."

I managed to keep my cool. "An affair, huh? Sounds like the perfect motive for murder."

Tab's neck got red. His face shot through with fire. He stepped back and pointed a finger in my direction. "Oh no. You can't say that. You don't have one bit of proof. You know I was at the movie."

"I know you have a ticket stub from the movie," I answered. "That doesn't mean you were there the whole time."

"I sure was." When he shot me a look, he narrowed his eyes. His mouth twisted with fury. "I was there, all right."

It seemed cruel to smile, but I wasn't sure what else to do, how else to cover for the fact that my insides were churning and my blood was racing and my knees felt like rubber. "But were you there the entire time?" I asked Tab.

He sputtered words that included, "How dare you?" and he would have kept right on sputtering if Oz didn't stroll up the aisle.

"You left the movie early," he told Tab and I'm not exactly sure how, since we hadn't discussed it, but with those words, I knew we were on the same page and the realization made me feel bolder, stronger. Just like me, Oz was trying to tease information out of Tab. "You came here to the club, murdered your wife, and—"

"No! No!" Tab's eyes bulged. "I didn't leave early."

Oz is a canny one. He unhooked his handcuffs from his belt.

That was all Tab needed to see to know he was in serious trouble. He swung around to point a finger at Agnes. "She came to the movie late. And when she did, she was nervous, out of breath. Sweaty."

Which explained that crumpled movie ticket I'd found in Agnes's office.

Before I had a chance to point it out, Agnes's silvery laugh cut through the tension. "That's crazy, Tab, and you know it. Why on earth would I want to kill Muriel?"

"Funny you should ask," I said. I set down the portfolio on an empty chair, took out that sheet of paper we'd found, and waved it in the air. "I think I finally figured it out." I cleared my throat, and I didn't read from the paper—not word for word—anyway, but I did home in on the pertinent details. "It's your birth certificate," I told Agnes and when she came at me, eager to snatch the paper out of my hand, I held it up higher where she couldn't reach it. "Your birth certificate, Agnes, that proves that Margaret Yarborough is not your biological mother."

The gasp from the crowd didn't surprise me. Margaret's low-throated chuckle did. "It's about time somebody figured it out," she said. "Come on, ladies, were you that blind? Or did you just not want to see the truth? I never could have children of my own. So when my stupid husband got that slut Dodie Hillenbrand pregnant, we made a deal. We sent Dodie away and paid for her silence. And I got to keep the baby I always wanted. Except the baby I always wanted . . ." She sneered at Agnes. "Always reminded me of my cheating creep of a husband."

Another gasp drowned out the rest of Margaret's story and I waited until it died down. "So that's what Muriel had on you," I told Agnes. "That's why you dropped out of the last election. She somehow found out about your parentage and she threatened to tell the world you didn't have the pedigree you pretended to have."

"And promised me she'd hand over that birth certificate if I let her win the election," Agnes grumbled. "She lied. Of course, she lied. That's what Muriel did. That's the kind of person Muriel was. She gave me one birth certificate and I thought that was that. Then she said she had others stashed away here at the club, in the books in Marigold."

Gracie popped out of her seat. "You started that fire on purpose! You wanted to destroy the books."

"Not the books," I corrected her. "Just any copies of the birth certificate that might be tucked inside them. It's the same reason Agnes broke into your house, Gracie. The same reason she tried to get into Jack's. She was so upset that Margaret wasn't her mother—"

The last thing I expected was a hoot of a laugh out of Agnes. "Upset that she wasn't my mother? You're kidding me, aren't you? Margaret never gave me the time of day. I wasn't upset she wasn't my mother. In fact, I was pretty relieved when I found out. I was upset that someone might find out that my biological mother was nothing but a cook." Her lip curled. "Nothing but a low-class kitchen worker."

"Watch what you say!" Geneva called out from the back of the room.

I ignored her and kept my eyes on Agnes. "You wanted to keep a secret. That's it. That's why you killed Muriel."

"She should have kept out of my way," Agnes growled. "She should have kept her mouth shut."

"And now . . ." Oz stepped forward. I've seen enough cop shows on TV to know he was about to read Agnes her rights, and I bet he would have done it, too.

If all the lights in the club didn't choose that exact moment to go out.

A couple people screamed, which would have been pretty silly, really, if it was just because the lights went out. But at the same time they did, Agnes must have realized this was her only chance to escape. She knocked the podium over, flung an empty chair out of the way. She grabbed the leather portfolio with the charter inside it and hurled it at Oz.

Then she took off running.

It was hard to focus on everyone and everything in the room in the weird half dark. People were out of their chairs, clamoring and shuffling toward the doors. Someone knocked over a tall stand with a flower arrangement on it, and glass shattered and water drenched the nearest guests. Patricia raced past me, the Finkinator at her best, but I couldn't take the chances of letting her get to Agnes before I did. Agnes was desperate. She'd killed before, and I had no doubt she'd do it again.

I pushed my way into the crowd just as Margaret Yarborough called out, "You go get her! That nobody doesn't deserve to be president of this club!" A couple potted palms had been overturned in the doorway between the ballroom and the hallway, and I jumped over them. No sign of Agnes.

But I did hear the sound of footsteps running up on the second floor.

I ran to the stairway and I was already at the top when I realized Oz was right behind me. Together, we raced from room to room, but wherever Agnes had gone, wherever she was headed, we couldn't find her.

"Upstairs!" Clemmie poofed up out of thin air and pointed to the stairway to the third floor.

"Upstairs," I told Oz and bless his law-enforcing heart, he didn't question it. He led the way and by the time we both got to the third floor, we were breathing hard.

"Ms. Yarborough!" He stepped into the hallway with its line of closed doors. Linen Room. Ironing Room. Shoe Polishing Room. All was quiet.

"Attic," Clemmie whispered in my ear.

"Attic," I told Oz.

"But why would she . . ." He looked at the closed door that led into the vast attic space. "There's no way out of the attic. How could she possibly think she could escape?"

My heart bumped. "Maybe that's not the kind of escape she's thinking about."

Oz pushed open the door, and though he tried to warn me back, one arm out, I knew right away that I didn't have to worry. Not for my safety, anyway.

Agnes had thrown open the large window at the end of the attic, and she stood on the sill, her knuckles white where she clutched the window frame.

"You don't want to do this," Oz said. He took a couple steps closer. "It won't help anything."

"It will help me." Agnes voice was heavy with tears. "It will save me the shame. The mortification of having to face everyone here at the club now that they know the awful truth."

"I honestly don't think they'll care who your biological mother is," I told her. "Fifty years ago, maybe. These days, it's like Patricia says, it's time to open up the club to the twenty-first century. People don't look down on cooks anymore. We're over that kind of class system."

Agnes managed a laugh. "Maybe you're over it. But you're not a member of the club, are you, Avery? You'd never be a member of this club. You're just a nobody from nowhere, just like Dodie was. You'll never understand how your betters live."

"I do understand that jumping out the window isn't going to help." I, too, took a few steps closer. "And Agnes, it's going to hurt like hell."

She hesitated, then tensed, and right then and there, I knew what was going to happen.

At least I thought I did.

The next thing I knew, there was a flash outside the window, right in front of Agnes. It wasn't so much a full-body apparition, not the Clemmie I was used to seeing when we passed the time together, or tried on clothes, or talked about men. This was an impression more than a clear image, a face, a body, a burst of luminosity like lightning, and it came along with a booming, good old-fashioned "Boo!"

Agnes screamed and fell back. She landed on her butt on the attic floor.

At the same time Oz raced over to make sure she was okay, he got out his cuffs. He put her hands behind her and secured her wrists before he dared a look at me.

"Did you see that?" he asked.

"I . . . uh . . ." I wasn't sure what I was supposed to say. What I was supposed to do. "What did you see?"

He looked at the window, empty now. "I thought I saw . . . It looked a whole lot like . . . I mean, it seems to me it was . . ." After he helped Agnes to her feet, he shook his head. "I think I need some time to process this."

He got it. His backup arrived and they took Agnes away, and they left other cops in the ballroom who took each guest there, one by one, and got a statement from every one of them.

By the time it was all over, the sun was about to slip below the horizon.

Oz rubbed the back of his neck with one hand. "You can tell everyone to go," he said. "We've got contact information. If we need to call them, we will."

"Except . . ." I looked at the chilled champagne, the uneaten food, our guests who'd been patient and waiting forever. "We might as well feed everyone, and Quentin tells me the band that was supposed to play after the swearing-in ceremony is in the kitchen eating us out of house and home. Union rules, we've got to pay them. They might as well play."

"They might as well," he said, and before I went to notify to the band, I stopped and talked to Clemmie, who was watching the action from the doorway of the Carnation Room.

"Good work," I told her. "Except I need one more thing from you."

B y the time the band set up and the food got reheated, we'd all had a couple glasses of champagne and everyone was in a better mood. I'd told the band which song I wanted them to play first and they didn't object.

Champagne flute in hand, I stood and listened to the first notes of "Bye Bye Blackbird." It sounded good. Once Clemmie joined the band on stage and started singing, it sounded great.

Since he was still working, Oz had opted for coffee. He

took a sip and nodded his approval. "Nice touch to add the recording of the voice to the music," he said.

I kept my gaze on the stage and the singer only I could see. Clemmie just about glowed with excitement. Her feet tapped out the rhythm of the song, and those big bows on her shoes jumped up and down to the beat. "You think?"

He kept his gaze on the band. "Something you want to tell me?"

"Not right now."

"Something that will explain what I saw up in the attic?"

"Maybe."

He set down his coffee, stretched his back. "I've got to get to the office and wrap this thing up. But not until—" He grabbed my hand and led me out on the dance floor and before he put his arm around me and swung me into the dance, I had just enough time to give Clemmie the thumbs-up.

She was the monkey's eyebrows.

# Acknowledgments

When it comes to plotting, writing, and getting a book onto bookstore and cyber shelves, there are always people to thank.

My gratitude goes out to Stephanie Cole, Serena Miller, and Emilie Richards, my incredibly talented and supportive brainstorming buddies.

To the staff at Berkley, thank you for giving me the chance to tell a fun tale, and to my agent, Gail Fortune . . . well, you know how much I love a good ghost story! Thank you for seizing on an opportunity to make this one come alive.

Mary Ellis and Peggy Svoboda are always willing to listen to ideas and offer advice, and I'm grateful for that.

My husband, David, puts up with my interest in all things paranormal. I can count how many times he's visited old cemeteries with me and gone on ghost hunting expeditions, too.

It's appropriate that this book is being published in conjunction with the time that Prohibition was enacted in the United States. Those years, of course, are the stuff of legend. Good guys and bad guys, folks just trying to eke out a living while others took advantage of every chance to make—or break—their fortunes. Before Prohibition became the law of the land, David's grandfather owned the largest bar in Ohio. And after? The man was a bootlegger who was arrested numerous times and even did a stretch in a federal prison. Someday maybe I'll have the opportunity to tell his story, too. For now, I'll just raise a glass in a toast to his memory—and his chutzpah!

Ready to find
your next great read?

Let us help.

**Visit prh.com/nextread**

Penguin
Random
House